JILLIAN DAVID

EVERNIGHT PUBLISHING ®

www.evernightpublishing.com

Copyright© 2023

Jillian David

Editor: Audrey Bobak

Cover Artist: Jay Aheer

ISBN: 978-0-3695-0806-5

JILLIAN DAVID

HIDDEN COMRADE

I want to wake up in the mountains,
Where the rhododendron grow.
Where the sun comes a-creepin' into where I'm sleepin'
And the songbirds say 'Hello.'
I want to wander through the wildwood,
Where the fragrant breezes blow.
And drift back to the mountains
Where the rhododendrons grow.

—The Rhododendron Song

JILLIAN DAVID

HIDDEN COMRADE

Project Morpheus, 2

Jillian David

Copyright © 2022

Chapter One

This so-called covert op had disaster written all over it.

No way could Saipele Tuitama execute this Morpheus Squad mission with any chance of success. One man couldn't do it.

Not even one man like Pele.

The entire team couldn't secure this Smoky Mountain location. Forget identification of exits and risk mitigation—everything was an exit, with multiple entry opportunities. Too many cabins, too many windows, too many constantly shuffling campers.

His brain struggled to process the numerous human patterns forming in front of him.

What about Pele's ability as a Morpheus operative to blend into the background? *Ti'o.* Shit. He couldn't be more conspicuous if he broke into a loud Siva Tau war dance.

He scanned the room, attempting to catalog every face and assess whether it was friend or enemy—his go-to calming technique when the mission went sideways or when the violent Morpheus Virus urges threatened to crush him like a tidal wave.

Target One: Approximately age eight, runny nose and potential contagion risk, screaming a song about a Little Bunny Foo Foo walking through a forest and bopping other animals on the head. Anticipate violence.

Friend. Or enemy?

Target Two: Approximately age seven, crying about a pet left at home. Given Target One's tendencies for violence, it was probably safer for Target Two's pet to stay at home.

Friend. Or enemy? His head swam, needing the comfort of processing threats.

He sucked cool, campfire-tinged air in and out of his tight lungs, willing the disorientation to recede. His brain craved patterns to function.

No. The virus craved patterns.

Unfortunately, before him existed utterly disorganized Brownian motion in the form of school-aged children. He patted his thigh to ensure the knife remained secured beneath his newly purchased hiking pants. A small breeze cooled his skin, thanks to the hole he had to cut in a cargo pocket for access to the hidden weapon. He shifted his arm, satisfied with the location of a small Sig tucked away near his armpit, anchored by a minimalist chest harness. One hiking boot hid a knife and the other boot stored yet another gun.

He could be clothed in nothing but munitions and it still wouldn't be enough to secure this situation.

Pele couldn't hear himself think over the din of chattering, laughing children streaming around him in the Camp Foxfire dining hall. He backed up until he bumped against a plywood wall, hung with pictures of random forest creatures and pithy descriptions beneath each one. He turned his head to examine a frame. *An opossum has scary, sharp teeth but likes to eat ticks.* Noted.

Tension lanced through his neck. A headache grew. Did these kids not know how to talk at normal volumes? Would it be too much to ask them to stand in one place so he could complete his assessment?

His gaze swept the room, over and over, seeking order.

Control.

His vision had tinged red. He needed control of the location.

His fingertips sank into the plywood with a dull creak of the wood's surrender. He scanned again. No patterns existed. His head throbbed. Sweat dampened his upper lip.

He ground his teeth. He needed to connect with his surveillance target ASAP. The sooner he initiated the next phase of this op, the sooner it would end. *Ti'o.*

How to secure this unfavorable location? He could tranquilize each child. Not permanently. Just enough to slow them down so he could do his job.

Monday morning. Where was Reagan McNeill? Mission files stated that she was punctual.

He lifted his hand from the indentations on the wall and glanced at his Luminox. 8:02. Late. So much for reliable intel. What other information was incorrect?

He scanned the room again. The floor was covered by linoleum, worn down by the scuffs of thousands of constantly moving children over many years. He stomped a foot. Hollow, thin plywood. Potential for ingress breach or for exfil. Potential munitions placement. His shoulder blades twitched.

Between the pictures of educational forest

creatures hung useless Plexiglas windows. Without locks. Unacceptable. Like this op.

A wooden screened door creaked on a hinge and then slammed shut. He peered through the wire mesh.

Acres of unsecured woods waited out there.

Damn it, this type of mission required multiple team members. The lead operator could directly monitor Reagan, and other teammates would patrol the camp and surrounding mountains. But dangerous circumstances required that the team cobble together protection duties ASAP. The team was spread too thin. Deviating from a standard op risked failure. Pele didn't fail.

So, Pele would improvise.

During his covert recon yesterday, he should have yanked Reagan out of here and kept her in a safe house until the danger passed. That action would technically meet criteria for felony kidnapping. Inconvenient detail. At a minimum, he should've curtailed her activities at this large, unsecured camp.

But Morpheus Squad did not officially exist.

If he operated conventionally, that meant outing his brothers-in-arms.

Risking recapture by the government. Or worse.

Ti'o. What a mess.

Pele was a glorified babysitter who still took the assignment seriously. His CO had set this mission up as a precaution, but Pele knew far too well that this job didn't come with guarantees. One lapse in his vigilance, and innocent people could get hurt. Case in point: Four nights ago, Reagan's sister, Kiera, had almost died escaping her Atlanta house to get away from an obsessed megalomaniac, Beaumont Lequire, the corrupt CFO of the Fallen Comrades organization. That company, Fallen Comrades, acted as a damned front, siphoning funds away from vets who needed help the most. The political implications for Lequire's senator father added more pressure to the situation. Throw in a hint of the Russian mob's participation, and Beau Lequire had every reason to silence any informant.

Even if it meant leveraging the informant's family members to secure cooperation.

Kiera was safe at the high-security Morpheus Squad compound in the North Carolina mountains east of here near Bryson City. If Lequire couldn't reach her directly, he would hurt her through her family.

The game had changed. If Pele lost focus, someone could die.

"Are you Pele?"

He whipped his head up to home in on that voice. The tone was bold and smooth like kava, with a hint of sweetness that made him want to lick his lips.

Eyes, blue as the Pacific sky, pulled the breath out of him. Tendrils of curly orange-blonde hair escaped dual braids that fell over her shoulders. She tilted her head away from him. Then a warm smile transformed Reagan McNeill from pleasant-looking into beautiful. The cacophony of forty-some-odd children faded into the background.

She was taller, like her sister, but unlike Kiera, Reagan's frame wasn't delicate. She carried herself with confident strength.

From her file, he knew that Reagan was twenty-eight. Engaged to be married, but the wedding had been called off in December, a little over three months ago. Merry Christmas indeed. He rolled his hands into fists as the ever-present Morpheus Virus rumbled to irritated life deep inside of him. *Ti'o.* With effort, he regained control with the go-to technique: *friend or enemy*? He knew the answer, but the familiar exercise centered and calmed him.

He studied her open, honest face. Lovely.

Friend.

Her fiancé was an idiot.

When she faced Pele straight-on, he could see the maroon birthmark that covered the side of her neck and jaw and continued up her right cheek. The pigmented skin stopped a few inches below her eye.

She didn't try to cover up the mark with makeup or clothing.

Why should she? The woman was beautiful. Her skin had created its own unique pattern, like many of his cousins who were born with blue-gray birthmarks on their lower backs.

"Um." She frowned, still holding out her hand.

Stupid. "Sorry, loud in here," he said. When their palms met, the heat knocked him back, the heel of his hiking boot bumping the wall with a crack. In a flash, he wanted to know whether the rest of her skin would be as warm and soft. The virus sent a wave of primal, possessive impulse that shot through Pele's core. What?

Stop. She is your mission. Nothing more. Stick with the job.

"Nice to meet you, R—" He almost blurted out her name. A rare mistake.

He withdrew his hand, needing to break contact so he could think straight. Officially, he had never met her before. Unofficially, he'd spent the last two days setting up surveillance equipment and mapping out this camp, especially near the cabin where she stayed. She had no idea about the tracking device secured on the underside of her truck, the tiny camera tucked in the crook of a tree near the craft shack, or any number of other hidden imaging devices scattered throughout the premises. After observing her from a series of blinds, he had noted her activity patterns. Not only did he have to get in sync with her for the mission objective, but he would use his virally enhanced ability to detect variations in her behaviors and keep her safe.

She flipped one of her long braids back over a shoulder. "I'm Reagan. They say you're the new guy." Her fingers drifted over her right cheek.

When a slight frown came and went across her smooth brow, a wave of raw need crashed over him, urging him to wrap his arms around her and shield her with every inch of his body. What the hell? How had his virus activity ramped up? It wasn't time yet. With a rapid calculation, he counted back. The last antidote shot had been six days ago. He typically went ten days between shots.

Had the virus changed? Damn it. He couldn't have anything else unexpected occur on this improvised mission. He might be dehydrated. He patted his back pocket with the small water bottle. Wouldn't hurt to drink some water.

He dragged his focus back to Reagan and the way she studied him. "Um. Sure am. New guy. Yes, uh. Are you training me?" If she only knew about his background in Special Forces. All the tactical training he'd completed. Wrangling kids on some hikes in the woods would be no problem at all. He glared at the teeming masses out of the corner of his eye.

But he needed to remain close to Reagan. So he would pretend to let her teach him about children's educational things.

"So, have you worked with kids before, Pele?" The rise and fall of her voice reminded him of the southern accent her brother, Brady, had. Except her brother's voice never hit Pele in the solar plexus.

"Oh, sure."

No. Never. I was the youngest child in my family.

I did visit my nieces and nephews a few years ago and they climbed all over me. Does that count?

"Done a lot of work with outdoor education or forest crafts?"

"Absolutely." If carrying out covert ops in Afghanistan while mortars exploded nearby counted as a forest craft, that was.

"Great." She smiled again, somehow making the entire room brighter. "Then working here will be a piece of cake."

Chapter Two

As Reagan stared up at the tall man, something about Pele didn't add up.

There was something familiar about him, but the idea drifted away like campfire smoke on a breeze.

It wasn't just that he was good-looking. He wouldn't be the first handsome man she'd met. By some miracle, she had clamped down on the sudden urge to run her fingers through his glossy, black hair to find out if it really was as thick as it appeared. Nothing like an inappropriate gesture to say *nice to meet you*.

But the whole picture with him didn't add up. Sure, he had all of the appropriate gear, like leather hiking boots, but they were scuffed on the sides and not the toes. He wore a dark-green flannel shirt over a black t-shirt and a black fleece vest. His tech pants fell well within the bell curve of normal outdoor attire. His golden-brown skin completed the perfect outdoorsy picture.

Did he seem rugged? Hell, yes. In fact, the guy's entire demeanor from broad shoulders to confident posture screamed *capable outdoor dude*.

So what gave?

"Did you have breakfast?" she asked, trying to break her spinning thoughts.

"Yes. Never miss it." The flash of his smile turned up the lumens in the room. Wow.

Seriously. What was he hiding? What did he want?

Not an opposition to breakfast. But still.

Now she had become cynical and suspicious of any man? According to the therapist who had helped her over the past several months, oh, yes, *cynical and suspicious* highlighted all of Reagan's trust issues.

Trust issues. An understatement, considering how badly her confidence had been shaken by her ex. Shaken. How about broken? Now all she heard were lies in Pele's straightforward answers. Kept sensing danger in each small movement of his arms.

How messed up was that?

Maybe she hadn't been in the company of a nice, kind, handsome—okay, hot—man in so long, that her brain cells no longer knew how to process the sensory input. Maybe her ovaries had finally ceased their boycott after last winter's strike.

She touched her right cheek out of habit. Covering the birthmark. Deflecting against criticism and rejection. Damn it. She shoved her hand back down and concentrated on the man standing quietly in front of her.

What about that flash of déjà vu? Something about the determined set to his jaw, his wide, vigilant stance, triggered a memory that was there one minute, gone the next. It made no sense. There was a familiar feeling about Pele and that grim press of his sensual mouth.

Great. Now she was thinking about his lips. It was all she could do not to wet her own in response.

Uh-oh. She hadn't said anything in what? A minute? An hour? How long had she been staring?

Recover. Say something appropriate, dammit.

"So, what do you say we round up our group of kiddos for the morning and go for a hike?" she asked.

Yup. Way to show your sparkling personality and completely professional demeanor.

His warm brown gaze flicked over the room teeming full of kids and then back to her. "Sounds great."

Judging by the tight lines around his mouth and flash of—fear?—it didn't sound at all great to him. What was this guy's deal?

Hey, maybe he needed the work. She couldn't fault anyone for taking a job to get by. Perhaps he had his own issues. Not like she had the corner on that market.

Reagan shook her head. She'd lost several years of her life trying to understand a guy. Trying to adapt to fit his needs.

See where it got her?

Pain. She rubbed her lower back. One of the places her ex had hit her where the bruises wouldn't show.

She didn't need to figure out a man. All she needed to do was her job.

Chapter Three

The next day, Pele couldn't hear anything in the woods over the squeals and shouts of the kids playing in the creek. Where had his surveillance target gone?

Someone flung a small fish net, and he tensed at the sudden movement.

Ti'o, everything around him involved sudden movement.

He peered downstream and shook his head. It was only Tuesday. This would be the longest week of his life. Or more.

He scanned the un-securable woods around him for the hundredth time. Assessments. Exfil points. Weaknesses. Defensibility. His head ached.

Steep hills rose from a rocky creek that burbled loudly in competition with the chattering voices echoing through the trees. Broadleaf green shrubs and short-needled evergreens provided a backdrop for the early leaf buds of deciduous plants sprouting up and down the small valley. The throb behind his eyes worsened. There existed no pattern.

Within the patternless environment, nothing seemed out of place. No flash of a scope, no dense shape of a human stealing through the woods.

His mind churned as he created escape routes to limit casualties for every new hike, every new venue, each new activity. Then he'd had to start over. Re-count the noncombatants, reassess the situation, account for variables, and formulate a plan.

He tugged up the long sleeves of his flannel shirt. One cuff was wet and frigid, thanks to retrieving the stream ecology net that had floated away from one of the students. He scowled up at the overcast sky filtering over the top of the ridges. He was an ex-Special Forces, dammit. He could infiltrate hostile territory and conduct dangerous missions.

Therefore, he could achieve competency in babysitting.

Peering past the ever-moving mass of splashing, net-wielding children, he caught sight of Reagan as she disappeared around a bend in the creek, trailing two students and the schoolteacher.

Leaving Pele with ten small children to wrangle.

Bet Reagan didn't have wet sleeves. The woman somehow avoided hordes of splashing kids and moved over the rocks as smoothly as the very water flowing in the stream.

His virus rumbled to life, fueled by Pele's irritation. Damn it. He clamped his jaw tightly closed.

Secrecy was everything. The Morpheus Squad didn't officially exist. If the government found them, the entire team would be locked away for testing. Again.

Those scientists had pushed the limits of what each of the virally-enhanced men could handle—heat, cold, pain, sound, light—all while taking diligent notes. The brass called it research. Pele called it torture.

He rubbed his thigh, checking for his knife. Wanting to plunge it into the heart of any one of those so-called researchers. The Morpheus Virus had been a great idea on paper: turn gifted soldiers into inexhaustible military machines. Simple enough. After their teammate Brady's injuries, each man on the squad had willingly volunteered for the experiment.

If the virus prevented soldiers like Brady from sustaining traumatic brain injuries that affected them long after combat ended, then it was worth the risk.

The experiment worked. At first.

Pele rolled his neck, assessing the virus's status.

Yes, still contained by the temporary antidote shot.

After the team escaped from the stateside testing facility, they regrouped in the mountains of North Carolina. The only thing keeping Pele free here? Total secrecy as to the team's existence and his nature.

Where was *here*? Camp Foxfire was located in the most unsecured location a solo operator could imagine: tucked into the southwestern corner of the Smoky Mountains National Park. He blew out a lungful of crisp mountain air, tainted with sour frustration and the imperative to get closer to Reagan. Closer for professional purposes, of course.

His concern had nothing to do with her hip sway when she hiked up hills and flitted through creeks. Nothing to do with the way her sky-blue eyes danced when she smiled.

If he was going to keep tabs on her, he would have to bring the herd of creek-stomping children down to where she was working.

"Come on, *isumutu*. Let's go see what Miss Reagan has found." He tried to strike a balance between friendly request and direct military order.

The children continued stomping and yelping. He groaned. In the cloudy March weather, wan sunlight struggled to make it to the ground.

Cold, wet fingers gripped his right hand. On instinct, he slid his hand up, gripped sweatshirt fabric, and dangled the child in front of him.

"Mister Pe—" the boy gasped.

Ti'o.

Friend. Enemy.

The virus rushed its fiery response through his veins. Pele's heart thundered.

He almost dropped the child but somehow regained enough control to lower the boy to a flat rock and step back. Pele yanked away the hand that had almost neutralized an innocent noncombatant.

He'd. Almost…

"Are you a superhero?"

Like it was his first day ever speaking, Pele shook his head and said, "What?"

"Like Thor?" The child made a whooshing noise and reached for the heavens with his fish net.

"No. Of course not."

"That was cool. Can you pick me up again?"

Raw, nasty horror congealed in Pele's gut. "No. I didn't—that's not—no. Forget it, okay?" he whispered the last part.

The boy attempted a wink that looked like a lopsided grin. "Like a secret?"

"Um."

"It's okay. I know the drill." He made a zipping gesture over his mouth.

If the child hadn't gotten close to the truth, this entire conversation would be laughable. He glanced around. Did anyone else see him? No curious stares or gaping mouths.

The boy stood, staring up at Pele for several long moments. Pele tilted his head and assessed the child. What was wrong? Was this boy hypothermic? A mute? The boy blinked. Had he injured the child? Did he require medical attention? Perhaps he needed water. Dehydration, then.

He peered down the narrow creek bed but couldn't see or hear Reagan. *Ti'o*. Gone from sight again.

He looked back down. The boy kept his lips clamped together.

Pele scanned the creek ecology teaching area, searching for something—anything—out of place. He quickly focused again on the possibly injured child. Cold sweat broke out on his forehead. With his attention split in too many directions, his head spun.

"What's *isthmoot*, Mr. Pele? Is it a secret code word?" The boy twirled the long handle of his small stream ecology net with his free hand. *Flicka-flicka, flicka-flicka.* Tiny drops of ice-cold water spun off the net-slash-fake Thor's hammer.

Pele wiped droplets off his face and suppressed an irritated growl. "What?" He blinked and concentrated. "No. No codes. *Isumutu* is a Samoan word. It describes a cheeky or naughty child."

"Oh." The child grinned. A tooth was missing. "I like that. *Isthmootoo.* Where's Samoa? Is that where Thor comes from?"

"What? No. No Thor. No super—no. Look, the proper name for where I was born is American Samoa. It's as far away from here as you can get and still be on the planet."

"Really? Is it cold there? Are there unicorns there?"

"Unicorns? No. There are brightly colored fish in the ocean. It's warm. It rains there. It's very green with beautiful beaches and a huge ocean around it." What he'd give to be walking on the white sands of Ofu Beach with the Pacific breeze soothing his skin right now.

He crashed back to his not-beach reality when the boy jumped with both feet into the creek, splattering Pele with more ice-cold water.

"Can we go find more crawdads?" the boy asked, tugging harder at Pele's sleeve.

In spite of himself, he felt the corners of his mouth rise. "Yes." He projected his voice. "Let's all of us go find more crawdads. We can see what Miss Reagan is doing." He clapped his hands once. "Form a line, everyone."

How the mighty had fallen. An ex-Special Forces, enhanced super-soldier, herding children.

They couldn't maintain formation. He gritted his teeth. Somehow, he got the gaggle of laughing, squealing children to follow him up out of the creek bed and hike along solid ground.

What about the children's safety? There hadn't been time to think through that aspect of this thrown-together mission. Too many targets. Not enough resources.

His instructions: protect Reagan. No guidance on how to accomplish that task.

Lequire would use anyone as leverage if it meant getting his hands on Reagan's sister again. He was that obsessed. That desperate.

With all the noise and constant chaos, this mission had become a nightmare with little chance of success. Failure could get Reagan or other innocent victims hurt. Or worse.

Pele never failed, and thanks to the virus, he didn't experience fear. None of that could change now.

Releasing the children from loose drill formation back to screaming and jumping at ease in the creek where their teacher and classmates worked, Pele peered over the bank seven feet down.

There, he got a front-row view of Reagan's rounded backside as she bent over, pointing out caddis fly larvae or snails or something else ecological he couldn't recall. He could only learn so much background information on the mission within a few days' time.

Well. He *had* learned that Reagan's faded jeans hugged her firm thighs, which were toned from miles of running in the mountains. He groaned to himself. Trail running—another intolerable security risk here. One of her hobbies.

Above the collar of her fleece pullover, her smooth skin peeked out, begging to be touched. Escaping the braids, pieces of coppery-blonde hair curled near her ears and forehead.

Reagan stood up and pivoted, locking her gaze on his. The flash of wariness that he'd noticed several times was replaced with a quick, tight smile.

"Good, you're back," she said, voice partially drowned out by the tumbling creek.

When he didn't answer, she frowned and turned back to the children, murmuring to them over their netfuls of rocks and insects.

Her curly hair glinted gold even in the low light.

His gut churned. She was everything he wanted, and at the same time, nothing he needed. *Palagi.* Foreigner. Non-Samoan.

What did he truly want? God only knew anymore. His life was no longer his own. He could never return to his real home. Never have a normal life.

He wanted to be done with his assignment and get back to the squad where he belonged. There, he knew how he fit in with his teammates, as close as a family as he could ever get thanks to the experimental virus.

A tiny voice whispered in his head that he didn't belong with Morpheus Squad, either. He didn't belong back in Hawaii with his family who had moved there when Pele was five. He didn't belong back in American Samoa, the island of his birth.

Nowhere. He belonged nowhere. Certainly not in this cold, damp mountain terrain.

Enough. He snapped back to his duty.

He surveyed the area once more. They were in a small, narrow gorge, a half-mile or so from the main camp buildings. To escape, they'd have to scramble up a hillside on one side or a steep bank on the other and run through the woods and then up a gravel road. This location was a kill box.

Although Pele had scattered trail cams all over the property, the cameras wouldn't defend against a bullet. The technology would only buy him time to respond.

For now, the best he could do was stick close to Reagan, which made his job both harder and easier. In addition to the file he'd been given a few days ago before beginning this mission, he did know a little about Reagan from the time he spent in Special Forces with her brother, Brady.

Before Brady got hurt. Before he died.

Pele knelt down, planted a hand on the bank, and dropped down to the streambed where Reagan and her class milled around. As he landed, a large three-foot-wide boulder at the top of the muddy bank got dislodged. With a soundless swing, he easily caught and rotated the rock away from its trajectory toward Reagan's head.

"What?" she yelped and stared.

"What?" He froze, boulder held in both hands.

"Wait. How are you doing that?"

Sweat dampened his back. He eased the rock down to the ground and shrugged. *Nothing to see here.*

"That must weigh over four hundred pounds, Pele, and you just … caught it?"

"It's, um, lighter than it looks, and adrenaline and all. Besides, I do kettle ball workouts, so. Yeah. Muscle memory. Like a kettle ball. And muscles. Um." He grimaced.

Smooth move, elite soldier.

One strawberry-blonde eyebrow rose. "Huh."

How had he ever passed the most rigorous training the Army had to offer? That training required subterfuge. Some Special Forces he'd turned out to be.

Then Reagan rested her hand on his forearm. Her touch should have steadied him. Grounded him. It should have reassured him. Instead, the light pressure of her hand on his arm branded Pele through the flannel fabric. The contact tilted his equilibrium. Worst of all, he wanted more of her touch.

"So, are you getting the hang of the class and handling the kids?" she asked. Her words reassured and soothed him, like an ocean breeze flowing over hypersensitive skin.

Soothed? A battle-tested soldier like Pele did not need to be soothed.

No. He couldn't have anything more than professional concern for the welfare of the woman he was entrusted to protect. Finish this mission, get back to the team, and then move on to the next mission.

"Love working with the class," he said between gritted teeth.

Her laugh blended with the sounds of the nearby creek. "Hey, I get it." She pointed a thumb. "They're exhausting. Especially if you're not used to working with kids."

Exhausting. That wasn't the problem. The problem in this isolated Appalachian valley was that Pele had too much time to think and no time to patrol. A terrible combination.

"No, that's not it—"

A glint of light on the hillside grabbed his attention. His eyes locked on the flicker.

A loud *crack* echoed.

On instinct, he spun Reagan into his chest, lifted, curved his shoulders around her with one hand cupped to protect the back of her head, and pivoted her away from the sound. He craned his neck to scan the area. His senses absorbed everything going on around him. The kids. Damn it. He hesitated, torn between duties.

One child jumped up and down, pointing at the stream.

"That was the biggest rock I've ever thrown!" the girl yelled, giving a triumphant fist-pump. "Wahoo! It went boom! Did you hear that?"

Pele's adrenaline seeped away. A damned rock in a shallow stream. The narrow gorge had amplified the sound. He re-scanned the area twice, three times. Nothing out of order. No human pattern of sound or movement detected. No glint of metal or glass. No shadows that didn't make sense.

After a few seconds, awareness shifted to Reagan's warm lips pressed against his neck. He sucked oxygen into his lungs to focus on his mission. Instead, the scent of fresh air, clean water, and pine trees drifted around her. Her tall frame curved perfectly against his body, her forehead coming right to where he could taste her skin if he turned his head an inch. Where her palms curled against his chest, he felt her touch all the way into his bones.

He kept the arm that protected the hidden gun clamped around her back. Hopefully, she wouldn't feel the knife in the leg holster or the chest strap under his shirt.

False alarm. No danger. He should let her go. Couldn't. Not yet. Even though she was a strong woman, her softness tucked against him fired up a driving need to use his entire body to protect her.

Which was ridiculous. It was a job. That was all. He was committed to his job.

"Um." She pressed harder against his chest. "Jumpy much?" Her muffled voice drifted up to him.

It took another five seconds to figure out how to remove his arms from around her head and back. When he stepped back, she straightened her shirt with a hand that shook. Her arms crossed in front of her chest.

"Still, uh, learning the new sounds out here," he mumbled.

"You sure?" Those light-blue eyes searched him then slid away. "You seem rattled." When she stepped back again, cold seeped into his bones.

"Thought you might fall for a second." Bad cover. Very bad.

"Well, then." Her cheeks colored a pretty shade of pink. "No worries there." She relaxed her arms and clasped her hands, then let them dangle at her sides. Gold-tipped eyelashes feathered her cheeks.

He checked the scene behind them. The children's elementary school teacher remained engrossed with the kids thirty feet away in the stream, his back turned to them. The kids collected minnows in buckets and stored them in the dams they built in the stream. Everyone was busy.

No one had seen him lose his shit. Except Reagan. And she thought he was simply a nervous guy.

Only he knew the danger that might be headed her way.

Chapter Four

When Pele hauled her into his arms, Reagan tried to play it off like no big deal.

But inside, her heart scampered like a tractionless Chihuahua unsuccessfully cornering on a hardwood floor. Her spark of pure feminine interest shifted gears right into full-on panic as a wave of nasty fear smashed into her. For a second, she fought the sensation of being held down and trapped.

Air lodged in her throat, suffocating her.

Not Clayton. This wasn't Clayton.

Pele was not her ex. He didn't deserve her baggage. Neither did she. She repeated the therapist's mantra: Reagan didn't deserve what Clayton had done. It wasn't her fault. Not her fault.

She was in Pele's arms. Not Clayton's.

With deliberate focus, she loosened up her muscles and talked herself back down from the emotional ledge. Adrenaline drained out of her body, leaving her muscles quivering and weak. Catching her breath, she leaned back to take stock of the situation and the man looking down at her like he held an irate snapping turtle.

Not Clayton.

Not by a long shot. For the first time in forever, she let herself be held. For the first time in forever, she let herself enjoy an embrace without fear.

Her nose was still close to Pele's thick neck, and good grief—he smelled like strong male, clean soap, and fresh creek water. Her body changed gears once again. Before she could deactivate her quivering ovaries, she fought the urge to lick his skin and see if he tasted as good as he smelled.

Her palms rested on top of his rock-solid chest, the firmness of his body softened only by the warm flannel shirt. His arms wrapped around her were thick bands of muscle hard as ironwood. She couldn't move if she wanted to. Her brain and her hormones dueled: run or sink further into his warm frame?

Hormones won. Barely. For a few seconds, she didn't want to be tough or brave. She didn't want to defend herself. She didn't want to worry that she'd be hurt. Good old responsible Reagan wanted to simply enjoy the sensation of being held.

The press of his warm torso against the area between her ribs and pelvis caused some serious fluttering deep in her belly.

All right, hormones, that's enough. Out of the pool. Swim time's over.

She pushed her hands against his chest. Nothing budged. Holy cow.

Moving her head back to look up at him, she licked her lips. "Jumpy much?" she managed to say.

If he answered, she didn't register the words. She'd gotten lost in his liquid brown gaze for a second there. When he set her away from him, stepped back, looked anywhere but at her, and rubbed his palms on his tech pants, she registered that clear action. Ah, yes. Rejection. Familiar territory.

"Uh, I thought you might fall for a second." Pele stood in front of her, his huge frame rigid. He searched her face then darted glances up the hillside and down the creek, past where the children tormented the aquatic life.

It wasn't the first time he'd had that scowl—grim, tight, like he expected disaster at any moment. Being this close to so much vibrating tension set her own nerves on edge.

Maybe she was edgy because of her younger

sister, Kiera. Reagan hadn't heard from her in a few weeks, which wasn't exactly unusual, at least not over the past year. Kiera had pulled away from the rest of the family after their brother, Brady, had died early last summer. Time went by too fast.

If Kiera wanted to have her own life? No rules against that. What didn't jive was the abrupt way she left, shortly after Brady's friend, Mateo, had visited. Kiera and Mateo were thicker than thieves, having quiet conversations that ceased when Reagan got close. Coincidence? Probably.

The scant communications from Kiera over the past many months had included some brief emails reassuring everyone that she was busy with a new job and doing just fine.

Just fine.

The opposite of the sum total of Reagan's life after Brady died. Then, after Clayton had…

She caught herself rubbing her birthmark on the right side of her neck. The instinct to cover it up was hard to resist, even now. *Quit it.*

"Well, then," she said. Pele's quiet scrutiny made her face heat again.

So much didn't add up about the guy, like the unclear circumstances of his hiring. It was obvious now that he lacked even basic knowledge or training in outdoor education and school-aged students. Well, except for when she and Pele took a group up to the high ropes course earlier today as part of his onboarding. Then he executed all the safety maneuvers and belay techniques with expert precision, like he'd been born to it. Or had previous experience.

Did that mean he deserved her distrust?

The way he occasionally called out commands to the students made her pause. He was never mean, but every so often, Pele transformed from Reagan's mentee to something more like a drill sergeant. Maybe he was ex-military with stuff like PTSD going on. Brady had similar issues. The explanation tracked, for the most part.

What about his age? This was no college grad, working his first job. Pele had a few lines around his eyes when he smiled which, dammit, made him even more handsome. She pegged him at around thirty. A thirty-year-old signing up to work at camp, sure. It wasn't typical, but heck, she wasn't too far away from thirty herself.

What about his body? Based on the way he carried himself, low-key and unassuming, it was obvious those muscles weren't for display. Every inch of his tall, solid frame seemed purposeful, ready for action, not for vanity.

For what purpose, at a camp for kids in the woods?

Nothing about Pele made sense.

She watched him until he dropped his gaze. It wasn't a show of weakness. More like he was hiding something. Strange.

The guy sure had Linda, the camp director, charmed. When he smiled with that dimple on one tanned cheek, Linda responded like a cat lapping up fresh milk. A twinge shot through Reagan's chest that for sure was *not* jealousy. One day, she might try for a meaningful relationship, but not any time soon.

Last Christmas had sucked twinkle lights.

She blinked hard. Enough reliving bad decisions. She should do her job. Time enough to deal with a Mr. Enigma later.

Rubbing her arms, she shivered. Glancing at her watch and then up at the overcast sky, she said, "Ready to call it an afternoon?"

"Looks like the kids are done," he said, the slight accent thickening his voice. The way he pronounced certain words, splitting vowels in that smooth tone, relaxed her.

Okay, seriously? Has your brain taken a vacation?

She struggled to refocus. "There aren't many more creatures in the stream that haven't been harassed today. We should leave a few crawdads for the next group."

Damn his dimple creasing that golden-brown skin. "We need to save the ecosystem from this group of second-graders?"

"That's correct." In spite of herself, she smiled.

"Roger that."

In record time, he had the kids out of the stream and lined up as close to attention as squirming second-graders could get.

****

The dining hall echoed with the cacophony of forty-plus children, teachers, and chaperones talking and laughing. Aromas of fabulous country cooking—greens, chicken patties, potatoes, and homemade gravy—had Reagan sighing in happiness as she leaned back in the metal folding chair. If blueberry cobbler got served up tonight, this mountain girl's day would be complete.

Chad and Jamila, coworkers and resident lovebirds, joined her. A few minutes later, Linda and Pele sat in the empty chairs across the table from Reagan.

"Who wants to lead the night hike?" Linda asked, passing the bowl of collard greens to Pele with an adoring smile and a bat of her mascaraed eyelashes. Since when did Linda wear makeup?

Reagan shoved down the flash of irritation. Hello, free country. People could like whomever they chose.

What grated was the fact that Reagan had been in his arms a few hours earlier, and she had enjoyed it

Which meant ... exactly nothing.

Pele studied the bowl of collards handed to him. A crease formed between his thick, dark eyebrows, then he shrugged and put a steaming scoop on his plate and passed the bowl. As Reagan took it, their fingers brushed, sending a jolt of warmth up her arm. Beneath the weight of his dark gaze, the air stuck in her throat, and she swallowed. Okay, these schoolgirl reactions were ridiculous. All women probably reacted that way around him, if Linda's unnatural giggles were any indication.

Chad and Jamila were deep in conversation at the other end of the table. They'd been together for all of three weeks and had that "new couple" glow about them. Reagan sighed, the action making her chest ache. She didn't begrudge them their relationship.

Reagan begrudged her lack of one. Or to be exact, *how* she had come by a lack of a relationship. Damn Clayton and his control issues. Damn how her incremental acceptance of his demands had reached that breaking point. Damn how he bent her to his will emotionally and physically. He claimed to have suffered from the breakup. Unlikely, but if true, then good. After all, misery should best be served up family-style, with all parties around the table sharing in the pain.

She rubbed her cheek.

She peeked at Pele eyeballing a Brussels sprout like it might jump off the fork and run away.

"Night hike?" Pele's baritone grabbed her attention as it cut through the din of chattering voices around them.

"Exactly what it sounds like." Linda shot him a big smile. "We take the kids out for a night hike so they can appreciate nature in the dark, with all the unique sounds and smells. Show them the things that we can experience in the woods at nighttime that you might not notice during the daytime."

"That's a horrible idea!" When he thudded his hand on the table, silverware clanked against the hard plastic plates.

Reagan flinched. An image of another yelling male flashed in her mind's eye. She shoved the memory away. God. Enough already with the flashbacks.

The table went dead silent. Everyone froze.

Linda patted his forearm. "It's perfectly safe."

Despite Reagan's best efforts to stay calm, anger flared when Linda touched him. Reagan pressed her hands to the tabletop, needing to get a grip on her careening emotions, pronto.

Hey, her emotions were multifaceted. She could totally experience fear, jealousy, and desire at the same exact time.

Pele answered, "I'm sure the hike is safe, but, um, it's still cold and damp. Won't it be too dangerous to hike tonight?"

Funny, Reagan read his angry, tense scowl. Nothing about his demeanor indicated actual concern about the terrain. Instead, he looked like a guy who had been delivered horrible news.

She had hoped for tonight off to … do what, exactly? Trail run? It was too late in the day. What other activities would she do on a Tuesday night? Nothing. Per the usual routine.

What about Chad and Jamila? Ugh. Their giggles and whispers to each other made it obvious neither wanted to volunteer for a hike tonight.

Fine. "I'll take care of it," Reagan said. She turned to Linda. "Can I finish up earlier on Thursday, then? I have plans."

Linda said, "Deal."

At the deepening scowl from Pele, Reagan's cheeks warmed.

"No," he said, jaw hard.

"Pardon me?" Heat flared from her chest as Reagan whipped her head up.

She had no patience to hang around guys who told her what she could and could not do. Been there, done that, got the t-shirt. She glared back at him. Right into his piercing brown eyes. Which were surrounded by dark eyelashes and dark brows, which made him appear even more mouth-wateringly attractive.

God *damn* it. What was wrong with her? She had gone through too much therapy and way too many mind-clearing trail runs for all that work to be blown to bits by a good-looking man with an attitude about her doing her job.

Not handsome, exactly. More like hot and intense. And controlling? Yes, but no. It was clear that he respected her work and seemed to enjoy learning from her. He followed her lead when it seemed that he might prefer organizing an activity. Not disrespectful at all.

The issue wasn't Pele, but Reagan. Something about him had opened doors to closets containing her carefully stored skeletons.

He brushed a napkin over his mouth and pushed back a few inches from the table. "What I meant to say was that I should go with you, to learn how you all do things here. So I can pull my own weight and do the hike on my own later on."

None of those words rang true.

Also, Pele tagging along exemplified a bad idea: Having the guy walking nearby in the moonlight, when the night goes still and all the sounds and scents become amplified, after her defenses would be down from a long day of chasing kids. Not good.

She couldn't trust herself.

Frankly, if she were to examine the adoring gaze Linda shot him and how he sat there and smiled over at the camp director, he couldn't be trusted either.

Reagan gripped the table edge. "It's okay, Pele. Enjoy the evening off. I bet you still need to get settled into your apartment."

"No. I'll go on the hike."

Linda nodded.

Just like that, it was decided. Pele's mouth twisted into a grim line, like he would rather shovel horse hockey. "When and where should I meet you?"

"We'll leave from the fire circle in forty-five minutes." A sudden thought had her grinning. "Bring a good story to tell."

His eyebrows rose. "What?"

Chad raised his head from mooning over Jamila and snickered. "Hazing the new guy?"

Reagan shrugged. "Hey. Rules are rules. He gets the full experience. He has to learn."

At Pele's frown, she felt her smile widen as she leaned back in the chair. Then she inhaled a lovely aroma.

Oh, yes. The kitchen staff was bringing out blueberry cobbler. This evening would shape up to be a great night after all.

Chapter Five

Pele's entire mission was to protect Reagan from bad guys tracking her down and hurting her. For his mission to succeed, he needed control over the situation.

A hike, in the night, without flashlights, in the woods, was the most FUBAR idea imaginable.

Forget all that dangerous, life-threatening stuff. Pele considered a much more important question.

What normal human *wanted* to go hiking in the March weather in the mountains in the darkness? He had performed his fair share of nighttime reconnaissance. A capable ex-Special Forces guy like Pele knew a night hike was a terrible idea, even without the potential for Lequire's cronies stalking through the woods.

Grumbling as he stood in his small basement room, which was tucked into the small staff housing building beneath the camp office a hundred yards or so from the dining hall, he stuffed his pockets with flashlights and snacks. And water. No Special Forces soldier would ever die of dehydration.

He patted his boot and left armpit. Pistols secure. Good.

The thought of having to use a gun anywhere near all these children iced Pele's blood. If Lequire's people attacked, Pele couldn't take care of everyone.

It was a given: someone would get hurt.

Ti'o. He shook his head and headed for the unlit campfire circle.

Man, this operation was far outside any safety tolerances. He could barely communicate. Cell signals were nearly impossible to find down in this densely wooded valley, despite his signal amplifier in the main camp. Even satellite communication struggled to connect. He should have called in to Morpheus Squad already and asked for extra help with this assignment.

Which would mean admitting he couldn't handle things on his own.

No. The team was stretched too thin. He would carry out his mission. Pele straightened up.

He would figure out how to keep Reagan safe, avoid collateral damage, and maintain Morpheus Squad's secrecy. All of it. Fake it until he succeeded.

Like this fake job—he'd gotten it due to the computer hacking ability of his teammate, Stumpy. The IT genius had created the perfect job application and shoved it into Camp Foxfire's director's email inbox.

When the director called a reference, lo and behold, Stumpy took the call, played the part of a gregarious camp director colleague at Camp Widjiwagan somewhere up north, and gave Pele a glowing recommendation that Linda couldn't refuse. Stumpy might have fibbed about Pele's experience in outdoor education.

Outright lied.

Pele had a college degree in communications technology, but he knew nothing about damselfly larvae and salamanders. He sure didn't know how to find a crayfish—pardon, *crawdad*—fast enough to maintain an eight-year-old's attention. He had zero understanding of child psychology or how to manage their erratic behaviors. Basically, he was unqualified for every aspect of his fake job, and now he was failing at the bare minimum requirement for the Morpheus Squad portion of the assignment as well.

Damn Beau Lequire. The thought of anyone hurting someone as nice as Reagan made Pele's gut tighten and amped up his damned virus's desire to protect or destroy.

So, Pele was stuck. He had to maintain his cover story, avoid detection, and guard Reagan. Now they were hiking through the woods in the middle of the night. Too bad his enhanced ability to see patterns didn't work when there was no freaking light to see by. He gritted his teeth.

The sounds of excited chatter led him to the unlit campfire circle. As his eyes adjusted to the partially moonlit scene, he made out the shapes of teachers and chaperones as well as children. Everyone huddled in small groups.

His back prickled. Far too many targets. The enemy could be anywhere in those dark woods. His virus perked up and took notice, eager to neutralize any and all threats. It wanted badly to break from Pele's tight control. He clamped his jaw shut and fought the viral impulses.

Scanning the crowd, he played friend-or-enemy over and over until he could think clearly. He needed to form a rational plan tonight, not uncork the virus and let the base impulses fuel his undirected rage.

Ducking into the woods about fifteen feet away from the crowd, he pulled out a small night-vision scope and scanned the surrounding hills. The experimental device, worth well over a hundred thousand dollars, provided him with both thermal imaging and night vision. Nothing but the best tech for the best-kept secret military experiments gone rogue. Commander Hunt would never give up the identity of his suppliers, but someone out in the real world was still a fan of Morpheus Squad. Long may it last.

In the gray-scale high-resolution images, he saw a few bright lights, consistent with small animals and birds. Why any woodland creature would come within a mile of the laughing, squealing mass of kids was beyond his understanding. He peered through the scope one more time. No human-sized signals in the woods. For now.

When his upper arm got squeezed, he whipped around for the second time in the day. Grabbing the wrist on a twist and a spin, he couldn't stop the instinctual act. He clamped his grip down hard.

"Yowch," Reagan yelped.

He dropped her fleece-covered arm as if it had burst into flames. *Ti'o*. He could not afford to lose control and hurt Reagan. Besides, he had felt the wild tension turn her frame rigid earlier today when he held her in his arms. That, combined with the memory of that terrified animal look in her eyes, had him considering carefully how he handled her. What happened to etch fear over her features? He needed to proceed with caution on more levels than one.

"Sorry," he said, easing the scope behind him and into a pocket.

With a shrug he sensed rather than saw in the low light, she said, "Most folks are nervous on their first night hike. Don't worry. We'll have a little more moonlight in a few minutes. It'll be fun."

Fun.

Overcast skies would give way to a clear, cold night with a sliver of moon rising above the trees. Better visibility for anyone who wanted to spy on them. Great.

He followed her to the empty fire circle, and she gathered the children in front of her. In no time, she had the kids lined up, with teachers interspersed every five or six children.

"Why don't you follow me, Pele?" she said. "You'll get an idea of where we're going and how to lead for when you take a group out."

"All right." He fell in behind her. His view of her backside would have been so much nicer in the daylight. A few remembered details and his imagination would have to be enough tonight.

The trip through the woods wasn't far but still took thirty minutes due to the maddeningly slow pace of the entire group. Before starting out, Reagan had encouraged the kids to feel the ground with their feet before stepping, and to roll their feet with each step to keep silent. Now, giggles and muffled whispers accompanied the shuffles of forty-plus sets of feet clomping through the forest.

In the emerging moonlight that filtered through the trees, Reagan's gray, shadowy frame floated across the terrain. If Pele weren't focused on the back of her yarn cap-clad head, she would have disappeared as she drifted in and out of shadows. Silent as a whisper, she glided down the path. He could make out the gray silhouetted sway of her hips as she walked with a soundless, smooth gait. His fingers itched to trace those curves.

The stomping hordes coming up the path behind him made him pause. He couldn't hear anything besides the children in line. He whipped his head back and forth, scanning the darkness and seeing nothing.

Any one of Lequire's men could be out there ready to attack, and Pele had no ability to detect them or respond right now. His heart slammed against his ribs.

What he'd give to stop and scan the forest for any unwanted observers who lay in wait. The hairs on the back of his neck stood up, and he patted the weapon on his right hip.

Small fingers noodled into his back pocket, and Pele turned and gently squeezed the hand, removing it from his clothing before the child encountered hidden weapons and stashed tech. Or the water bottle. That was his.

"Are we almost there?" the girl whispered.

Did she need water? Food? He tamped down Special Forces instincts and patted the back of her hand before letting go. "No idea," Pele murmured. "Miss Reagan?"

Her disembodied voice floated back to him. "Almost there, y'all. Good job."

As they emerged from the woods to an open, flat patch of ground, Pele's heart sank. He dropped his forehead into his palm. No way could he secure this area.

"I'll be back in a sec," he whispered.

"Drink too much Kool-Aid at dinner?" Laughter sparkled beneath each of Reagan's words.

"Something like that."

As she gathered the kids and talked about the night sky and how the rods and cones in the eyes adjusted to the darkness, Pele melted back into the woods.

Fishing in his pocket, he pulled out his scope and swept the area, expecting to see more little sparks of animals.

A bright light signature flashed across his field of vision at the top of a nearby rise. He froze, focused on the image.

As he watched, the spot faded. Either a large animal had left or a human had backed away.

Chances of a large animal hanging around a crowd of chattering, moving kids? Nil.

Sweat beaded then chilled on his forehead. He lifted the instrument again and stilled his breathing. Nothing. Damn it, he wished it were daylight when his visual pattern recognition skills could help him. He ran inventory over his stashed weapons, starting at his ankles and working his way up. Everything strapped in and ready to go.

He scanned the clearing. Friend versus enemy.

Friend. Versus. Enemy. *Destroy. Protect. All of it.*

His grip on the tree trunk shredded under his fingertips. He sucked in the crisp night air and slowly let it out with a misty cloud of vapor. Numerous bright heat signals sat on the ground. One taller signal stood in front of the crowd. Reagan.

In plain sight, she made a single, tempting target. Every nerve in his body buzzed, ratcheting muscles down tight. Ready. The wood trunk creaked as he pushed.

He could take no action without blowing his cover. All he could do was pray that anyone out there didn't want to make a scene. He backed away from the tree.

He had to play the odds that anyone out there wanted Reagan alive and wouldn't want witnesses when they snatched her. If he was lucky, they didn't want to kill her. Good God. That was his plan, to hedge every single bet?

As he focused on the bright figure in front of the small crowd, her clear voice cut through the night.

Kefe. Fuck. Was she telling a story now?

Yes, and it sounded like it would be a long one. All while standing in the line of fire.

She had no idea that she was in danger. He curled his hands into fists and fought down a wave of the impulse to spirit her away. With nothing else to do except let dread churn divots in his gut, he returned to stand off to the side of the group of kids. He was twelve feet away from her. Too far.

Reagan's story had the children riveted. A few gasps and giggles accompanied the tale.

He rotated like a lodestone until his internal magnetic north locked in on the rise and fall of Reagan's voice flowing over him in the cool night air. She had a light southern accent like his teammate, Jake, who had brought Reagan's sister Kiera to the compound a few days ago. Jake had grown up around the McNeill family, so Reagan would know him if he became involved in this op. What a strange, braided mess this family and the Morpheus Squad had become.

Without being able to see Reagan well, Pele's senses focused instead on the cadence of her words as she moved from character to character, her tone changing from playful to foreboding as needed. Her enthusiasm drew everyone into the tale.

"… so the hideously ugly woman who was snot-nosed, pimple-faced, and awful-looking said, 'King Arthur, if you let me marry the hunky Sir Gawain, I will give you the answer to complete your quest and save your kingdom. Here is what you must know: Far and wide, the world over, the one thing a woman desires is … sovereignty—the right to choose her own destiny.'" Reagan paused.

An owl hooted, and Pele froze. He turned around and scanned the forest with his scope. Nothing big.

Yet.

She continued. "So then King Arthur returned to the giant in the forest, ready to meet his death if he gave the wrong answer to the giant's riddle. The giant pointed his sword and asked, 'Arthur, what is your answer to the question: Far and wide, the world over, what is the one thing a woman desires?'"

The children didn't move. Even the woods were silent.

Pele sure as hell wanted to know the one thing a woman desired. The one thing one particular woman wanted.

A light breeze rustled leaves above them.

"King Arthur thought for a moment and said, 'Far and wide, the world over, the one thing a woman wants is sovereignty—the right for the woman to choose her own destiny.'" She paused and her shadowed fists rested on her hips. "Well, that big giant howled in anger! King Arthur had given the correct answer. The giant had to let him go."

Giggles and little claps broke out across the open area.

With her voice full of laughter, she continued, "Then King Arthur, not one to go back on a promise, found the snot-nosed, pimple-faced, awful-looking old hag of a woman who had given him the correct answer and heaved her up onto his beautiful white horse." She waited for snickers to die down. "He led her on the horse back to the castle."

"As promised, the handsome Sir Gawain waited to do his duty. He would marry this lady because his king asked it of him. When the minister said, 'You may kiss your bride,' Gawain nearly passed out!"

Another wave of giggles streamed across the clearing. Pele felt the corners of his mouth lift. For a split second, the tension in his spine dropped a few notches.

"Well, Sir Gawain, being the honorable knight he was, pulled himself together and managed to kiss the warty cheek of his bride. As tradition dictated, he took her back to his chambers. Night fell, and he slowly turned around. There, standing before him, was the most beautiful woman he had ever seen in his entire life."

A collective gasp. Even Pele held his breath.

"Gawain rubbed his eyes. 'Where is my bride?' he asked. The woman answered him, 'I am your wife.' Gawain said, 'How is this possible? You are nothing like the woman I married earlier today.' With a sad smile she said, 'My husband, I am cursed. I must spend half of the day as that creature you saw earlier today, and the other half as I am now. Since you are my husband, you can choose whether I shall be ugly during the day and beautiful during the night, or ugly during the night and beautiful during the day.'"

Reagan's voice chimed across the clearing. "Well, which do you think Gawain chose? Warty woman in the daytime when everyone would see her and regular woman at nighttime when he had her to himself? Or warty at nighttime and regular during the day?"

Murmurs and votes returned to her. Pele chuckled at one intrepid kid's option of alternate days.

Her voice dropped as she launched back into the tale. No one moved. *Ti'o*, she had the kids eating out of her hand. As his world tunneled in on the woman spinning the story, he almost forgot about the mission. Almost.

"So, Gawain hemmed and hawed. Finally, he gazed upon the woman standing in front of him, his cursed bride, and said, 'It is not for me to decide. You must choose what makes you happy, and that is what will make me happy.' With a giant clang of a hidden bell, the woman blinked and tears filled her eyes. 'My husband,' she said. 'By letting me choose my own destiny, you have broken the spell laid upon me. I will no longer be hideous again. You have given me sovereignty, the right to choose, and that was the key to breaking the curse.' And so they lived happily ever after. The end."

Pele grinned despite himself. Of course, Reagan would tell a story about a woman's right to choose her own future. A perfect story for such a strong woman. The clapping died down.

Before he could step back outside the clearing to do another sweep of the forest, her clear voice stopped him in his tracks.

"Pele?"

His heart paused. "Yes."

"Hey, kids, would you like to hear something really cool? Pele is going to tell you one more story before we go back tonight."

Murmurs, chatter, and claps sealed his fate.

His mouth went dry. Not only did he hate the limelight, but he hadn't taken her instructions earlier seriously in the evening to prepare a story. He'd been too busy prepping his body to be a defensive weapon if Lequire's men attacked. Now he had to tell a story. This was not in the mission file. There had been no spec ops intel involving folk tales. He stared up at the moon which was now visible through the trees—as though the heavens could bail him out.

The heavens had nothing.

He searched his memory. He had to come up with something.

Then, a recollection of another clear night sky, glinting with the stars in different constellations came to him, and he could hear his grandfather telling a story from when Pele was a boy.

Yes, that one would do.

Chapter Six

Maybe Reagan felt a tiny bit of remorse at Pele's hesitation, but she had given him fair warning at dinner, with witnesses present. To be fair, storytelling was part of the job at Camp Foxfire.

When she stepped aside so he could take her place in front of the group, he murmured, "I'll get you for this."

Not so much a threat but a promise. One that sent a shiver all the way down to her toes.

He unzipped his fleece vest and shifted from foot to foot, a large shadow in the scant moonlight.

The children whispered and moved around.

An unpleasant sensation of guilt crawled through Reagan's gut. He didn't have a story, did he? Oh, no. As she stepped forward to help the quiet, proud man, he cleared his throat again.

And began.

"I'm from American Samoa, which is an island in the Pacific Ocean. It's far from here, in a place that's sunny and warm." He chuckled. "I'm going to tell you a story passed down through generations. It's about the most beautiful woman in all the islands in the ocean. Her name was Sina."

His warm voice evoked the feeling of sun-heated sand and tropical breezes, and Reagan's internal temperature rose a few degrees. "One day, the King of Fiji heard about Sina and went to Samoa to win her as his wife. He used his special magic to turn himself into an eel and swim to Samoa. Do you know what an eel is?"

Mumbles and suggestions.

"It's a type of fish, long and narrow. One day, Sina was collecting seawater in a bucket and noticed an eel in the lagoon. She placed the eel in her bucket and took it home. Sina put the eel in a village bathing pool near their house and continued to care for it."

The shadow form of Pele relaxed as he took several steps to the side and punctuated his words with his hands.

Almost reverently, he continued. "Everyone used the pool, but no one saw the eel except Sina. When she would come to the village pool, the eel would come out of hiding and wind around her in a sort of eel embrace. She tried going to a different spring, but still, the eel would appear, as if by magic. Sina became scared and left her village to escape the eel."

The melody of his voice felt like the roll of gentle waves on a protected lagoon. Reagan leaned against a tree trunk.

"When Sina escaped, what do you think happened? Every village she went—the eel followed her. Every time she stopped at a spring to take a drink, the eel was there. Finally, she went to a village meeting. A huge eel approached across the open ground to stop in front of Sina. The eel said, 'Beautiful Sina, I am the King of Fiji. I came here to try and win you as my wife, but my magic is gone, and now I cannot change back into a man.'

"Sina realized that the persistent eel was the king trying to show his affection for her all along. He said, 'When I die, bury me in front of your home. A tree will grow and provide you comfort. When it is warm, use the leaves to make a fan and cool yourself. When the tree bears fruit, you can drink from it when you are thirsty. When you drink from the fruit, it will be like you are kissing me.'"

On instinct, Reagan touched her own lips.

"Even though Sina was sad that her love had died, she did as the king told her. Sure enough, a tree grew and provided many benefits to Sina, and later to the Samoan people that we still use today."

Jacket fabric shushed as some of the children shifted.

He paused. "Have you all ever heard of a coconut?" He acknowledged correct answers. "Well, that's the fruit from the tree. Because of his love for Sina, the eel became the palm tree, the gifts of which Samoans now use for all sorts of things in their lives. True love can live on in many different ways. The end."

Images of the island legend danced in Reagan's imagination. The kids clapping broke the spell. She swallowed a lump in her throat.

Do your job. No getting sappy. Whatever you do, don't get sucked in by another handsome man.

"Well, let's thank Mr. Pele again for telling us his story." Her voice didn't sound as sure as it did before. Had to be because of the long day. She waited until the kids quieted down. "Okay, it's getting near bedtime. Time to head on back. Before we go, look around and tell me if you are able to see and hear better than before."

Happy exclamations returned.

"Now do you understand? If you let yourself get used to the nighttime, it's not so dark after all, is it? Even at nighttime, your senses still help you." She waited a few more seconds. "All right, let's get going."

She lined the kids up and walked to the front of the line. Turning to Pele, she asked, "Do you want to lead us back? I can bring up the rear."

"You shouldn't be in the back of the group." All of a sudden, his voice had that hard edge in it again. It made her shiver, but not in the same way as his story did. Was he upset that she had put him on the spot?

The tension in his frame fairly vibrated through her. "Okay."

"I mean, I'm happy to lead," he added. "But you could follow me, to make sure I get everyone back where they need to go."

She darted a glance around the woods. Why was he so worried? She'd worked at Camp Foxfire for years. Nothing dangerous was out there. Maybe he had a hang-up about the night, or some bad experiences in the past. Maybe the PTSD theory was accurate. People could react in various ways that seemed illogical, but often they had good reasons for doing so.

She should know.

"Well, okay." It was pretty much a straight path back to base camp, but if it made him more comfortable, she'd walk behind him. She would also breathe in that scent of strong male and mountain air. Sure thing.

Within a half hour, Pele deposited the entire group back at the dining hall where the lights were lit, and she blinked in the glare until her eyes readjusted once more. Under the bare bulbs of the main building's porch, she and Pele sat across from each other on wooden benches. She relaxed while the voices, creaks of door springs, and echoing bangs of doorframes coming from the various cabins off in the woods reached her ears as everyone settled in for the night. Good sounds. The normal rhythm of camp activities.

With a deep breath, she inhaled the cool night air, the dew-covered grass, and the wood scent from the benches and porch. Weariness seeped into her bones. Worry about Kiera, the rush of—whatever it was— earlier with Pele when he had his massive arms around her, and the late-night camp activities left her wrung out.

Although he sat motionlessly, Pele didn't relax. His legs remained planted as he leaned forward, hands pressed to the edge of the wood bench. After darting a glance out into the woods, he slid his gaze to her with a dark intensity shadowed by the stark overhead light. Her twitchy skin had nothing to do with the cool glide of air sweeping over her neck.

No. She refused to give in to the moonlight or night air or whatever the heck caused such a squishy feeling when she was around the guy. Getting all googly-eyed over Pele would be a big steaming cup of... Nope.

What she wouldn't give to talk with Kiera. Damn it. She missed the close ties they'd once shared. Missed the advice.

Reagan sighed. Enough. She needed rest.

When she pushed to her feet, Pele stood as well. Not exactly stood, but unfurled his large body in a smooth motion until he was right in front of her. Her heart stuttered a beat.

"Well, I'd better turn in. Workday tomorrow." She pivoted on her booted heel.

Pele placed a hand under her elbow. She startled, then melted as the warmth of his big palm seeped through her fleece jacket.

"Can I walk you back to where you're staying?" he asked.

"Uh." Sure, he had a masculine strength and appeal. No one could argue that point. But why waste it on someone as unavailable as Reagan? He could have any woman he wanted.

In her experience, guys with charm usually wanted something and used their powers of attraction to get it. Once they had it... She shook her head. Not going to go there.

She watched him as he waited, unmoving, supporting her arm. Quiet but not still. His head cocked from side to side, as if he picked out sounds coming from different areas of the woods.

No one had ever offered to walk her to the small

apartment she called home at the upper end of the main base camp. Seemed like quite a formal request for such a casual setting. "Sure, I guess." *Real smooth there, Reagan*. She mentally smacked herself on the forehead.

"Good." His rich voice whispered over her, like a finger caressing her cheek.

What would his actual fingers feel like on her skin? Would his touch be gentle and filled with restrained power, or demanding and rough? Would his touch hurt like in the past or slide smoothly over her body like a balm?

Enough already.

When he moved closer, she zipped her long-sleeve fleece and crossed her arms. Without a change in expression, his hand dropped to his side, and the air between them thickened.

With the overhead porch light throwing his features into shadow, she couldn't read his expression. A shudder worked itself down her spine. It wasn't fear, which surprised her. For whatever reason, Pele in all his muscle-bound, tall presence didn't scare her. He intrigued her.

Stop it.

She needed to get a grip on reality because nothing was going to happen. Couldn't happen. The wounds on her heart were too raw. She'd erected too many walls.

She'd been wrong about Clayton. She couldn't risk being wrong about Pele, too.

If he wanted to walk with her in the night, then fine, but that was all that would occur.

Gravel crunched under their boots as they strolled up the road the half-mile to the large outpost cabin. Until summer camp began, Reagan had this building all to herself, even though she only lived in the small one-bedroom apartment just inside the main entrance.

During the walk, it took a few minutes for her eyes to readjust from porch light back to ambient moonlight illumination. A rustle in the leaves nearby made her jump. Pele sucked in a breath. The woods never scared her. What the heck? She blinked until her night vision improved.

An owl hooted up in a nearby tree.

"What was that?" Pele asked.

She could barely see his profile. The moonlight speckled his skin with black and gray.

She listened for a moment. "Barred owl."

"How can you tell?"

"You can tell because when it hoots, it sounds like someone is saying, 'Who cooks for you? Who cooks for you all?'"

"Really?" He stopped and lifted his chin. After another few hoots, he smiled, his even teeth visible in the dim light. "Hey, you're right."

She continued walking. "I love the sounds out here. Can't wait for it to warm up. The tree frogs will start calling. When those frogs get going, it's like a crowd of people all talking all at once."

"Sounds loud."

"It's a good type of loud. Then if we have a season with cicadas, it gets super noisy! But the tree frogs talking means summer's coming. We always loved the summer, my sisters and—" A lump formed in her throat. She stumbled a step on the gravel.

"And?"

"Nothing."

After a pause, he asked, "What about your sisters?"

Damn his sincerity. She shouldn't be rude to him. Besides, something about being around Pele made her want to share instead of keeping her feelings bottled up inside.

She scuffed her feet a few paces. "My family had … a hard patch over the past few years. Mom died just over a year ago. Dad's trying to move on with life. My brother died a few months after Mom. I had some tough things going on recently."

If you could describe calling off the wedding to an increasingly abusive fiancé as *tough*. *Humiliating but necessary* was more like it. Didn't matter. The outcome still stunk. "The younger of my two sisters is running amok in Atlanta, wreaking havoc on the fashion world there."

"And?"

"My other sister, Kiera, I don't know. I haven't heard from her in weeks. It's like she doesn't want anything to do with us."

He paused. "I'm sure that's not the case." Spoken with confidence.

Relaxing the fists she'd formed in her pockets, she stifled the snapped response that threatened to erupt. This guy might have ulterior motives, but he didn't deserve her anger.

He hadn't done anything wrong.

Yet.

"We've always been close. But after my brother died, Kiera changed. Heck, we all changed. Who wouldn't? But she and one of my brother's friends started hanging out together. Wanting to find out why Brady died. I never heard what they learned because she moved away."

"Maybe she was ready to move? Needed to move."

Reagan stopped and stared at his imposing figure. His big frame blocked the scant moonlight from the night sky. "What reason is good enough to run away from your family and communicate only in little email bursts? No calls, no visits, nothing. For almost a year." She fingered the hem of her jacket. "Sorry. It's … we were close, and I miss her. That's all."

He turned toward her. "I understand. My family is far away and I don't get to see them as much as I'd like."

Shame warmed her chest. Of course, he knew. The guy grew up halfway around the world.

"Are they in American Samoa?"

"Most of my family is in Hawaii now, though I have some cousins in Samoa."

"Still pretty far away."

"Yes." The calm of his voice cut through the night sounds in the woods.

"How come your family left?"

He rubbed his upper thigh, the movement more of a shadow she sensed rather than saw. "My parents didn't think that us kids would have quite as much opportunity if we stayed in American Samoa. I'm sure it was a gut-wrenching decision for Mom and Dad. The pull to live a traditional Samoan life is massive."

"They put that aside for you and your siblings?"

"Well, my parents continued teaching us the traditions, but of course it wasn't the same as growing up there."

"How was Hawaii?"

The way his low voice flowed through the night air comforted her, relaxed her. "We were bullied in school by the *kanaka* kids, the native Hawaiians."

"Really?"

He barked what passed for a laugh. "You'd think all Polynesians are one big happy group of islanders, right? Not even close. On the island of Hawaii, there was a surprising amount of prejudice against non-Hawaiians."

"Is that why you moved away?"

"No." An odd undertone in his voice had her glancing sideways again. His profile shifted and tightened in the low-level moonlight, but the sensation of his intense focus on her remained constant. "I had a need to belong somewhere. After I got a degree at the University of Hawaii, I spent a year back in Samoa with relatives."

"Did you find what you were looking for?"

A boot crunched the gravel as he shifted from foot to foot. "That's an interesting question. Not sure." He rubbed at his thigh again. "Not exactly. I joined the Army."

"Kind of an extreme move to find yourself halfway around the world, isn't it?" She regretted the words the minute they came out. It wasn't that she wanted to be insensitive, but Reagan always knew where she belonged—in the mountains near her family.

That was until her entire life and family all went to pieces over the past two years. As it turned out, she had no room to talk.

"In the Army, I received a purpose." He clamped down on the bitter last word.

"What about now?" Waving a hand in front of her, she said, "Now you're working here. Is this what you like?"

The long pause caught her attention. "People change. Situations change."

"That's a pretty vague non-answer." She shoved her hand back in the fleece pocket and continued walking.

He matched her steps. "What I'm saying is I can understand your sister's situation. She had a good reason to move away."

She stopped and reared back. "What did you say?" For a split second, it sounded like he knew something Reagan didn't, which was ridiculous.

"I meant that she *probably* had a good reason to move away." Gravel under boots filled a few seconds of silence as they walked again. "What if she was searching for something she needed in her life? To do something she felt she had to do?"

"Sure," she mumbled. "Possibly."

The large cabin appeared as a shadow growing from the stand of trees, and they left the gravel road to walk up a short dirt path to the porch stairs. When full, the structure could hold thirty kids and camp counselors, plus Reagan in her small apartment in the basement. Tonight, the building was silent and dark in the middle of the early spring forest.

At the bottom of the steps, he stopped, his face a low gray glow in the moonlight. He turned his head from side to side. "I don't think you should be staying out here."

Pulling her head back, she said, "Are you serious? Camp Foxfire is the safest place around. I've worked here for years. Know every nook and cranny. We've got critters from the National Park next door that like to wander over now and then, but nothing dangerous."

"You're far away from the other staff, and phones."

She paused for a moment. Stared into the dark woods. Imagined what else could be out there. Second-guessed herself.

Damn him. Damn the manipulation. Something about how his tone changed along with the rigid set of his shoulders put her nerves back on edge again. "It's fine."

"What about—"

She cut him off with a swipe of her arm. "Stop. Just because this is a new place for you and it's in the mountains and you're uncomfortable, that doesn't make it dangerous for me."

He leaned back and crossed his arms over his massive chest. "Huh."

Okay, that was a little below the belt, pulling the rookie card. For all she knew, he'd been frolicking in the mountains for years. Way to jump to conclusions. God, she could be insensitive.

"If you say so." Bitterness and—anger?—dripped from every word. How strange. He didn't strike her as an angry guy at his core. But there it was vibrating the air between them.

She lifted her foot to the bottom of the three porch steps and turned back to him. "Pele, I'm sorry. That wasn't an appropriate comment."

"It was accurate."

"It was a stupid assumption." It was quiet enough to hear another barred owl call from a nearby tree. The soft rush of water in the creek near the gravel road tinkled through the air. Damn her mouth.

He hadn't moved, but somehow his broad shoulders and tall frame took up all of her field of vision.

Planting her other foot on the step, she faced him squarely and tried for a solid statement to end the evening on a positive note instead of this awkward silence. "So … okay, then. Thanks for your help with the hike tonight."

"Reagan."

She froze.

Son of a gun, when he said her name, it made her libido do backflips and warmed her faster than a roaring campfire. "Yes?"

She could make out his jaw working the muscles of his thick neck. "You didn't need my help. You're capable of taking care of everything yourself." His Adam's apple bobbed. "I don't want to give the impression otherwise"—he rotated his shoulders briefly—"out here. You've got your life all locked down."

Strange choice of words. That was the problem, wasn't it?

She'd keep right on taking care of everything and everyone, to the detriment of herself, if need be. To the exclusion of allowing anyone else entry into her locked-down life, if that was what it took to protect her heart.

Even when things with Clayton went south and she had been hurt? She'd still kept what happened private. No one else needed to know how badly she had misjudged her fiancé. No one would ever learn the extent of how he'd knocked the supports out from under her. No one needed the burden of her misery. The shame. She rubbed her neck. So, yes, to any casual observer, she could take perfectly fine care of herself, thank you very much.

"Well, um, that's nice of you to say." When he moved in her direction, he came to her eye level, shifting her equilibrium.

Not eye level. Lip level.

Come on. You know better.

She was still working on step eight of the Twelve-Step Recover from the Controlling Asshole Program. Tonight was not the time to jump back in the game. Even her baggage had carry-ons. She couldn't risk making another bad decision. She couldn't handle another failed relationship.

What the heck? Now her walk from the dining hall to her cabin had become a relationship? Good grief.

Time to start over with her Twelve-Step plan. Back to the beginning. *Step One: Admit that there's a problem.*

The waves of his thick, black hair gleamed in the moonlight. He leaned close enough that she could smell his spicy, masculine scent. His hands curled into mighty fists, like he could hold back all the water behind a dam, one crack away from bursting. Like he could fight all her demons and win.

Yes, Step One, there was a problem.

How good would it feel to run her hands through that hair? To feel the hard muscles of his shoulders bunch up when she touched him. He could touch her as well. How would it feel to have his big hands roam over her body?

How much counseling would she need if she got in over her head with someone like Pele? Technically, she needed to finish dealing with her lingering issues from her ex. Seemed like there should be a rule about one at a time or something.

She had no idea how long she'd been staring at him. She clamped her open mouth closed.

He hadn't made any kind of move, but for the love of all that was holy, her nipples had become points of quivering attention, focused on him. A whisper of air separated them. He closed the space. She held her breath.

A loud crack echoed over the narrow valley.

Pele dove, knocking her onto the top step and sending a burst of pain to her lower back. In the space of a second, he had her wrapped up in his arms, her spine pressed against the wood slats on the porch wall. Anything that would harm her had to go through the cabin wall or a wall of Pele.

"*Kefe*," he muttered as he lifted her with one arm and crawled while dragging her across the porch ten feet to the door of the cabin.

How was that even possible?

Reaching up from the crouch, he grabbed the door handle, turned it, and pushed her inside the cabin.

"What the heck?" she sputtered, her heart pounding triple time.

"Stay here. Keep the lights off. Please."

Then just like that, he was gone.

Chapter Seven

Kefe. Fuck. Cold sweat broke out on Pele's forehead.

He pulled his Sig out of the hidden chest holster as he slid off the side of the porch and knelt in a shadow. Hiding might not work. Patterns, patterns. Friend. Enemy. He blinked at the moonlight shadows, trying to bring order to the chaos in his brain.

Protect Reagan.

He'd been about to do more than protect her.

Focus, dammit. Patterns. Patterns. Assess, plan, adapt.

Weaknesses?

If someone out there had infrared detection, then he had zero advantage in the darkness. Easing behind a large tree to reduce his visible heat signature, he fished out the compact thermal night vision scope from his back pocket. He needed to find the threat to Reagan. Now.

The virus flared, clawing at his mind, wanting to be let off the chain. Air strafed his lungs in and out.

He deployed training techniques to slow his breathing and heart rate. Friend versus enemy, friend versus enemy. Adrenaline coalesced into laser focus.

Pele was calm, focused, and in control—for now. He held the instrument up and studied the hillside across from the cabin.

Ten seconds ago, he had come *this close* to having his lips on Reagan. His hand shook. He had needed to kiss her more than he needed air. Every inch of his body strained to touch and taste her. Once he wrapped her in his arms, could he have stopped?

Ti'o, this mission had gone to hell at a ridiculous pace.

For a few seconds, he'd shifted his attention from the mission to Reagan. So had his hungry virus. Damned thing responded to Reagan like Pavlov's dog on steroids. If the virus had assumed control, Pele would have taken her on any surface available.

Concentrate. Protect.

Patterns. Find the patterns.

His jaw ached. There were no patterns in this unlimited chaos.

A light *thunk* of a footstep sounded within the cabin behind him. Reagan. Every sense homed in on her movements.

This woman. With nothing more than her kind, calm, sexy self, she had somehow triggered the brutal power and raw instincts of his Morpheus Virus. His inability to focus could get both of them killed. Actually, he had no problem focusing—on her.

An ex-Special Forces soldier who couldn't concentrate on the assignment wasn't merely useless for mission ops. He was flat-out dangerous.

Damn the night. If it were daylight, he could better use his virus-augmented senses to detect unusual patterns in the woods. At night, he was equal to any other of the Morpheus Squad teammates. Strong, amplified, but without Pele's own extra edge required to outmaneuver Lequire and his men in this environment.

Still gripping the Sig with one hand, he lifted the scope and squinted into the eyepiece. A few bright spots popped up here and there. Squirrels or rabbits maybe. Nothing big.

He gritted his teeth, squeezed his eyes shut and open, and looked again.

No one could completely evade infrared detection unless they built a structure and covered it with materials isothermic to the environment. Even then, a faint diffused heat signature might remain. Creating such a space took time and required the surveillance target to stay in one place. Made no sense to go to that effort in the large camp, where Reagan could be anywhere.

So any warm-blooded *puaaelo* out there doing their typical job? Pele should be able to see with the scope. Creeping around the cabin, he scanned the woods another time. Nothing unexpected. No large heat signatures.

Maybe he'd heard a large branch falling? Or a bear crashing through the brush.

Or one of Lequire's people coming to hurt Reagan.

Ti'o.

Anger bubbled up into viral pops of irritation that prickled his scalp.

Calm down. Contain it.

How could one woman make him forget the skills he'd worked so hard to hone? His control? Unlike some of his teammates, Pele possessed the best control over his virus out of the entire Morpheus Squad.

He rubbed his hand over his head. How could an assignment to protect one person be so difficult?

He rested his forehead against the rough bark of a nearby oak tree. Part of the problem was that he needed to remain close to Reagan to do the job. But being around her made it hard to do the job. Also, at some point, he needed a mandated rest. The virus would only take him so far before his brain and body crashed. Sure, he could camp out in the woods near her cabin and go psychotic from the lack of sleep. Wouldn't be the first time. He could handle a good six nights with little sleep and still function.

He was already on day five. He needed to stop and recover.

If he stopped to recover, Lequire's men might hurt her.

What if there was a better way to protect her, make his job easier, and allow him to rest?

A way that both parties might even enjoy. *Kefe.* Was he so tired and desperate he'd try a tactic like this? Worth a shot.

Time to see if he could improve the … security of the assignment. How great would it be if he could get some sleep tonight, with Reagan right next to him. Massive bonus.

Conflict of interest? Sure.

Did it make him a *ulu'ela'ela*? A total bastard?

Yes. He pulled out his phone and ran through the video feeds from camera traps. Nothing out of place. Satisfied that the terrain was safe for now, Pele stowed the scope in his cargo pants pocket and replaced the gun into the holster.

After striding up the stairs of the cabin, he knocked, paused, and pushed open the door.

Reagan stood next to the moonlit window. He lurched forward. Not smart. If someone had night-vision goggles, they could see her well enough to take a shot. How could she not know this?

How could he complete his mission if she couldn't make safe decisions?

Because she doesn't know you're on a mission and that the mission is Reagan. She's not a trained military asset whose brain has been rewired into something cold and calculating.

She'd never lived in the world Pele had experienced with explosions, screams, and body parts. Reagan had no firsthand experience with what horrible things humans could do to each other.

Come to think of it, judging by the flashes of pain

and fear that flitted across her shadowed, sweet face, maybe she did have an idea of how cruel people could be. Each time he saw that wariness, Pele wanted to be the man to take her pain away. *Ti'o.*

Comforting her was not. His. Mission. His jaw ached as he ground his molars.

God help them all if Reagan ever had to personally learn about the extent of human cruelty on Pele's watch. Someone would die.

Half of her face glowed in the beam of partial moonlight coming through the window. Her lips remained downturned. When he closed the door, she didn't move. With the fleece now off, she wore a long-sleeved thermal shirt that hugged her curves. Her knit cap was off, the tendrils of curly hair escaped from braids creating a moonlit nimbus.

"You're not safe there." He caught her by the upper arm and pulled her away from the window. He loosened up his grip at her sharp breath. *Gentle. Be gentle.*

Hard to remain gentle when concern for her safety and his flashes of desire flogged by a hungry, savage virus overrode what remained of his good judgment. He studied her face: friend versus enemy. Friend versus enemy? *Click. Click.* Familiar patterns fell into place. Another deep breath pushed the virus back behind the trap door, and he mentally closed it. Safe for now.

"What's going on, Pele? Seriously."

He grasped her other upper arm. Even in the low light, he saw her eyes, wide and fixed on him.

She bit her lower lip. "I'm never scared of things that go bump in the night, but you're making me nervous."

If she knew his secrets, she would be more than

nervous. Pele *was* the thing that fucking went bump in the night.

When he let go, he slid both hands up to rest on her shoulders. Like he had to stay in contact with her, to be reassured that she was okay.

Unable to meet her raised-eyebrow challenge, he studied the floor instead.

He rubbed his thumbs across the smooth skin under the shirt collar. "There are things I can't tell you, Reagan."

"Try again."

"You have to trust me."

The stubborn jut of her jaw made him smile.

Until she took a step back. He moved with her. "Trust you?" She barked a laugh. "I barely know you. Why don't you pick the few things you *are* able to share, then? Like the weird strength or jumpiness. Throw me a bone here. This is strange behavior."

"I can't say." Honesty left a sour taste in his mouth. Frustration, concern for her safety, the damned virus cranking up its activity, and lack of REM sleep made him twitchy. His mandate was clear: keep her safe *without* exposing the team.

Kefe. At what point would he have to decide between the Morpheus Squad and protecting Reagan?

"Is this about your military service?"

He reared back. "What?" Was his cover blown already?

She reached up and patted one of his hands still resting on her shoulder. "Um, my brother Brady had some PTSD issues after leaving the Army. He got startled easily. Kind of overreacted to certain situations." She studied him until he trembled. "Is that maybe part of what's going on here?"

"Huh." He gave the best non-answer he could

come up with. She had no idea what he'd experienced in his military career as a virally enhanced guinea pig for the Army.

Tonight's alarm wasn't about PTSD. But she wouldn't understand, and he couldn't explain the truth.

This mission. It was damned naïve to operate on sheer hope that Lequire's people would only focus their efforts on Reagan here. What was to say they wouldn't try to hurt the children and teachers in the camp, too? Lequire had no problem threatening anyone, including pregnant women—case in point, Kiera.

The only thing that kept this many soft targets safe? Lequire's risk of exposure and bad publicity for Fallen Comrades and how that would harm his father's senate reelection campaign. And luck.

How long would Lequire maintain a circumspect approach? At some point, the madman would escalate his efforts and risk exposure. Was Pele ready to do anything to protect Reagan if that happened?

He ground his teeth until his head hurt.

Too many secrets, too many moving parts. He needed to simplify the situation. Damn it, he hated manipulation, but there weren't tons of options in his playbook right now.

Blowing out a lungful of air, he got sucked into the vortex of Reagan's shadowed gaze. He couldn't walk away from her if his life depended on it, and that feeling had nothing to do with the mission.

Irritational fear, doubt, and exhaustion swirled until she became his anchor.

She leaned away, but he couldn't lose contact with her. Wouldn't. Not yet.

"Pele?" That worried voice cut through the morass in his mind.

"*Ti'o.*"

"What—was I right about your past?"

"Maybe. Yeah. Kind of." He'd bend the truth if it provided him a way to carry out his mission. He shoved air in and out of his lungs, heart pounding. "I want—"

Her mouth opened on a whisper of sound. "Pele."

"Please."

Leaning forward until their lips were mere millimeters apart, she breathed, "Yes."

Sliding his hand up and around her neck, he cradled the back of her head. With a guttural sound he'd never heard coming from him before, he crashed his mouth down on hers, pressing against the soft skin, consuming her. The second their lips touched, Pele's brain zapped until all he knew was Reagan's mouth, smooth against his.

He wanted so much more of her.

At a whimper from one of them—who?—he lifted his head a few inches. Her damp, swollen lips, visible in the moonlight, tempted him to taste more, but gently. So gently. Each of her tiny gasps blew warm air over his hypersensitive nerves.

He was an out-of-control bonfire, and she was like a refreshing, mountain rain shower. He needed more of Reagan.

Moving the other hand off her collarbone, he traced the line of her neck up to her jaw and then over her chin. With the smallest pressure, he opened her mouth and inched his thumb forward. Her eyes widened.

When she nipped at his fingertip, his instant erection tried to punch a hole in his pants. He had never responded like this to anyone before. Shifting to open his stance and relieve pressure, he leaned into her. It didn't help the pressure situation one bit. He didn't care.

Her hands slid around his torso and under his vest until they branded him on the small of his back, and he groaned. How amazing would her hands feel on every inch of his bare skin?

One remaining rational part of his brain hoped that she wouldn't let those hands drift up or down and encounter his stashed weapons. He lifted her hands until they draped around the back of his neck, stretching her out and arching her into his chest.

Bolts of desire bulldozed through him until his world boiled down to how badly he wanted her. The hungry virus roiled, like an animal straining against a chain. He clamped down control. No way would Pele unleash the full force of his passion while fueled by a poorly controlled virus.

Turned out the hardest part of this mission would be taking care with her and going slowly. He didn't know if that was even possible with his altered nature.

He brushed his mouth over hers, another light touch, holding back, keeping his body as still as he could. His leg and back muscles quivered, so badly did he want to crush her to him, surround her with his body. After each feathered kiss, he pulled back a few millimeters, ensuring she wanted this, letting her respond.

Which she did. With interest. *Ti'o.*

When he dropped a kiss across the bow of her upper lip, then retreated, she followed, increasing the pressure and intensity. He tried to hold still. He tried to keep the kisses light.

Honestly, he tried.

Until she slid her fingers into his hair and pulled him closer with a rough, desperate movement and a sexy groan.

The kiss exploded into a firestorm of angles and pressures. Her soft mouth had unchained the beast. He entered her lips and tangled her tongue with his until he couldn't tell where he stopped and where she started. Her scent had become his. Her warmth. Those little gasps. His. The rhythm of his mouth aligned with the rocking motion of his hips.

She was the perfect fit for him. Tall enough that the top of her head came to his eye level. She was strong and unassumingly sexy. She met the thrusts of his hips with her own until a ringing in his ears began.

Leaving her mouth long enough to nip his way over her jaw and neck until she shuddered, he traveled back up to her ear and swept his tongue over the sensitive skin there. She moaned and squeezed the skin at the nape of his neck. The pinch heightened his desire, and he brushed an unsteady hand down, cupping her breast through the shirt fabric.

When he lifted the hem, she kissed him with a fierceness that drove his need even higher. Trailing his fingertips over her silky skin, he drew his hand up until he encountered the simple bra. He slid the material to the side and cupped the weight of her breast in his hand. Perfect.

The virus burned its way through every one of his cells. *Want. Need.* Pele was in so much trouble.

This mission... He was making the worst decisions for the best reasons. He should stop.

Should. Stop.

He nipped her lower lip, rolling her hard nipple between his thumb and index finger until he inhaled her moan as she arched into him. With his other hand, he palmed her lower back and pressed her hips against his. He was hard. Hungry.

He couldn't get enough of this woman. Couldn't kiss her enough, couldn't touch her enough. Couldn't complete his mission if she distracted him. Couldn't control the damned virus. *Ti'o.* He'd lost the ability to think.

All he could do was react.

"This is nice," he mumbled against her sweet mouth. "It's so much easier to keep an eye on you now."

Her breathy voice whispered over him. "What?" She bit off another moan as he moved his hand to the other breast and worked the nipple until she ground her hips against him.

"So much better, Reagan."

She leaned back. "Wait. What are you talking about?"

His brain had left him, and his throbbing, stupid body remained. Oh, yeah, and a stupid mouth that was running on viral instinct. "I wanted you safe, in a place where I could watch over you. This is perfect. Here. Together."

"The hell?"

He didn't register her pushing against him until she turned her head away from his eager mouth.

When he didn't let go, she rammed a knuckle into his chest, hard, the jolt of pain getting his attention in a hurry. Damned instincts from Special Forces, augmented by the vicious virus, fired up, and he spun her around and slammed her back flush against his chest, his arm looped tightly over her breasts.

"What are you doing?" she gasped.

Ti'o.

He released her like she was a live grenade, and he backed up. Damn his training. Damn the virus. Damn the asinine words that came out of his mouth. He was drowning. Glancing around the room, he tried to find something concrete and familiar. He couldn't find patterns. Couldn't focus.

"What did you say to me?" Her chest heaved as she adjusted her bra and tugged her shirt back down.

Think, man. Think. "Only that I wanted you safe.

With being out here alone in the woods and all." He gulped air. *Kefe*. The more he talked, the deeper a hole he dug. "And that I could watch you better if you were next to me."

"Next to you?" Her chest heaved. "You thought we were going to be next to each other tonight?"

"I hoped?" Was the attraction not mutual? He'd missed something important.

"Your plan for me…" she murmured. "Dammit. Not again." Staring at him until his knees shook, she finally said, "Why do you need to watch me?"

"Because it's not safe here."

"What are you talking about?" She rubbed her temples. "What the hell did I expect from a guy that told a story about a stalker eel. God, my life." Groaning, she raised a hand. "Okay, you know what? I'm not doing this. Screw it all. I'm done. Get out."

Now it was his turn to be confused. "What?"

"Get. Out." Her voice quivered. "PSTD or not, I don't know what kind of freaky game you're playing, but I'm not your pawn to manipulate into doing whatever you want."

The virus churned his brain to mush. "Um. I don't want to mold you. I want you to be yourself." He needed to stop saying words, now.

"The hell. You were seducing me … to keep me safe? That's the dumbest thing I've heard in a while." She pointed. "Don't ever try that move on me again."

"What?"

Her shoulders rose and fell as she pointed. "You do not get to mold me into someone I'm not. You don't get to control me." Her voice shook.

Whoa. He froze. Where did that statement come from? "Wait. What? You don't understand."

"Yes, I do. Perfectly. Good night."

He hooked her elbow, and she spun around, pulling away from him and pointing a finger at his chest. "Touch me again, Poindexter, and that'll be the last time you use your hand."

With superhuman effort, he clenched his jaw and suppressed the howling viral rage that wanted to both possess her and enter combat.

Where had sweet Reagan gone? The woman who told stories to the children. The woman who sighed at his kisses. The woman whose touch soothed him.

This furious woman quivering with stark terror written across her face had replaced her. Thanks to his ham-handed attempt to make his job easier, combined with his loss of control over the damned virus, this evening had turned into a downhill lava flow of bad decision-making.

"I wasn't going to—" Well. He wanted to. "You don't understand."

Her empty laugh chilled him. "I understand perfectly. You're no different than the other guys. You try to get what you want. You'll manipulate and hurt me to get it, and damn the consequences. Guess what? Not falling for it. It's not going to work." She held open the door. "Good night."

"But."

With a light shove that he could have easily overcome, but thank God his stupid brain knew enough to comply, she pushed him out the door and slammed it behind him.

Well, *kefe*. He was no Casanova, but this had to rate highly on the all-time seduction fails.

The bolt on the front door *thunk*ed into place, paltry protection against the force he was capable of wielding. He could go back in there anytime. He rolled his hands into fists, ready to break down the door. *Stop.*

No. What a disaster.

He exited the porch and stood in front of the cabin. A light came on in the cabin's great room window, then the blinds flicked shut.

That about summed up the night. Locked out.

Speaking of night, it was going to be a long, cold one, because he still couldn't leave his post here at the cabin. Why had he said what he was thinking? First rule of survival: *don't let women know everything that's on your mind.*

The first rule of the Morpheus Squad: *never lose control of the virus. Ever.*

Two missteps.

He spun on his heel and began the evening's patrol circuit as the quarter moon continued across the sky.

Chapter Eight

Reagan leaned against the cabin door as Pele's footsteps faded.

What the hell? Had she truly had an existential meltdown in the arms of a sexy man she had met a day ago? Way to go with the self-promise to not make rash decisions when it came to men.

But those kisses. A warm blast coiled in her chest, followed by a wave of terrible ice.

For a split second, she had been in a time warp. Instead of Pele's tanned skin and dark hair, she had inserted an image of her snarling, sarcastic ex. Complete with him yelling and pointing at his diplomas hanging on the wall of his fancy office. What a tool.

Okay, so that might not have been the healthiest of substitutions. Pretty unfair to Pele.

Those kisses.

She touched her tingling lips. She didn't dare touch other areas of her body that still pulsed. Damn it, his sexy mouth and demanding hands had transported her to a different place. For a moment, she had been under his spell, floating on a cloud of pure bliss. For a moment, she would have done anything for more of his kisses, more of those amazing strokes of his strong but gentle fingers over her skin. Her nipples tightened.

She swallowed an acidic taste that rose in her throat.

Her blissed-out feelings? Part of the scam that was All Men. Pele was no different than her ex. He wanted something from her and used his obvious charm to get it. Granted, Pele's M.O. might not have been for as cruel as a purpose as her ex's manipulation, but at least she recognized the pattern when she saw it this time. Still hurt.

The whole danger thing he rambled on about? This was Camp Foxfire. What the hell was he talking about? The worst creatures she had seen out here included a grumpy momma bear with two cubs, a skunk with a spray-control problem, and some mice that insisted on chewing through her tent a while back.

It had to be a ploy, a way to make her vulnerable enough to let Pele maneuver her emotions around. She had been used again. Damn it.

She paused. Her gut clenched.

What if he truly had PTSD like her brother? What if his actions were driven by sincere fear and personal hang-ups?

Clamping her lips together to hold back a sob, she paced the main room of the group cabin, her footsteps scuffing the worn carpet. She couldn't handle being confined in the small apartment downstairs. For now, she wanted to really wallow in this pissed-off state and walk around.

Because for a second there, she had trusted Pele's smiling, handsome face.

Because this might not be about Pele at all. This disaster could all have to do with her trust issues. Damn it.

Hopefully, a close call would scare the lesson into her, once and for all. Maybe not every handsome face hid an agenda, but damn it, she couldn't trust her judgment. She rubbed her cheek.

It was stupid, anyway. Hoping to find something that didn't exist: a guy who accepted her for the person she was, imperfections and all. A man who didn't interfere with her own choices. Like the story she told tonight, she wanted sovereignty. Shouldn't be too tall of an order.

Right?

Wrong.

A crackling sound outside the cabin made her jump. She listened, heart thudding. Another few crackles. Probably some deer wandering through or a squirrel foraging in dried leaves.

Damn it, she was safe here at camp, physically and emotionally.

Her coworkers accepted her. No one at Camp Foxfire wanted to change the person Reagan was deep down inside.

A sigh caught in her chest and twisted there.

She flicked off the main light and trudged down the stairs.

****

Pele scanned the woods with his IR scope once more before dialing the satellite phone from his position in a brush thicket. He kept staring into the shadows while the connection booted up. He adjusted the wireless earpiece. A few rings and security clicks came through the line as the call went through secure routers and bounced off multiple orbiting objects. A beep. A pause.

"Boss?"

"Pele. Situation?" Typical CO Hunt, cutting to the chase.

Pele tried not to laugh, but that was what this disaster of an op had boiled down to: a laughable mission. "Area is impossible to secure." He shifted, relieving the cramp in one thigh as he crouched. "What's the real likelihood of Lequire coming here? Because if he shows up, we're screwed."

"We're assessing fifty-fifty chance."

"*Kefe.*" Fuck.

His CO Hunt ripped off an orderly and proficient string of curses. "Since we last spoke over forty-eight hours ago, Kiera was kidnapped out from under our noses."

He gripped the phone. "What?"

"Right off our compound."

"With Stumpy's bulletproof security system?" If Lequire had no problem breaching the Morpheus Squad compound, then the residents of porous Camp Foxfire were in real trouble. He flipped the screen back to the dark cabin. Reagan was in her apartment below the cabin, preparing for bed.

He swallowed hard and blanked the screen.

"Didn't say I was happy about the breach." Hunt wasn't happy about anything these days.

"Is Kiera okay?" Pele peered up at twinkling stars through the treetops. "The baby?" Reagan's sister had been pretty far along. He held his breath.

"Baby came a little early during the wild ride back to the Ashe County compound. But mother and child are secure. Doc's got them taken care of."

"Wait. We moved?" Their Plan B compound was set in the extreme northwest corner of North Carolina, deep in the woods. Good for hiding the team but not for Pele. That meant backup was much further away than it had been. Great.

"Yep. Plan B."

"The Bryson City compound?"

"Ashes."

Just like Pele's mission. "So Lequire didn't get what he wanted. Bet he's pissed now."

"It's even worse."

What the hell could be worse than a power-hungry, wealthy CFO embezzling funds from veterans and using his senator father's clout for resources to take revenge on Kiera and her family?

"Okay, I'll bite."

"Lequire took a dose."

"Of *what*?" Pele's ears buzzed. *No, no, no.* He knew the answer to the question.

"He injected the virus. He's like us now."

Ten disciplined soldiers with the Morpheus Virus coursing through their veins was bad enough. An unhinged asshole with a nose for cruelty now possessing superpowers and an unlimited bank account? *Ti'o.* They were all in trouble.

"He'll never be like us." Pele whistled low. "What extra goodies did the virus give *him*?"

"Too early to tell."

Virus plus unhinged power-grubbing narcissist with impulse control issues. Terrible combo. "Does he have the antidote?"

"No idea."

"*Kefe.*"

"Took the word right out of my mouth. Assume that he's a ticking time bomb."

"Just as hard to kill, too." Each of the Morpheus Squad guys was durable. Not impossible to kill, given that one of their own, Mateo, had died in an exploding house in Atlanta less than a week ago. But in general, when the virus was on board, everything sped up—reaction times and healing ability.

Apparently, not the common sense to keep one's mouth shut. Damned virus helped exactly zero with that skill.

"Believe me, we tried to end him," Hunt gritted out. "It didn't take."

Suddenly, the pleasant forest hid every kind of evil imaginable, all aimed at Reagan. "So."

"Stay sharp and be ready for anything. He's got men out actively tracking in Atlanta, so Red has asked for help protecting Britt McNeill. If things get worse, I might send Rodeo down there." Another curse. "If Lequire isn't successful in Atlanta, it doesn't take a rocket scientist to guess where he's headed next."

"What about Mr. McNeill?" Reagan's widowed father was a tempting target, too, for a corrupt Lequire who would use anything and anyone as leverage to get to Kiera and the Morpheus Squad.

"Safe and hanging out with his new BFF, Rivera. They are a pool-shooting match made in heaven." A few taps on what sounded like the table. "Rivera has the situation locked down there."

Unlike at Camp Foxfire. "All right."

Back to the only person Pele needed to focus on at this time: Reagan. How much damage could an average supercharged madman bent on revenge rain down on the average environmental educator whose most dangerous days involved taking kids on hikes and teaching them crafts and stream ecology?

The image of Lequire's hands on Reagan iced Pele's blood. He swallowed around a hot lump in his throat. Tucking the phone between his jaw and shoulder, he checked his stashed weapons for the thousandth time today. It wasn't enough. None of it would be enough. "You have another five or fifty guys to spare? If Lequire's crew shows up here, we've got way too many soft targets and a total inability to secure the property."

"You'll have to improvise."

Pele shook his head. "And hope like hell he goes for Britt in Atlanta? Or that I can get lucky with an early warning and keep Reagan from ending up dead?"

"Something like that."

"Bad plan." He rubbed his thigh. "Sir. Can I take her out of here? Tell her what the hell is going on? Maybe she'll listen and go hunker down somewhere, like Maine. Or Antarctica."

"And expose Morpheus? Negative. The team has to remain secret. Too many people know about it already. It's our lives at stake. Our freedom. It's the safety of everyone in the world that's at stake, if that virus ever gets off the leash."

"So that's the plan: Do the best I can do with zero backup and minimal resources. Do not extract the target because of team security? And what? Hope for the best?" The tension in his shoulders ratcheted up a few more notches until his bones creaked. "We are in the middle of a slow-moving disaster. Sir."

"Be happy it's not a fast-moving disaster. It's shitty, but this is the only viable plan right now." The harsh breath followed by a juicy swear shot through the phone. "I'll mobilize help as soon as is feasible, but we're busy securing the Ashe County compound right now. Hadn't planned on using it this soon."

"Hadn't planned on a lot of things happening."

"Got that right, soldier."

Chapter Nine

Wednesday morning came way too early for Reagan's liking. She had slept two, maybe three, hours. Her hip throbbed from where she'd hit the step when Pele barreled into her with his metric ton of solid muscle last night. Her lips were sensitive to even the lightest touch, also thanks to a certain man's heady kisses. Worst of all, an empty space in her chest ached like the air had been vacuumed out.

What bothered her wasn't that she might have been played. She could deal with that betrayal—heck, she had a master's degree in being used.

What hurt most was that she had lost control and projected all of her baggage on him.

Hey, she had wanted him, fair and square. She responded to their mutual interest. Then she second-guessed herself and overreacted when he misspoke. That fact scared her more than anything.

No question, he'd come on too strong and that was on him, even if his actions were somehow driven by PTSD. His past was not her responsibility. However, she could have handled herself better. Her treatment of Pele had been unfair. The guy had gotten a double helping of her still-raw insecurities. Pele didn't deserve half of her reaction, and she never gave him a chance to explain himself.

Talk about a knee-jerk reaction.

For the past year, she had been continually told to change and how. Clayton's encouragement and support had eventually turned into prodding and snide remarks that eroded her emotionally and physically until she complied. Death by a thousand papercuts. Damn her messed-up brain and hating herself for falling for her ex's manipulation.

She pulled her braids forward and flipped up the hood of her sweatshirt. As she exited the cabin, the puffs of vapor when she exhaled and the frost on the leaves put the temperature right around the freezing mark. Cold morning for Kids' Archery and Outdoor Survival 101, but things would warm up quickly. At least teaching classes should take her mind off Pele. Unless Linda assigned him to Reagan again.

Reagan's stomach twisted into knots.

He had to own his actions, yes. But she wasn't innocent in last night's supernova. She needed to be an adult and try to smooth things over with him to maintain a professional working environment.

She did want to figure out why he had a weird hang-up about safety at camp. His jumpiness was wearing on her. Reminded of her brother after he came back from the Middle East. A different flash of déjà vu made her stumble. Something about Pele *was* familiar. She concentrated, but nothing tangible came to mind.

His hypervigilance had her looking over her shoulder in the one place she felt safest. Damn it. No. She would give him a chance to explain. Maybe he had his own fears and insecurities. What a concept—other people besides Reagan had issues.

A knot grew in her belly. She didn't want to face him.

The cold, damp morning air stung when she inhaled as she walked down the dirt path to the gravel road toward the dining hall. Already, she could hear the distant din of chattering kids getting ready for family-style breakfast.

With every step, she came closer to confronting Pele. She stuffed her hands into the front pocket of the hoodie. At least after today's classes, there were no more groups in the camp until Monday.

Four full days to think. Great.

Thank goodness she was meeting her friends tomorrow night for a well-deserved girls' night out. Reagan had been eagerly anticipating this date since Kate had emailed a few days ago and suggested it.

"Good morning."

She jumped out of her skin and spun around.

Pele had appeared as if out of thin air. He rubbed his thigh, and then froze and put his hand into a cargo pant pocket. The line of his massive shoulders nearly vibrated, he had such a rigid stance. He flicked his gaze around and behind her, like he expected the boogeyman to jump out of the woods at any moment.

"Hi," she said. After swallowing a lump that tasted a lot like shame, she began again. "So. I need to apologize."

"Ah, that's my line."

"Fair." Her chest hurt. "We can trade apologies. I'd like to go first."

His jaw dropped, then snapped closed. His dark gaze slid over her and away. "Want to go to the cabin to talk?" He lifted his head as if he smelled the air.

"No. Here will be fine."

His gaze darted in the direction of the gravel road and the trees. "It's—all right," he said. The lines of fatigue etched around his eyes and bracketing his mouth mirrored how she felt inside.

"You didn't deserve the full force of my personal issues."

Thick brows drew together. "What?"

"Long story short, I was burned by a guy emotionally and am still working through things. When you and I got close, my brain short-circuited. My baggage has nothing to do with you."

"I kn— Uh, what happened?"

Could she tell him? Heck, the people who'd been invited to her wedding didn't even know the truth. Only her friends and her younger sister, Britt, knew pieces of what happened. Not like telling the story could make things worse.

Worse? Like ripping open barely healed emotional scabs.

She stared at Pele. She was risking judgment.

Damn that sucking sensation again. Her entire chest wanted to cave in. "My ex and I broke up several months ago."

Please don't let him give the pitying look. Anything but that.

Only a hard glint to his brown eyes. "Why?"

"Why?" Few people had the guts to ask that question.

She rubbed the right side of her neck. Damn Clayton. With a conscious effort, she lowered her hand. "Well. It's complicated. Long story short, we were engaged to be married. A few weeks before the wedding, we called it off."

"Both of you?"

"Yes, for different reasons."

"Why?"

She brushed her fingertips over her cheek. *Quit it.* No way was she sharing the whole story. Shame warmed her neck. "My fiancé, Clayton, wanted me to change a few things, then it became more things. Then it became too many things. Big things."

A muscle in his cheek jumped. "Like what?"

"Well, a couple of months before the wedding, he had gotten a hell of a promotion from the Knoxville branch of a national finance firm. He was under a lot of pressure to present an image of corporate success ... both in the office and outside of it."

Damn it, she was still making excuses for him. Hadn't that been thoroughly addressed during counseling? "My job out here in the boonies didn't fit with his ideal picture of the society wife of a rising-star financial analyst in one of the Big Five accounting firms. He was taking a huge step into a high-powered position. His job meant that he had to wine and dine clients. Project an image of corporate success in all aspects of his life."

"All aspects of his life." Pele's controlled, low voice scared her. The guy held still like a calm puma a split second before it pounced and ripped the head off a small animal.

"He needed a certain kind of wife, and I didn't fit the profile. It wouldn't be possible to do this"—she motioned with her hand at the camp in general—"in those social circles." She shrugged. "I was prepared to find another job. But it wasn't enough. He wanted me to attend a kind of finishing school so I would gain 'more refinement' around his rich clients."

"Are we in the 1800s?" Pele spat.

"Nope. We are, however, in the south. In certain circles, there are unspoken rules and expectations of what constitutes an image of success."

"Sounds ridiculous."

"It is what it is." She toyed with the strings at the collar of the hoodie. "What's bad is that I considered changing for even a minute."

"Wait. I don't get it. *He* asked *you* to marry him."

"Yes, but after he got the promotion, he started dropping hints about how I could improve. Sure, he wanted me, but he made it clear he'd want me more with some … significant upgrades." She brushed her fingers over her neck. God, she recalled how he'd slapped her right on the neck that one night, when they had argued about the procedure to treat it.

"What?" He growled. "The birthmark?"

"He wanted it gone." She took a shaky breath. "Actually, he said he wanted to marry me, 'no matter how I looked,' which somehow felt worse. Then he explained how he wanted to be proud to have me by his side at corporate events, which meant I needed to do something about my job and wifely image and the birthmark, so that I wouldn't, as he said, 'distract clients.'"

"What a *puaaelo*." He pressed his mouth into a hard line.

"A what?"

A hint of a dimple, then it was gone. "Samoan word. Roughly means *stinking pig*."

She giggled in spite of unhappiness prickling her gut. "That's similar to what my younger sister, Britt, called him."

"She's right." Pele frowned. "I'd like to have a word in private with this ... man."

"Dad covered that base already." Her laugh came out wrong. All grim, bitter, and empty. Forced.

"Were you going to remove the birthmark?" he asked. "Not that you should. It's part of the person you are."

"It's okay. You don't have to be nice. I know what it looks like." When he opened his mouth, she cut him off with a slash of her hand. She didn't need platitudes or sympathy. She'd had her fill of atta-girls and was sick to death of them. "My type of port-wine stain doesn't respond well to laser treatment. They tried it when I was a child. Very painful, but no improvement."

He winced.

God, please don't let him feel sorry for me.

Crossing his arms, he said, "Where I'm from, birthmarks are considered blessings from the gods."

"Too bad I was born here, huh?"

He didn't laugh.

She barreled ahead. "Anyway, Mom and Dad taught me how to respond when people asked questions. My brother, Brady, was great for managing bullies." A stab of sadness hit her in the chest. With his death following closely after Mom's, then canceling the wedding, she still reeled from all of it.

"Other kids made fun of you?"

"Well, of course. Pretty easy target." She shoved her hands back into the front hoodie pocket.

"I can relate, but still, that's horrible."

"Let's say I learned who my friends were." She tried to remain objective. "Anyway, Clayton really wanted the birthmark off. The only other procedure available for me was a large area skin graft."

"Sounds painful."

"Painful, dangerous, and with risk of complications. At one point, he demanded that I do the procedure as a condition of getting married."

"No." His hands curled into massive fists. His eyes darkened.

She leaned away from the hot wave of anger rolling off him. "It's no excuse, but I do think the pressure of his job drove a lot of his bad behavior."

"No. That's not an excuse." He studied her until her knees shook. "What else happened?"

"Anyway, to wrap up this pathetic story, we had a … rough conversation." Her back still ached after the blows he had landed there. "Then we agreed to call off the wedding two weeks before the date."

"You're not telling the whole story," he said with

a growl. His quiet, low voice held the promise of retribution. For a moment, Reagan fantasized about how Clayton would fare against Pele. Poorly.

"It's my story to tell."

A pause. "You're right." A muscle jumped in his jaw. "Still. What a bastard."

She shrugged. "Hey, my bad for sticking with him as long as I did."

Pulling his head back, he said, "Wait. You think his bad behavior is somehow your fault?"

"Not exactly." She waved her hand. "Whatever." Anything to end this uncomfortable talk. "He did say he wanted to work things out."

"Like how?" he spat. The fierce edge to his voice had her taking a full step back. "Like, if you got the surgery, then he could see how it turned out and make his decision?"

"Well. That's the gist of it." When he opened his mouth, she raised her palm again. "I don't want sympathy. God knows, I'm sick and tired of people feeling sorry for me. I don't need solutions, either. I'm only telling you this so you understand some of the background to my super-sized meltdown last night. I'm sorry. You were the recipient of a lot of baggage that had nothing to do with you."

"It's understandable." His scowl deepened and he flicked another glance behind her. "Everyone has things they have to deal with."

Another weird déjà vu flash hit her and then dissipated.

"Yes. True. Well, um, I hope we can still have a good working relationship." Her cheeks felt way too warm as his gaze landed fully on her.

He didn't move.

She didn't move. When he stared at her like that,

she wanted to hide.

"Of course, Reagan. Apology accepted. Everyone has a bad day." Then he smiled, and heaven help her, but the dimple that winked on his cheek somehow made the morning sky brighter.

She stood there, speechless.

After kicking a piece of gravel and clearing his throat a few times, he finally met her eyes, and the dark intensity in his stare made her breath catch.

"My turn," he said. "I was in the wrong last night." Another pivot on one foot. "Someday, I'd like another chance, but this time without me screwing things up. Like I said, everyone has things they have to deal with." A crease to his brow came and went. "No excuses. I moved way too fast."

"No, but—"

He raised his hand, and somehow she didn't flinch at the action when it was Pele doing it.

"It's okay," he said. "I own my part and apologize for my own … baggage … that makes me act differently."

Despite herself, Reagan grinned. The tight vise around her heart loosened a tiny bit.

With a lift to one shoulder, he added, "*Ti'o*, but you're a hard woman to resist."

Right. Now he was patronizing her. "Stop it. I said no sympathy. You don't have to be nice."

"I say what I mean, Reagan. Sympathy?" His barked laugh echoed in the cool morning. "That's the last thing I feel. Being nice? When I'm around you, *nice* is the last thing I want to be." He licked his lips and took a half step forward. "What I desire has nothing to do with a good working relationship."

Something coiled, delicious and warm in her belly, and honest to God, she leaned forward. "What?

Why are you saying this?"

He rubbed his thigh. "I thought we were being honest."

"Yes, but—"

"You don't think that's the truth?"

"I..." She shivered, despite herself. "I want it to be the truth."

"One day, I hope you'll let me prove how much I believe my words." He slowly raised his hand, gaze watchful.

She didn't move as he brushed a rough fingertip over the birthmark on her cheek. His eyes darkened as he took one step back and then another, curling his fingers into his palm and cupping his other hand around the fist.

Then he blinked and the thick emotion dissipated like Smoky Mountain mist in the sunshine.

His big chest rose and fell. "For now, let's educate some kids. Then tonight, maybe you would be open to having a meal together. Deal?" He stuck out his big hand.

When he closed his hand around hers, the warmth went straight through her all the way down to her toes. Which was ridiculous, because it was only a meal with a friend. It wasn't a date. Was she jumping from a frying pan into the fire?

God, she hoped not.

"Deal," she agreed.

Chapter Ten

He hadn't completely destroyed all of his chances with Reagan.

But he'd have to be more careful. For such a tough woman on the outside, her fragile heart still needed protecting. There was more to her story that she wasn't telling him, judging by the lines between her eyebrows and the twist of that sexy mouth.

The virus roared, begging Pele to find that ex-fiancé and ram a fist through the bastard's face. He held his breath and reached for his calming technique. He studied the archery students: friend or enemy? Friend or enemy? Laughing girl? Friend. Runny-nosed boy? Friend. He went down the line of children until the impulses receded.

How could that *puaaelo* hurt such a beautiful and strong woman? Another wave rose up.

What? Now you've become both her physical and *emotional protector? This is a job. A mission op. Nothing more.*

For his mission to succeed, he needed her to trust him so he could stay close to her. For safety reasons. Successful completion of the op. That was all.

No, that wasn't all. He needed to check his camera traps. There was no time to do his job. His real job.

He guided a girl in how to use the bow and arrow. Her small hands wrapped around the grip, pulled the string back, and let go with a *twang*. Miss. Pele handed her another arrow, trying to stay attentive.

Would Pele ask Reagan to change, like her ex-fiancé had?

His first instinct? No, he would never ask her to

change.

But hadn't he complained years ago about dating *palagi* women? *Palagi*. Non-Samoan. His parents always encouraged him to marry a Samoan and keep with tradition. So long ago. Before the experiment with the virus.

Before he became who he was today. A different person. An incomplete person.

Would Pele be happy with a woman who had no connection to his culture? He wasn't in a position to make demands of anyone. He wasn't even part of his own culture anymore. He rubbed his thigh. Not after taking the virus. His current family was now the motley bunch of mutant brothers-in-arms.

Besides, what fantasy did he live in, thinking there was a chance for something real with a woman like Reagan? He had nothing to offer.

Pele technically did not exist. A life lived off the record, and any partner would have to disappear their entire life, too.

With his body and mind altered by the virus, no sane woman would want Pele and his chained monster inside. Even if a cure could be developed, no one knew if it would work. No one knew how long the antidote shots would keep the virus from pushing the men over into madness. If he lost control, he could hurt someone.

None of that mattered. He had a job to do.

His job? It had become one huge, deadly joke.

He surveyed the vulnerable open field with the hay bales and targets set up, then assessed the surrounding forest. His virus-enhanced vision didn't find any abnormal patterns in the light and shadows, but that didn't mean they were safe. The temperature had warmed up into the sixties. Thermal imaging would be less effective. He patted the sat phone in his left pants pocket, right next to his knife strapped flat to his leg. Moved his ankles, feeling the bump of weapons in the boots.

Even armed, there was zero way for one man to secure the area.

Reagan's coppery-blonde braids and sun-blushed skin glowed in the mid-morning light as she walked behind several budding archers, giving instructions and encouragement. She'd pulled the hood of her jacket down, which meant he could better see her smile. Suited him fine.

Focus on the job.

The child in front of him picked up a plastic arrow.

Not this job. The real *job.*

Here was what Pele knew: Last night's patrols and last night's kisses had left him exhausted, edgy. He was losing focus. All his efforts to get closer to Reagan had crashed and burned like a chunk of ejected lava exploding in the night sky. He needed help.

His virus raged against the invisible chains. It sure as hell didn't like the idea of sharing Reagan's protection duties. Pele wanted to do it himself.

Because he was a professional? Yeah. That.

He ducked as his buddy from the stream ecology class turned around to ask him a question, with the nocked plastic arrow aimed at Pele.

"Whoa." He put his hand on the top of the bow and aimed it at the ground. "Remember, never point this, or any weapon, at anyone. You could hurt someone."

"Yes, sir," the boy said. "Can you help me? It's not working."

Pele spent several minutes correcting the boy's stance and pull. The child let the arrow fly and managed to hit the bale.

"Wahoo! Thanks, Mr. Pele."

"Good job. Keep practicing, and you'll be a champion shot." He patted the boy on his head and paused. He had lost his chance to have a child, thanks to the Army's offer of complimentary vasectomies after receiving the virus. Offer. More like a high-pressure mandate. An ache grew in his chest. He'd never have a son or daughter of his own with whom to enjoy outdoor activities.

He'd never risk passing on the virus to his offspring.

When he stood up, Pele scanned and homed in on Reagan. She had a thoughtful tilt of her head as she watched him. Then she knelt down to help another student, and the rise and fall of her voice moved like the breeze over the archery range.

He passed a hand over his face and rubbed hard. Now was not the time to get googly-eyed. He had to maintain Reagan's safety. Nothing more.

What if he wanted more?

Ti'o. Didn't matter. There would never be a good time, with his obligation to the team. His schedule didn't look good for any long-term plans. Hell, the schedule didn't look good for short-term plans at the rate his mission was tanking.

****

When the school bus full of shouting, laughing kids pulled away after lunchtime that same Wednesday, complete with lots of little hands waving out the windows, Reagan breathed a sigh of relief. Normally, the staff of Camp Foxfire rolled from one school group into another with a quick turnaround of the facility. However, they had a rare break until Monday. Thank goodness.

She sniffed. The scent of wood smoke lingered in the valley. Her outdoor survival class involved teaching the kids to start fires. Always a dicey activity with second-graders, but they loved it. Then together, they all built an emergency shelter out of dead tree limbs and leaf litter, which each child crawled into to test it out.

Put a fork in her, Reagan was done for the day. She pulled a twig from a braid, gave one more weary wave at the bus, and lifted her face to the sunshine. The temperature had warmed up to the seventies. Perfect.

The week wasn't done. Not quite yet. Tomorrow, she and the rest of the staff had cleanup duties as they transitioned the camp from winterized cabins to warm-weather-ready facilities. The to-do list Linda had was a mile long, but at least Reagan had dibs on leaving early tomorrow for the evening out with her girlfriends.

She sighed. What she'd give for a nap. But she couldn't rest. She needed some breathing space away from Pele before her head and heart imploded. Fortunately, Linda assigned him along with Chad and Jamila to inventory the arts and crafts cabin and clear brush on the trails, and the trio headed off to do so for the next few hours.

Should be enough time. Earlier in the day, Reagan had thought over what Pele had said about being away from his home. His culture. Pacific islands must feel way different than the landlocked Smoky Mountains. A literal entire world away.

Sitting in the office, she clicked through a website. She leaned forward, studied instructions, and took copious notes. An ingredient list. Yes. She could pull off this project. She Googled another query. Good. A specialty store in the nearby town of Maryville should have most of what she needed.

Hopefully, she was looking at a two-hour trip, leaving the camp and going up and over the winding road on Chilhowee Mountain to get to Maryville and back. Barely enough time.

As she swung her backpack over her shoulder, she surveyed the gravel parking lot in front of the office and dining hall. Empty. Perfect.

Why sneak off? Because Pele had been sticking with her like stink on a hog since his first day here at camp. Not that she minded his company—when he wasn't upsetting her equilibrium—but today's trip needed to be a solo endeavor if she was going to pull off the … peace offering.

Hurrying to her old brown Ford, she tossed the backpack on the front seat and fired up the truck's engine, saying thanks when the temperamental machine turned over on the first try. With the shriek of an unhappy engine belt, the truck bounced down the gravel camp road onto Happy Valley Road.

A few minutes later, a dark-blue truck appeared in the rearview mirror. Toyota, judging by the silver logo on the front grille. Odd, only because there were about ten houses in Happy Valley and she was familiar with what most folks in this small valley drove.

No one in the mountains drove a Toyota.

Fine, some folks did drive Toyota trucks, but they got razzed for it by die-hard Ford and Chevy owners. She wasn't saying that was right, it was just the way things were.

Tourist? Wrong season for it. She squinted, but the tinted windshield didn't reveal anything about the occupant.

Taking a right, she maneuvered up switchbacks to the gap in the ridge of Chilhowee Mountain. The shiny truck trailed her. Not a crime. This was the most direct route to town from the valley. Yet, she kept an eye on the vehicle. Was it too close? Not close enough?

Great. Now Reagan imagined danger all around her, thanks to Pele and his paranoia.

She rolled down the window and continued down the mountain, through the curvy roads until the terrain flattened out on the final stretch to Maryville. As she passed by more homes, a minivan pulled out of one of the neighborhoods and tucked in behind her. Another glance in the rearview a few minutes later revealed the van only, no truck.

She exhaled.

Why the stress and relief? Because Pele projected his issues onto her. Good grief.

After several weeks in the mountains, the suburban houses on manicured green lawns giving way to the busier streets and stores in downtown Maryville always jarred her senses. Soon, she had concrete and traffic all around. She pulled into the World Foods parking lot.

A promising name for what she wanted to accomplish. She was doing this for Pele because she wanted to be nice and because she felt bad about his situation and her overreaction. Making peace. No other reason.

Heart light, she hummed along to the radio as she turned off the vehicle and glanced around the parking lot. No blue trucks. See? Imagining things.

She checked her phone.

Solid five-bar cell phone signal. About time. A red dot appeared, indicating a text message. Probably from one of her friends regarding tomorrow's girls' night out.

She tapped on the screen, still humming to herself.

Call me, please. I want to try again. I'm sorry. I will do better.

Clayton Carpenter.

What. The. Actual. Hell?

She couldn't breathe. Anger, bizarre laughter, and disbelief stunned her stupid. Unable to move, she gaped at the phone.

Then the screen showed dots. He was typing. Of course, because if he was monitoring closely, he could see the minute when she read a text. Damn it.

Sweat broke out between her breasts despite the mild spring day. She shrugged out of her hoodie and clutched her phone in front of her.

Can we get coffee and talk?

Her stomach knotted. How could Clayton do this? Now? Her back ached and her eyelids burned.

She paused, heart hammering away beneath her ribs.

Then reality hit her like a one-two reminder punch. His so-called love had come with a boatload of conditions and a dinner-sized helping of pain. Even if he'd changed his mind and even if he said all the right things, he would never be satisfied with Reagan as is. She would always know he wanted her to be different. "Improved."

She'd never stop wondering when he'd hurt her again.

Nope.

As much as she would love to have someone to call her own, this guy wasn't that person. Never would be. To hell with Clayton.

Hitting the *delete* button on his messages was a pleasure. Blocking his number—pure bliss.

Speaking of almost being married, she still had her wedding dress packed up in a box somewhere. Trissa and Kate, her friends she was meeting tomorrow night, might have a ritual for burning the dress in effigy while also putting a hex on her ex. Or maybe she could sell that crinoline and satin monstrosity. The lace train alone needed its own zip code and extra handlers.

Her friends had been awesome when Reagan and jerk-pants had called the wedding off, with the timing about as close as a gal could come without actually getting to wear the dress. After today's boneheaded text from Clayton, she was hoping her friends could come up with another voodoo doll, complete with a penis, all the better to stab with needles.

She shut off the phone and tossed it in her purse.

Good riddance.

She'd rather be alone than be tied to a guy like that.

So, she did what any red-blooded woman would do when life threw her a curveball. She fished out the list and went shopping.

After splurging on an organic latte with extra cream, she browsed the store. The act of wandering the aisles soothed her nerves, and she worked on her project list.

A zip of excitement went through her as she collected items. Would Pele like it?

She reread the list. When she couldn't find all the ingredients, a helpful clerk suggested substitutions. She paid the bill and jumped back into her truck a few minutes after two o'clock.

If she hurried, she could get back, start the fire, and hopefully have food ready by dinnertime.

Dinner.

But not a date.

Chapter Eleven

Where had Reagan gone?

The minute he could leave the arts and crafts inventory without completely blowing his cover, Pele raced to his small room beneath the large group lodge near the dining hall. He grabbed the laptop, shoved it into a backpack, and ran up the hill to an empty, open gravel parking pad. A quick scan of the area confirmed that he was alone. His shoulders knotted.

Where was she?

At least he had a decent satellite signal in this spot. Damned cold at nighttime, but this location had worked in a pinch when he hadn't been able to leave the premises earlier in the week. The screen blinked on, and the map centered on a glowing dot.

The muscles in his back relaxed.

There. The tracking device he'd planted on her truck appeared as a blip on the screen. He leaned forward and zoomed out the map. Maryville? Why hadn't she told him she was leaving?

Because she didn't know she was in danger. Also, Reagan was a grown woman who did not need to check in with him when she did normal adult activities. Or any activities.

He rechecked his trail cams. Nothing in the traps. No patterns out of the ordinary. He turned in a circle again. Green shoots and a few buds pushed up from under the leaf litter nearby. Tiny green leaves emerged from trees. Birds chirped as they flitted from branch to branch. A normal, pleasant March day in the mountains.

With deadly potential.

At least his trail cams worked. Earlier today, his phone had buzzed activity alerts a few times, all for animals passing by. No humans.

So far so good. Maybe Lequire wouldn't come after Reagan after all. And maybe Pele's balls would turn into coconuts and fall from trees.

The blip on the screen followed a switchback road slowly up toward the top of a mountain ridge, heading back in the general direction of Camp Foxfire. His gut churned. What if she got in an accident on the steep terrain? What if Lequire's people ran her off the road or cut her brake lines?

Here he was, in camp, cooling his heels. Needing something to do, he activated the satellite phone and called in to work.

"Hunt," came the brusque voice on the other end of the line.

"Checking in," Pele said.

"Update." Static crackled. Still not great reception.

"No sightings. Any news on Lequire? Or the other targets?"

"You haven't told Regan anything, have you?"

He rubbed his hand over his thigh. "No sir. She's completely in the dark." He paused. "Though I don't think withholding this information is appropriate."

"If nothing comes of this op, then exposing us would have been the wrong decision. Understand?"

"Yes, sir."

"Sure as hell no one gets to be privy to information that could destroy *my* life and the lives of my team members," Hunt said with a growl. "If the wrong person squeals about Morpheus Squad and the virus, our existence ends. Finito."

"Roger that. Still don't like it."

"The less Reagan knows, the better, in case she's compromised."

Pele froze and ran a hand over the small Sig tucked into the waistband at his lower back. "Compromised?"

"Kidnapped. Or worse."

"What's worse?" Tortured. Made to talk.

"Someone tried to kill Britt last night."

The youngest sister? *Ti'o.* "Lequire's men?" He kept one eye on the tracking signal on the map. Reagan's truck was still heading in this direction.

"Who else?" Hunt barked.

Good point. "Is she okay? Did Red stop them?" His buddy had some impressive skills in the silent and deadly killer department. But even virally enhanced soldiers had their limits.

"Yes, they're fine for now. Rodeo's heading there to help."

"Everything else all right at the base?"

"Affirmative. Kiera and baby are doing fine. Doc's checking them every day."

"What about Jake?" His team member had been key in rescuing Reagan's sister.

A pause. "We haven't seen Jake since he took off once Kiera and the baby were safe."

"He's coming back?"

"Unknown. I'm giving him space for now. He's got personal shit to work out. I may need him to shelve the issues and help out soon."

Pele filled his lungs and let out the air in a whoosh, continuing to monitor the sights and sounds around him. "When he returns, maybe he can give me a hand."

"Even if I could spare someone, I can't send Jake. Reagan knows him from high school and his friendship with Brady."

"I meant for the covert portion."

"Too risky."

"Anyone else free?" The blip on the screen had crossed over a saddle high up on a nearby mountain and was traveling down more switchbacks. He gritted his teeth and glanced at his watch. She should be here in twenty minutes, tops.

Hunt exhaled what Pele knew was a barrel chest full of air. "Negative. Too many moving parts with this Lequire problem. We can't spare anyone. I'm monitoring the situation in Atlanta."

"Do you think he'll ignore Reagan and try to take Britt?" He gripped the phone. Not that Pele wanted anyone to be harmed, but if Lequire's focus was on the younger sister, Pele could ease up on the one-man job here.

"I assume nothing. Lequire's a snake in the grass. I don't trust anything about him, other than he's a lying, cheating son of a bitch."

"Sounds like I'm on my own. Maybe it's less likely he'll target Reagan."

"You know what they say about assuming." A growl.

"End point for this op?"

His boss laughed, the sound like that of rocks tumbling. "Hopefully Lequire's death and soon. We threw these three surveillance and protection ops together at the last minute. You'll have to stay blended in over there and maintain readiness."

"Roger, sir. Will try to make the situation work."

"That's why I put you on this mission. I trust you being there on your own."

Pele ran a hand through his hair and then made a fist. "The vote of confidence is appreciated, but this is not a one-man job."

"If all I have is one operative, then you're the one

I want on this assignment."

"Thanks, boss."

"Hopefully this will end soon. The boys miss your home cooking."

Pele chuckled as he shut off the satellite phone and stowed it. With one more recheck of the blip on the map—still moving steadily closer—he turned off the equipment.

Not quite three o'clock. He would give Reagan a little time and space before casually dropping by her cabin for more surveillance. He needed to grab an hour or so of shut-eye before he went psychotic from the lack of REM sleep. He patted his pocket holding the alarm device.

There were enough cameras and sensors around her cabin in several concentric detection circles that he should have enough time to get there if anyone breached the perimeter.

Chapter Twelve

Ninety minutes later, Pele strolled up the gravel road toward Reagan's cabin. When he smelled smoke, he picked up the pace.

A pop like a gun being fired was followed by a scream.

His pulse pounded as he sprinted at full speed. Glancing at the woods, he didn't see any movement or abnormal sounds. Just Reagan jumping up and down. Had she been shot? In a split-second assessment, he scanned her from head to toe as he ran toward her. Where was the wound? Blood?

"Ow, ow, ow!" she yelped.

Sweat broke out on his forehead.

Kefe. He'd failed. Lequire's people had gotten to her while Pele had let down his guard. Why hadn't the motion detectors alerted him? Air sawed in and out of his lungs. How badly had she been hurt?

He skidded to a stop close to her.

Reagan hopped on one foot while waving long, metal tongs in her hand. A few ripe curses escaped her downturned mouth. Her braids flew as she spun around.

Several feet away, a fire blazed in a pit about three feet wide.

On top of the burning wood was a clump of sizzling rocks.

Kapow!

Another stone rocketed down the hillside. Reagan ducked and shrieked, covering her head. The tongs quivered like lopsided antennas as she kept her hands on top of her head.

Still jumping on one foot, she looked like a deranged alien, dressed in a short-sleeved t-shirt and jeans, metal tongs perched above her bare head.

"What's going on?" he roared. "Are you okay?"

"Sort of." She panted and cringed.

"Hurt?" He surveyed her body. No visible blood, no obvious head injuries. Arms and legs appeared unharmed.

"Not really."

The fire. The noise. *Ti'o*. This scene broadcast her position to anyone who wanted to find her.

Her wide blue eyes locked onto his. "Stay back!" Limping over to him, she grimaced and gave him a lopsided smile.

"Are you okay?"

Another rock cracked and she flinched, her cheeks flushed. "Oh, sure."

His redlining stress level receded a few points, and the muscles in his arms loosened. Pele stepped between Reagan and the fire. "What are you doing?"

When she rubbed her nose, a sooty mark remained. It took all of his willpower not to wipe the mark away. Despite the op procedures and the adrenaline still coursing through his veins, he smiled at her flushed face and singed hairline.

"You said we were having dinner tonight." She pointed the tongs at him.

He paused and took in the entire scene. "Yes. But not exploding dinner." Another low crack came from deep inside the fire pit, and she ducked. "What is this?"

"So you know how you mentioned missing American Samoa?" She winced at another deep, grinding pop, then glanced at him from under her blonde eyelashes. "Yeah. I tried to make an *umu* to use for cooking. Thought you might like it." He had to strain to hear the last bit as she mumbled.

"A what?" His jaw dropped. How would she have

known? His heart paused for a solid five seconds until his head swam.

"*Umu*? A traditional earth oven on hot rocks?" She shrugged with a wary half-smile.

"Holy crap, you're cooking Samoan? For me?" Security concern warred with frank astonishment and admiration.

She lowered her hands from her head. "Quite badly, it would appear."

At another whistle and pop from the fire pit, a chuckle started low in Pele's gut until it rang out in a belly laugh, a sound he hadn't made in years. He wrapped his arms around her and turned so his back faced the fire. At least he could protect her from the steaming rock grenades. The happiness rose up from his soul and burst out like the rocks flying off the fire. He couldn't stop, the laughter felt so good as it shook his entire body and Reagan's as she remained in his arms. Glancing over her head, he spied the brown bags of groceries on the porch, as well as cutting boards and knives.

Another crack preceded the ping of a rock off his lower leg. Damn, that stung. Why were so many rocks exploding? Normal *umu* rocks didn't have this volatile behavior. He frowned as he studied the fire over his shoulder.

The rocks sizzled and hissed.

He glanced toward the bottom of the narrow valley at the burbling creek, then back to the fire pit. She had used soaking-wet river rocks.

The steam building up inside each rock was creating mini bombs, but damn it, she had tried. Of course, they were both going to have concussions before transferring any actual food onto the stones. Didn't matter. He couldn't stop chuckling.

"I hope you're not laughing at me," she mumbled against his neck. The motion of her mouth on his skin sent a warm swirl deep into his belly.

"Not at all," he said. "Okay, a little bit." He inhaled the combination of mountain air, her fresh scent, campfire, and the faint mixture of spices from the bags of food.

She leaned back and scowled at him. That smudge mark drove him crazy. He used his flannel shirt sleeve and wiped the soot off. With effort, he stepped away from her.

Her shoulders slumped in defeat. The tongs dangled from her hand. "Setting up an *umu* sounded easy from what I read on the internet."

"You researched how to do this?"

"Yes."

No one had ever done anything so thoughtful before. Unfortunately, the timing sucked, along with the exposure. "Wow. Okay. Then let's see if we can salvage this *umu* you worked so hard to build. Safety first. Do you have anything like a grill or barbeque grate?"

"Behind the cabin, there's an old rusted Weber."

"Pull off the cooking grill. That will be fine for now. We need to direct the explosions away from us until the rocks are done steaming."

As she ran behind the cabin, he whipped out his phone and checked on all the security feeds, ensuring that the furthest perimeter traps were armed and would notify him immediately if anything tripped them. This outdoor dinner had *bad idea* written all over it. His skin crawled.

What could he do? He could shut it down now and devastate her after all the effort.

Damn it all, he'd like a traditional meal. He'd like one night of a normal existence. That wasn't too much to ask for a guy who had sacrificed his entire life to the Army and his teammates.

Loud metal clanks and muffled curses made him laugh again. She returned with a round, rusty grate, the metal tongs still extended, like a medieval knight ready to do battle with a shield and sword.

He accepted the grate and made a fire-pit-plus-grate lean-to where the open end faced out away from Pele and Reagan. Much better. At least now they were less likely to die if another stone launched itself out of the fire. Other than the risk of death, this was an excellent fire, burning hot and clean. Perfect *umu* temperature.

When he walked back over, the eager lift to her eyebrows had him smiling again. She still held the tongs.

"So, let me mention a couple of items of cultural interest," he said, gently extricating the tongs from her clutched fist. "First of all, wet rocks for an *umu* are dangerous." He held a hand up in surrender when she planted a fist on her hip and scowled. "Don't blame me—it's the truth. Second, you have no idea how much I appreciate you making this meal. But did you know that the men in Samoa prepare the oven and do all the cooking?"

"That was not in my admittedly cursory Google search."

He grinned at the cute, perplexed quirk to her mouth. "Being able to prepare food and provide for one's family is a key part of what makes for a strong man. Not only did my dad teach us everything he knew when we were growing up, but when I spent time back in American Samoa, my relatives turned me into an expert on indoor and outdoor cooking."

"Oh, so this isn't that big of a deal for you then."

He dropped his empty hand on her shoulder and

gave a light squeeze. What he really wanted to do was haul her into his arms and kiss her until she couldn't stand. But he needed to handle her with care. He didn't miss the wary fear that still flashed when he touched her. Like she expected him to betray her trust. Understandable, since his entire presence here was a lie.

Or she expected him to injure her.

Never going to happen.

"Reagan, thank you." He paused to swallow. Must be allergies from the woods making his voice rough. "This is the nicest thing anyone has ever done for me."

"Except for the part where you might die." Her wry smile and tilt of her head made him chuckle again.

He patted her shoulder, then stepped away. "You know, I've always felt that *abject fear* was the ingredient missing from my cooking all these years."

Now Reagan laughed in earnest, and the uninhibited, effervescent sound that echoed in the woods erased the fatigue and stress he'd been trying to manage. What an amazing woman.

Her blue eyes danced as she held her midsection.

"You should stand back while I work some culinary magic." He felt lighter. The modified earthen oven, the wood smoke, her laughter—it all blended into a great combination.

For the first time in years, he felt truly accepted by someone outside of his team. He was as comfortable as a hypervigilant, virally altered soldier on a covert mission could be, right at this moment.

After rearranging the stones and the protective grate, he went over to the porch, Reagan trailing behind him. It was four thirty in the afternoon, so he would have enough light to prepare food outside. Exactly how he preferred it.

He excused himself for a few minutes, on the pretext so that he could duck around the back of the cabin and sweep the area with the thermal scope and check the trail cam alarm again. Nothing on the cam. No alarms going off. He scanned the area visually. No patterns. He checked all of his hidden weapons for the hundredth time today.

For the next hour or so, he could feel normal. They could enjoy this treat as long as he stuck close to her.

Which would be his pleasure.

Returning to the porch, he laid out the contents of the bags and gave a low whistle. "How did you get all these things?"

"Specialty store in Maryville. I, um, had to substitute a few things that they didn't have."

He lifted a can. "Coconut cream! My favorite. Ripe bananas and banana fronds! You even got a tuna steak and real coconuts? How did you find taro leaves? You're amazing." The words were out of his mouth before he could stop them.

She froze, gaze locked on him. Then she blinked and shot him a shy half-smile. "Glad you know what all the ingredients are for. I wasn't exactly sure what to do with all of it."

He made an exaggerated sweep of his arm, widened his stance, puffed out his chest, and made a show of stretching out his arms and rolling his shoulders. "Step back, madam. Give the chef some space."

"No problem. I mean, I already did the hard part, getting the fire going." Flinching at another loud pop, she dropped her forehead into her palm.

He laughed out loud. Peering into the last bag, he frowned. "What's this?"

"Dessert."

His brows drew further together. "Graham crackers and marshmallows?"

"And chocolate bars. To make S'mores." She tilted her head. "No? Never heard of them?"

"I've heard the word, but never had one."

"You're kidding." She gasped and pressed a hand to her sternum. "S'mores are campfire staples around these parts." With a pause, she glared at the food. "I have no idea how they pair with Samoan cuisine."

This mission had gone off the rails long before she lit a dangerous *umu* and then gifted him with that beautiful laugh. Disaster had occurred the minute Pele had shaken Reagan's hand.

He prayed that he wasn't making the biggest mistake of his career. "S'mores and Samoan cuisine will go perfectly together."

Chapter Thirteen

Reagan's mouth watered at the aroma of the food packets sizzling beneath the banana fronds. The supplies for the meal had cost a pretty penny because these products didn't grow anywhere close to east Tennessee, but the expense had been worth it when she saw Pele's astonished, happy smile. He had gone from a wary, vigilant, hard guy to a heart-melting softie in the space of a few seconds.

His response made something inside of her melt. Damn it.

The sun had gone down. Light came from glowing stones and embers as well as the Coleman gas lantern she'd lit on the porch. Pele knelt near the edge of the pit, lifting some packets and checking items. At least the rocks had stopped blowing up.

He joined her on the tarp she had laid on the ground. It allowed her to stay close enough to enjoy the heat from the fire but kept the damp earth from seeping into her jeans. While working near the fire, Pele had unbuttoned his flannel shirt and rolled up the sleeves to his elbows. The tight t-shirt hugged his chest and outlined a faint horizontal strap over his lower chest. Kind of like a heart monitor similar to one she sometimes used when running. She ventured another glance under her lashes. Wow. The guy was a solid mass of muscles. Now, when he reclined on his elbows, the cords on his forearms rippled and shifted with the movement.

Watching Pele counted as an appetizer. Her mouth watered.

Nope. She mentally shook off the feelings. This was simply dinner. A dinner with two coworkers. Fine, a dinner with a hot coworker.

Besides, there was a moment a while ago when he stared at her that she got the weird déjà vu experience again. Like they'd met, or she'd seen him before. It wasn't like he had "one of those faces" with the unique combination of his golden-tan skin, deep-brown eyes, and dark, wavy hair. You didn't see someone from Polynesia every day of the week. Well, at least, not in east Tennessee. Too bad. She peeked at him again.

Yet. Something familiar. An idea whispered past her, then was gone, like a tendril of smoke from the fire. She'd figure it out sooner or later.

As he relaxed, he turned his head toward her. "So, when we have the S'mores, how are they cooked?"

"On a stick."

His dark brows drew together. "Huh?"

"I'll show you." She put her hand on his hard chest. "Ahem. Pardon me, but I am the S'more expert in this forest."

Lifting his hands, palms up, he chuckled, the sound low and rich. "Fair enough. I'm man enough to admit I have zero S'more experience." His grin gleamed in the glow from the fire.

He was man enough for quite a few things that she had no business thinking about.

"You're in for a treat, then." She paused and glanced at the cabin. "Uh, at least, I hope. Do you have a knife handy? Mine's on the porch."

He reached inside a pocket and pulled out a compact but lethal-looking blade with a glinting and finely honed edge. He handed it to her handle first.

"Wow, fancy." She brushed a nail over the edge. "You're not kidding around with this knife. What else is hidden in there?" She pointed toward his cargo pants.

A flash of intensity lit his eyes, then he blinked and it was gone. "Well." The sound came out as a light growl.

"Oh. *Oh.* No, that's not—" Her face flushed far hotter than the fire, and it took a solid minute before her brain quit trying to generate inappropriate answers to her question.

One corner of Pele's mouth rose.

Well, indeed.

She made a big show of selecting the appropriate roasting sticks and whittling for a few minutes.

After her hormones calmed back down, she asked, "You mind me asking a question?"

"Of course not."

Was that hesitation? Lack of enthusiasm, or simply her own paranoia?

She kept her eyes on the knife. "I'm curious. What's your full name?"

He paused for a moment, then faced her. "You ready for it? Saepele Mata'ala … Tuitama." She caught a hesitation before his last name.

"Sounds cool. Does it mean something?"

"*Saepele* can be translated a few ways, but it loosely means *machete.* My family all called me Pele. Unfortunately, though, in Hawaii, *Pele* is the goddess of fire and volcanoes." At his self-deprecating snort, something girly and giggly fluttered in her chest. Not much about the guy suggested *goddess.*

"Interesting."

"Not if you're a boy nicknamed Pele who attends a Hawaiian primary school. Then it's fodder for bullies."

"Ouch." She laughed. "If it makes you feel any better, my name is a little different."

"Really?" He loved her name. The feel of it on his tongue when he said it.

"It's actually an Irish name, but also the last name of a president."

"We both have mixed-up names, then."

She shaved little pieces of wood into a pile in front of her.

"Is it different dating non-Samoan women?" Where the heck had that question come from? Her cheeks burned. "Oh, wow. Sorry. None of my business. Bad question."

"You can ask me anything." The hooded expression suggested that while she could *ask* him anything, he might not *tell* her everything.

She babbled, "Because with those cooking skills, you know you're head and shoulders above a lot of guys. You could date any woman and she'd be thrilled to be with you. Not only because of the cooking. Um." Just like that, she had turned this pleasant conversation into a slow-moving train wreck. Amazing.

All of a sudden, his gaze felt heavy, assessing. Her scalp prickled. Unable to face him, she concentrated on whittling the sticks. At the rate she was going, she'd have toothpicks in a few minutes.

"Cooking is one of my many abilities," he said.

Oh, God.

His smooth voice sent a tingle down into her pelvis as she imagined what other skills he possessed. She'd sampled some of his … abilities, which only whetted her appetite for more.

He sat up and tossed a few hemlock pinecones into the fire. Crackles followed a few seconds later as they caught. "So, to answer your question, yes, I've dated both Samoan and *palagi* women."

"You used that term earlier."

"*Palagi.* Means foreigner, non-Samoan. In the culture, it's not considered a derogatory term. Merely descriptive. To answer the unspoken question, no, I don't have a preference."

Her head snapped up. "I didn't—"

He raised a hand, palm toward her. "The question is a point of contention in my family. Some traditional parents prefer their kids date Samoans. That pressure has faded away over the last generation. Some. My family would have wished for me to marry a Samoan woman, but now they've abandoned all hope, given that I'm still single at thirty now."

He didn't seem to notice her wince, thank God. That "single" comment hit close to home.

Shrugging, he continued, "Parents are parents. They'll support me no matter what, but they would be happier if I settled down with a woman who grew up with our customs. Probably not going to happen." He frowned and glanced off into the woods with a hard glint in his eyes.

"So, what do you want?"

He swung his dark gaze on her for a full ten seconds. "Let's just say I understood your story on the hike last night."

She swallowed and thought. "Sovereignty?"

"Yes. Women aren't the only ones with pressure regarding who they can be with and how. All I want is the right to choose."

"Makes perfect sense to me. Why can't you?"

"Oh, I can choose, but it's clear which choice is preferred. That pressure has been enough to mess up a few relationships over the years."

"Really?"

"I can't believe I'm telling you all of this." He rubbed his thigh. "You really want to know?"

"Absolutely, if you want to share."

Peering at the *umu*, the glowing embers reflected in his eyes. "Okay. It's not that I've dated hundreds of women. I haven't. But in general, I've found that it doesn't make a difference where the person comes from."

"Oh?"

"The problem has been with me. I've been pulled in different directions for, um, a lot of reasons. There's pressure to continue tradition. I want to create my own path. Then life has thrown a few, uh, curveballs, which I'm still dealing with." He paused, brows drawn down, mouth pressed together. Only half of his face was visible in the firelight. "Still don't know what the correct answer is for the future." He blinked, pushed to his feet, and clapped his hands together, breaking the quiet spell. "But the answer now is to have dinner!"

"Always a good answer." Wow. He had bailed out hard from that conversation.

Not like Reagan didn't understand.

Chapter Fourteen

Using the tongs, Pele moved all the food to cooling rocks he'd placed several feet away from the fire pit. The savory aroma of tuna that had cooked inside a half coconut weakened his knees. How long had it been since he'd had such a treat? He pulled out the taro leaves marinated in coconut cream and laid out the cooked bananas on the utilitarian plates she had brought. He was dishing everything up like a normal meal, eaten in safety. It was a terrible idea.

So was telling her his name. He was proud of his name and its meaning. He took a chance that Brady had never breached confidentiality and shared his teammates' identities with his family. At least Reagan didn't respond as if she recognized his name. Close call. He was having too many close calls with Reagan. Honesty and a three-course meal made for more bad decisions.

But ... coconut cream.

Was he really going to keep hedging his bets that Lequire wouldn't attack here? On this particular night? Half of his virally driven brain screamed at him to stop the buffet, move her into the cabin, and return to his surveillance.

The other half of his brain convinced him that his security systems were in place, and that he needed the poached tuna and coconut. Now.

"Yum, that smells so good," Reagan said.

His attention focused on the way her tongue darted out to moisten her lower lip. "You bet."

She motioned toward the pile of wood next to the banked fire. "Do you mind?"

The sun had gone down and the last glow of twilight was fading. "Not at all, I'm done with my recipes. Do what you need to for the dessert course."

While she stoked the campfire, he excused himself again and swept the area once more with his thermal scope. A quick scroll through the camera feeds showed no human action. Still clear. He grimaced.

Returning, he loaded plates with the food. True, this didn't work exactly like a traditional *umu*, which was built in more sand than earth, and the food contained different spices and fresh taro root. Still, this evening's feast brought back memories of home and Hawaii and of time spent with his family in the backyard. Add in a unique twist of being in the Appalachian Mountains and having Reagan at his side, and the whole scene worked.

"Careful, it's hot," he warned her as he passed the plate.

"Wow, thanks. Looks great!"

"I'll say. It's all due to one hundred percent fire-pit building skill, by the way."

"Ha." She lifted a taro leaf and frowned at it. "Do I eat this?"

"Yes. And enjoy."

She nibbled a bite. "Yum."

His gaze was riveted to her mouth as she chewed. He wanted her to enjoy the food of his home. Not that it mattered in the big picture of his life.

Couldn't matter. Never would matter. "It's perfect," he agreed, chest tightening when her tongue darted out to lick a morsel from her lip.

The corners of her mouth rose. "Thank you for cooking. My version would never have turned out like this."

"My pleasure." When he cut into the coconut-infused tuna, the meat fell apart, it was so tender. "Oh, man, this is so good."

"I'll say." She swallowed. "How come no one

here knows about Samoan cooking? This meal is fabulous."

"Must be another secret that only a select few local *palagi* get to know." He took a bite of the cooked unripe banana. The savory and sweet flavor with the chewy texture was perfection.

They ate in silence for several minutes. The pop and crackle of the stoked fire and a few owls in distant trees provided peaceful background noise. He finally set his empty plate to the side, lay back on the tarp, rested his hands on his stomach, and let out a sigh of happiness.

"Is relaxing under the stars part of the traditional meal?" Reagan's face entered his field of vision sideways as she leaned over him, her braids dangling down.

A flash of her body above him for less innocent activities shot a bolt of desire into his groin. *Ti'o.* Pressure immediately started to build, and the damned virus growled its demand for action.

He tugged on one of her braids. "No, but it should be."

"I agree." She glanced toward the roaring fire. "Such a good meal. The S'mores would ruin it now."

"No!" He sat straight up, startling her into sitting back on her heels. "I want to try it."

"You sure? After all this amazing food?"

"Is it traditional for you?"

"S'mores? Well, they're traditional campfire snacks, especially here at Camp Foxfire. No camping trip or fireside gathering is complete without them."

"Then it's decided. We're having them." He held out his hand. "Teach me."

With a nod, she handed him a stick with a tapered tip. "Okay. You put two marshmallows on the end of the stick and roast them."

He immediately thrust the white sugar puffs into the flame and they caught fire. "I don't think that's the way it's supposed to go," he said as the sugar turned to black carbon.

"Actually." She leaned over and blew out the blue flame as he got a whiff of charred caramel. "Some people like the burnt flavor and gooey center. Try it. Be careful, it'll be like molten lava inside."

With a flaky crunch, he took a bite of the marshmallow, getting a smoky, thin crunch and a hot, gooey sugary center. A little charcoal-y. Not bad.

"Now, if you want to do it the expert way, ahem, then you must learn patience and proper technique." She knelt on one knee next to a bed of glowing embers on the edge of the fire pit.

He laughed out loud. "I'm listening, professor."

"The color you're going for is light caramelized brown, which is the most perfect color for a roasted marshmallow."

"I'm light caramelized brown, does that count as perfect?"

The snicker that burst from her lips had him grinning again. "Sure, if you are getting paired with melted chocolate." She clapped her hand over her mouth. "Oh, wow. Fine. Never mind. Er, back to the marshmallows."

What he'd give to see her blush again. Maybe mutual feelings still existed. A flash of Reagan licking chocolate off of his body sent another inappropriate jolt straight to his throbbing pelvis.

Focusing on the task at hand, he followed her lead and kept the marshmallows well above the heat until all of the outsides were bubbled and brown. The cooked sugar smell filled the air.

"Here, hold both of our sticks," she said, reaching

into the other packages. "So. Right now, all you have are roasted marshmallows. Next step is turning them into S'mores." She held a graham cracker piece with a square of chocolate on top in her palm. "One slab of chocolate or two?"

"Two, of course." He studied her smiling face. "Right?"

"Bold choice, but not wrong." She sandwiched the steaming marshmallow between another cracker and chocolate combo and pulled back until the stick slid out. Then she handed him the final product and took her own stick back. "Okay, go for it."

He bit down and got a burst of warm sugar, semi-melted chocolate, and crunchy graham cracker. After swallowing a bite, he said, "I've never had anything like it. This is really good."

"I know." She took a bite of her own creation and sat back down on the tarp. "Simple but fun." She chewed and sighed.

Finishing up his treat, he joined her on the groundcover. "Thank you for all of this. For the company and the food."

"Your cooking skills saved the day." The last bit of her S'more disappeared, and he followed the line of her neck as she swallowed.

"What?" she asked, concern etching a furrow between her light brows.

"You have marshmallow on your face."

She swiped at her nose and cheek. "Got it?"

The tiny piece of white remained on her lower lip. "Not quite." He leaned forward and licked his lips.

She froze.

Gently. He could approach her gently. He would be careful with her. Shoving aside the drive to consume her, mark her, take her, he concentrated on Reagan's sweet face instead. "May I?" he asked. It would hurt, but he would stop if she said no.

"Okay," she whispered.

He rested his hand on her jaw and focused on the hitch in her breathing. With a little bit of suction, he nipped her lower lip and a tiny shot of sugar combined with the taste of her lips burst on his tongue. *Ti'o*. Perfection. In a flash, his damned viral-driven lust infused every cell with a blinding wave of need. He wanted to possess her right now. Here, under the stars and in front of the fire, with no one but the barred owls as witnesses. Primitive and perfect.

No. He would take his time and go slowly, even if it killed him.

"Mmm," he murmured, tasting her mouth again. He nipped at her soft lips, tasting, and licking, like sampling a rare treat.

Angling his head, he slid his tongue along the seam of her mouth before slipping it between her lips and stroking her tongue with his. His senses were overloaded with wood smoke, sugar, coconut cream, fresh air, and Reagan's soft skin. Nothing else existed.

A warning alarm chimed, too faint to fully register.

Trailing his lips down one side of her face, then the other, he enjoyed the tiny sounds she made as he found sensitive skin under her jaw. He eased her back onto the tarp and lifted her chin, exposing her smooth neck. With his finger, he traced the jumping pulse on each side and dropped light kisses on her skin until she moaned.

Her fingers gripped his bare forearms, stoking his desire. Damned if that simple pressure of her hands on him didn't send urgent signals to other areas of his anatomy. Areas that demanded immediate attention from

Reagan.

Tough. Those areas would have to take a number and wait in line. He had other work to do, other parts of her body to explore first.

At a gentle swipe of her fingers across his jaw to the back of his neck, he groaned his pleasure. She drew him down to meet her lips for a sizzling kiss that made every muscle in his back clench. Maybe he wouldn't have to wait much longer to address all of the pressure building.

Bracing his hands next to her head, he half crouched over her but kept his lower body to one side. She'd be less likely to encounter the knives and guns strapped to and hidden on his person. Also, *ti'o*, with all the throbbing going on, the minute he got fully on top of her, all best intentions to take things slowly would fly out the window. As it was, the need to grind into her shifting hips was becoming a priority. A wave of desire, amplified by his virus, rushed over him until a buzzing sound started in his head and traveled through his chest.

When she slid her hands under his shirt and caressed his belly, his abs tightened. He hissed his pleasure but couldn't risk her finding the chest strap or the Sig. He eased her hands away until they rested next to her head. Lacing his fingers in hers, he tried to sell the move as part of the seduction.

Nudging her mouth open wider, he swept his tongue deep inside, wanting to possess her, wanting to mark her as his own, wanting so much more. For a few seconds, he forgot his other life. At this moment, his existence narrowed down to Reagan. He ran his hands down her sides and squeezed her hips and thighs through the denim until she whimpered. With a force of will, he loosened his desperate grip. What would it feel like to hold on to her bare skin as he drove into her, over and over, until he lost his mind?

He was one foot over the precipice already. He retained the barest sliver of control.

Reflected firelight made her eyes dance.

When she licked her lips and lifted her head to brush her mouth against his, what scant restraint he possessed fled. His body vibrated with a roaring, activated virus and flaming desire for her that burned hotter than the fire. Vibrations of hunger for her body made his body shake.

Vibrations.

On his leg. Vibrating.

His leg?

The buzzing sensation continued as he kissed her. Through the fog of lust, he registered the source and woke up in a hurry, like cold water thrown on hot stones.

Kefe. The motion detectors had activated. Sudden cold sweat dried in the heat of the fire.

Now he positioned himself on all fours, but this time it was to shield her as he cursed the bright fire that knocked out his night vision.

He scanned the dark woods. Enemies? Where?

Valea! He was stupid.

He kept his body in a human bracket around her and flipped into mission mode—what he should have been in all afternoon and evening.

Error: An assumption the enemy would not come here.

Potentially fatal error: A lapse in personal behavior standards and failure to follow mission op protocol.

He had to get her to safety, and fast. Assess the threat. Eliminate the threat.

The buzzing continued. Her kisses continued. He groaned.

With a single, smooth movement, he jumped to his feet, pulling her with him. She was unsteady, and he tucked her into his side. Her wide eyes glazed with lust, and her swollen lips made him want to lose himself in her for weeks.

They didn't have weeks.

Might not even have minutes.

"Come on," he said. How the hell would he play this one off? *Think.*

"Wh-what?"

Over her head, he studied the forest. Any noise? Shapes? Damn it, he needed to use his scope and eliminate whatever set off the alarm.

Protect Reagan.

This entire evening had been a horrible misjudgment. What had he been thinking? He knew exactly what he'd been thinking, and it had zero to do with his mission. His desire for Reagan might be the biggest threat to this assignment.

Urging her up the steps to the front door, he guided her inside the cabin.

"Didn't we do this last night?" she asked, planting her feet and facing him. "What's going on?"

"Uh, Samoan tradition. The men are supposed to take care of the food and fire. And cleanup. We can't leave it out there. Bad luck." Lame. "You have to stay in here while I put everything away. Rules."

"Really?" In the darkness, he could sense rather than see her frown.

The buzzing in his pocket had become more insistent. *Ti'o.* Such a bad mistake. "You don't want to mess with my culture, do you?"

"What? No. But what's gotten into you?" Her eyebrows rose. Then she frowned as the hopeful expression crumbled. "Oh, because you don't want to…"

"What? No. God, no. Not even close." He wanted to reassure her in the most definite way possible, but first, he had to keep her alive. "I'll be back, okay?"

"Yeah. Fine. Got it." The light faded from her eyes.

"No. Damn it, Reagan. You don't get it."

"Uh, yes. I get it. All of it. I think I have a real good handle on what's going on." When she crossed her arms, he mentally slapped his forehead. "Go ahead and finish up with the 'tradition' you need to stick with."

"You don't—"

"It's okay, Pele." She bit her lower lip, and he licked his own in response. "Really, I understand. You're right, this was a bad idea. Nothing good would have come from us doing anything."

He snapped his jaw shut. No time to explain or beg forgiveness.

The hardest thing he'd done to date was stepping out of the cabin and closing the door.

Chapter Fifteen

Fool me once, shame on you. Fool me twice ... damn it. She rested her forehead on the door. With shaking fingers, she touched her sensitive lips. Even now, even with that ridiculous disaster, she wanted to run out of the cabin and claim more of his kisses.

Damn, damn, damn. She slid along the wall until she crouched, legs pressed together in an attempt to ease the throbbing there.

Such a mistake. She'd fallen for it twice. Of course, he didn't want to take things further. She'd responded to him like a woman in the desert seeing an oasis after days of walking on sandy dunes.

Pele had done her a favor by bailing out. Less emotional fallout to deal with later.

Oh, God. She had been willing to do the thing she vowed never to do again. Change for a man. She had learned about his culture and attempted to make a meal specifically for him. What would she do next, try to grow a coconut tree here in Tennessee?

He had been kind to her out of appreciation. Then when she took it too far, he kept them in the friend zone. As they should be.

At least he hadn't hurt her physically. Pele wouldn't. If anything, she knew she was safe in his presence.

Emotionally? His hot-and-cold maneuvers and rejection hurt. Cut far deeper than it should have because her wounded heart hadn't recovered from her ex yet.

Similar issues, different guy. Only now she was learning Samoan terms and figuring out how to cook with an *umu*.

Ha. Turned out in his culture, the woman didn't

cook. She pressed her palm to the ache in her chest. God, she couldn't even get the simple parts right.

What business did she have even considering that there could be a thing with him? A few meaningful glances from a handsome guy, and she went back down the proverbial rabbit hole again. She didn't even know the guy.

She peeked out between the blinds. No sign of Pele. Of course. He had used his flimsy excuse and disappeared already.

What she wouldn't give to talk to Kiera. Her sister would help Reagan sort through the facts and feelings. Britt would step up with advice, too, but it might not be helpful or relevant, with her youngest sister's head in the clouds.

Brady would have been a good option, giving his "dude perspective" as he often had to with three sisters. He was dead. Her chest clenched.

Mom? Dead.

What about Dad? Poor ol' Dad hoped his daughters would get married one day and enjoy happy, fulfilled lives. Beyond that, he was still sorting through boxes of Mom's stuff and avoiding looking at Brady's personal items.

Which left no one to talk with about her mistrust in herself. No one to call. Reagan looked around the empty, dark cabin.

Good grief, if she had been ready to assimilate into a different culture, what had kept her from changing for Clayton? Besides the abuse, of course. Never would forget that part.

She stopped dead still. Maybe she should have taken Clayton's request to meet again more seriously.

No. Absolutely not.

No.

She'd rather be alone than under the thumb of her ex. That much she knew with complete confidence.

There she had it. Decision made: Reagan had her sovereignty.

And nothing else.

****

Pele knocked lightly on the cabin door, but no answer. After checking the camera planted in her apartment to ensure she was indeed safely in her basement apartment, he cursed himself as a creeper and turned off the screen. As much as he'd love to watch her sleep for hours, that would be an invasion of privacy—beyond what he'd already done. Also, he couldn't let her distract him from the op.

Again.

Ti'o, he had handled the entire situation tonight all wrong. Again.

Handled the person he was supposed to protect, that was where things went wrong. He continued his circuit in the woods surrounding her cabin.

The recollection of Regan's soft mouth and eager moans stopped him in his tracks and woke up the virus. He had come within seconds of ripping her clothes off and taking her on the tarp next to the campfire. How amazing would that have been, her sexy body lit by the flickering flames as he licked his way over every inch of her skin. That experience would have been one for the ages.

His penis agreed, as it eagerly pushed against his trousers no matter how he shifted to try and relieve the pressure. Another rush of desire hit him like a tidal wave, and he lurched three steps toward the cabin before regaining control.

Focus on something else. Anything besides Reagan.

He raised the scope and slowly scanned the terrain. Breathe in and out. *Friend versus enemy.* Find the pattern. Breathe in and out. *Friend versus enemy.*

On autopilot, he performed another compulsive check of his weapons in the various holsters and straps on his body. All readily accessible.

Food and water? He patted pockets. Check.

Time for another check of the trail cams.

Flipping on the small screen, he scrolled through recently captured images.

First image: deer, with its eyes glowing.

Second image: opossum foraging for a midnight snack.

Third image: human, large.

He backed up a step, kicking a chunk of bark out of a thick tree trunk.

Kefe.

Pele stared at the profile visible in the lurid pale-green image. The cruel twist of the man's mouth wasn't reassuring.

Lost hunter or hiker? Could Pele be that lucky?

Didn't act like a lost hunter. People couldn't hunt in the National Park adjacent to the camp.

Looked more like a man on a very different mission than Pele's.

How many others waited in the woods?

He needed to call this in to Hunt. Then what? The team was spread too thin. No help would roll up in one of their kitted-out black SUVs anytime soon. Pele and his ability to do a very specific job were all that stood between Reagan and death.

He'd swept the area around the cabin and didn't detect any heat signatures, which made sense. The trail cam that had been triggered was located at the other end of camp, above the arts and crafts cabin, the area where they had taken the night hike. While it wasn't near her cabin, it was still too close. If someone searched for Reagan, then it was only a matter of time before they came here.

A prickle of cold air had him lifting his head. Could he keep her safe without revealing the Morpheus Squad secrets while also avoiding recognition and capture by the government? He refused to go back to being a lab rat.

If she found out about his Morpheus Virus status, she wouldn't want anything to do with a man with a monster inside of him.

A decision crystallized in his mind. If it came down to it, he'd compromise the mission, his team, and his entire existence to save her life.

Chapter Sixteen

The only good thing about this morning was that it wasn't last night.

Reagan's heart felt like it had been run over by a Mack truck.

Damn Pele. She'd fallen for the handsome man again.

Her face burned despite the cool morning, thinking how stupid she'd been to research recipes for him and shop for the man. Heck, she flipping built an earthen oven for the guy.

The part that made her eyelids sting? She had fixed the meal out of kindness and friendship.

Well, that backfired. Time to change her standard operating procedure when it came to men. She zipped her fleece jacket and trudged toward the office.

How about now? Her heart rate sped up as the guy at the top of her *persona non grata* list walked toward her on the gravel road. Her hands curled into fists.

"We should stop meeting like this," he said. The smile was way too tight and didn't reach his dark eyes.

"Couldn't agree more. I know a bad pattern when I see one." When she blurted out the words, he flinched, but she didn't care. Today she was a new Reagan, and the new Reagan would call things like she saw them, and damn the consequences. If Mr. Bronze and Buff's feelings got hurt, then so be it. Not her problem.

"About last night—" he began.

Cutting him off with a chop of her hand, she said, "Also part of the bad pattern, this whole conversation. We're having *Groundhog's Day* all over again, and I don't love it. About last night, hey, it's past history.

Nothing else to discuss. Done."

He flinched like she had slapped him. "Don't you want to talk about it?"

"Won't change the past or alter the future, so, no." She walked quickly, making him keep up with her. Which he did, easily, much to her disgust.

"Reagan."

"Are we going to discuss work? Because that's the only topic that is open at this time."

Damn it, her temper had gone from simmer to boil in ten seconds flat. She knew that her anger involved more than Pele, but she didn't have the energy to separate out all the hurts. So she piled them at his feet.

Her ex's treatment of her, Reagan's fractured family, the bad patterns of her life, Pele's lame excuses to get away from her. Her shame at not seeing the same mistake being made over and over again. It didn't matter whose fault all the issues were, the mess needed to be dumped somewhere. Pele was reckless enough to seek her out this morning. Natural consequences of his decision. Too bad. Time to back up the dump truck to Pele.

No more being the oldest sister and worrying about everyone. No more trying to adapt to what a man wanted her to be. No more letting a guy hurt her in the name of the relationship. No more hope that someone would accept her for who she was, because even a blind woman could see that wasn't going to happen, ever. Done.

Ping, ping, ping. Bubbles of irritation burst inside of her as his chest rose with a big breath.

God help him if he opened his mouth to say anything else.

When he touched her arm, she smacked it away, shocking herself to tears. She'd never hit anyone.

He shot forward as his face twisted from placid to tightly focused in a split second, and he manacled her wrist with his massive hand.

Yelping, she pulled away.

He let go like he'd touched a hot poker, and she stumbled but kept her feet. With visible effort and a roll of his shoulders, he reset his facial features back to neutral and studied her beneath his dark eyelashes. What the heck was going on with this guy?

"Damn it. Sorry," he muttered.

"Me too. Look. We're done here, Pele. No more stories about Polynesian stalker eels or traditional cooking. No more yanking me around by my feelings while you run hot and cold. I don't deserve any of it. I don't want any part of it. Just stop."

He closed his gaping mouth with a *clunk* of molars. His eyes turned stony and cold.

Guilt clawed its way through her chest, but she shoved it back. *Sorry, not sorry.* She couldn't spend her entire life worrying about the feelings of others. For once, she needed to take care of herself. Because no one else would.

The rest of the walk to the office took far too long for her preference, especially with Pele staying at her side the whole time. At least he would be maintaining the trails today while she caught up on office duties and summer camp curriculum development. She didn't have to deal with him through the whole day.

Stop it. He had to learn the job. She couldn't punish him for working with her. The part where he kept showing up for non-work activities and trampling on her confidence? That behavior she would be happy to correct.

Maybe he didn't have a lot of friends. Or past trauma was part of his deal, like the PTSD he alluded to having. He had personal issues of his own. What if being here at Camp Foxfire was a chance for a new beginning?

She stumbled a step. Imagine that. What if someone else had problems, too? What if another human being was as wounded as Reagan?

Shame, a nasty, oily sensation, grew in her gut.

That look on his face, the flashes of it she'd seen the past few days. So similar to when Brady had a flashback.

His vigilance and over-the-top reactions. He was ex-military. Could have PTSD, like Brady did. Might explain the déjà vu feeling she had around him.

Damn.

Seriously, guilt? Now?

Forget it. Now wasn't the time to analyze his behavior. Wasn't her job to figure him out, and if he wanted her to know about his past, he would have told her.

She checked the clock. Ten o'clock. Six hours until she could start getting ready for girls' night out. With any luck, she'd be decent company for her friends, despite her foul mood. Trissa and Kate always cheered her up.

Reagan needed to lose herself in the nice evening and forget all the crap that this week had unearthed.

****

On the hill high above the arts and crafts cabin, Pele checked the trail cam that had flashed the image of that man. Sure enough, it was the camera closest to the National Park boundary. The man could have entered from any of the millions of acres of wilderness. An un-securable border.

Now Pele was going to have even more trouble staying close enough to Reagan to do his job, if this morning's outburst was any indication.

He deserved the tongue-lashing, and then some. He was surprised she spoke to him, if only to chew him out.

He had a very legitimate reason to walk away from Reagan's passionate kisses, twice in as many nights. It was a shame he couldn't explain it to her. Still, he felt like a chump for hurting her twice like that.

Sure, he had hang-ups regarding his identity and cultural background. Valid issues. Then he had been infected with a virus that had taken away his identity and freedom while turning him into a creature with superhuman strength he could call to bear with the snap of his fingers. Obviously, not a selling point in the dating circles. Also, not his fault.

He studied the footprints in the soft earth and followed them toward the ridge. Climbing a rocky draw, he lost the track. On the ridge, no sign of new treads.

Standing utterly still, he turned in a slow circle, trying to guess where that man might hide and who else would be with him.

Instead, his brain played images of Reagan in front of him.

What about almost losing all control with her earlier when she had smacked him? He had come within a hair's breadth of breaking her arm. Unacceptable. *Ti'o.* He needed to get his head screwed on straight for this mission, to say nothing of any future relationships with anyone.

Not anyone. He froze, hand on a tree trunk.

Wait. Did he want a relationship with Reagan?

Not an option. Couldn't think about it now. Wouldn't.

The last time he lost focus with Reagan, he'd put her life in danger. That lapse would not happen again. Period.

What about her emotional needs? It was clear she dealt with far more than a simple break-up right before the wedding. If staying away from her meant that her bruised heart could heal, then he would also leave Reagan alone. Forever, if that was what it took.

A spike of pain lanced his chest. The virus welled up in protest. Damned virus needed Pele to be closer to her.

He studied the woods, taking slow and even breaths, calming down. Friends versus enemies? Patterns. Patterns.

Friends.

Enemies.

What lengths would he go to keep her safe?

All answers led him to one conclusion.

There was no future with Reagan. He would sacrifice everything to keep her safe.

Chapter Seventeen

Reagan let out a deep breath as she pulled into the parking lot at the Cotton Eyed Joe at 8:00, right on time. The tight muscles in her shoulders didn't relax. She double-checked her appearance in the truck's rearview mirror. Vichy Dermablend in Opal 15 hid most of her port-wine stain. Her hair, worn long and curly today, came forward to cover the rest of the birthmark. With a quick swipe of lip gloss, the corners of her mouth lifted.

See? Normal.

She tossed the tube into her small purse, along with the keys to the truck, and the concealer stick for touch-ups. She rattled her keys and smiled. On her keychain remained the thumb drive with photos of Brady. It stayed with her no matter where she went. Her last connection to her brother. With a sigh, she rolled her neck and tried to focus on an enjoyable evening ahead of her.

Despite the fact that she loved spending time with her friends, large social events and attention made her tense. Fortunately, she liked her friends more than she disliked the nerves. Even after all these years, she still didn't want people staring and asking questions. Didn't like the judgment.

The pity.

The sign for the largest country dance club in Knoxville glowed neon pink as she hopped down from her truck. Cool air perked her up in a hurry. Other vehicles poured in. A flash of chrome blue caught her eye, but when she glanced around the cars and trucks, nothing seemed out of place. As she crunched over gravel at the edge of the club's packed parking lot, she was thankful for her tooled Ariat boots absorbing the bumpy ground under her feet. She smoothed her cap-sleeve denim shirt tucked into a layered cream-colored lace skirt. The breeze chilled her bare knees, but she'd be inside soon enough.

Passing the guy at the front door who barely looked at her ID—yeah, she understood no one would question whether she was twenty-one, thanks—she maneuvered through the press of people and wove past tables of denim- and boot-clad men and women. Upbeat country music beats made her ears ring as she passed by the main floor's speakers. She avoided avid stares, laughter, and shouted conversations all around her. On instinct, she pulled the hair on her right side forward. Damn it.

"Reagan!"

She hurried to the high-top table where her friends sat on stools. Hugs all around, and Reagan hopped up on a chair. The server came by and took Reagan's order.

"How are things going, sweets?" Trissa asked, patting her perfect, tight curls. Natural. Effortless. Just like her smooth, dark skin.

Unlike Reagan, whose neck itched under the foundation.

"Good." Reagan relaxed and smiled. "How about y'all?"

Kate tossed her glossy brown hair off her shoulders, exposing her considerable tanned cleavage and attracting avid interest from several nearby patrons. "Honey, you have no idea. Here's the low down..."

Trissa rolled her eyes and sighed after Kate finished her story. "God, my ears are on fire. Yes, we've got it. You and your fabulous boyfriend are doing the nasty, Cirque du Soleil style. Seriously. I'm calling bullshit on those details. No human can be that flexible.

If I tried that, I'd be in the hospital with a dislocated hip."

Reagan snorted her drink.

Kate somehow managed to look both beautiful and chagrined. Even in the lower light of the club, a tinge of pink brightened her cheeks as she shrugged.

"Huh." Trissa pinned Reagan with an arched eyebrow. "So. What about you? Anything exciting in your life?"

"Not much," she demurred. If you didn't count S'mores and heavy petting under the stars with a sexy man who changed temperatures faster than she could turn a faucet handle.

Trissa rubbed a hand over her neck as a handsome guy in a cowboy hat tipped his brim at her. She winked back and then focused on Reagan. "I don't buy your boring story for a minute. How about some good stories about rugged mountain men up in them thar hills?" Trissa squinted one eye and pushed her tongue under her lower lip.

Reagan raised her fingers. "Number one, not all the men in the mountains use tobacco. Not even most of them. Ew. And two, didn't I tell you to never attempt a hillbilly accent again? You're from Cleveland. Your accent is as wrong as a Kool-Aid mixed with moonshine."

"Seems to work pretty well for me, according to stretch over there." She waved at the man in the tight jeans and he headed over. "You should try it." She glanced over at Reagan's footwear. "Use the accent while wearing your big ol' boots. And nothing else!"

Trissa leaned back and crossed her arms while Reagan choked on her beer and Kate giggled.

The interested cowboy who personified a "tall drink of water" sauntered up and lasered his blue-eyed gaze onto Trissa.

"Hey. Wanna…?" He nodded toward the crowded dance floor.

"You bet, bucko." She cocked her head. "Ladies, if you'll excuse me? Zach Brown Band is playing, and this fella looks like he wants to boot scoot."

Kate scowled and then smiled. "Impressive."

"You know it." With a wiggle that kept the man's attention firmly on her toned backside, Trissa led the man to the dance floor and they joined the line dance for a minute, then blended into the two-stepping couples as the next song started.

"She's good," Reagan said. How amazing would it be to have that much confidence that everyone could sense it? So much confidence that men rushed over to experience it?

"She never misses an opportunity to check out a new pair of Wranglers." Kate sipped her rum and Coke. "Camp going okay?"

Aside from the exploding *umu*, a new hire who kept pulling emotional bait-and-switches, and kisses that consistently ended in a disaster? Peachy. "Yeah."

"Heard anything from Kiera?" Kate asked.

"No calls recently. She emailed a few weeks back, telling me about her job." Reagan leaned forward. "I'm worried." She consciously removed her hand from her neck and pasted her palm on the table. "Dad and Britt think we should give her time. Last time she wrote, she said she was doing fine."

"So?"

"So, I miss her. It's not like her not to visit over such a long time."

"Well. She might have a lot going on in her life right now. Your Mom. Brady's passing last summer."

"I know. We're all still dealing with their deaths.

It's just"—Reagan played with the corner of the beer label—"with all the stupidity with Clayton and the wedding going down last Christmas, it would have been great to talk with her. Get some advice."

"What am I? Chopped liver?" Kate scrunched her nose. "Trissa, too. We were totally ready to knock some sense into that dummy." A pause. She glanced around the room, then back to Reagan. "Do you ever wonder if he's changed?"

"He'd have to have done a complete one-eighty for me to even consider talking with him again." She grinned as she took a sip of beer. "I'm sorry I didn't give you and Trissa more credit. You guys definitely had my back."

Her friend drummed her pink lacquered fingers on the table, making the rings on her fingers flash sparks of light. "Are you thinking about getting back into the dating game?"

"Um." Ha. A certain camp employee's intense expression inserted itself in her mind's eye. She crossed her legs. "Not really." As in, never.

"No way. You totally should get back out there." She shrugged and glanced over her shoulder. "Unless you're not over … Clayton." With a frown, she took another long swig of her drink.

With conscious effort, Reagan pushed down a wave of irritation. Kate didn't know about the worst of Clayton's bad behavior. No one knew. Reagan had kept those awful details to herself. Her friends thought he called the wedding off and was a jerk. Nothing more. He had begged Reagan not to tell the whole truth of their situation, and she had allowed the lie of omission so he could save face and she could get out. "No. We're done. That boat left the dock when I had to contact two hundred guests and explain that our wedding was canceled."

She rubbed her face, then stopped, worried that she might have removed some of the makeup. Clayton had drilled it into her: it wouldn't do for anyone to see the birthmark. She froze. Damn how his manipulation had changed her behavior. Changed who she was and how she thought. Even now, she still second-guessed herself. "Nothing like reliving the humiliation with each and every phone call. Canceling the minister, flowers, venue, the limo. Talking with aunts and uncles. Good times."

"To our credit, Trissa and I helped with the guest calls."

Reagan leaned over and rested her head on Kate's shoulder for a moment. "You have no idea how much I appreciated that." Another swallow of beer produced a warm, relaxed feeling in her gut and some of the tension seeped away.

"Ever think about getting back with Clayton? I mean, what if he's a better person or grew more mature or something?" Kate's gaze darted all over the place. She kept checking her cell phone.

Maybe she was meeting someone here later or checking for messages from her boyfriend.

Reagan waved her hand. "For a second there, I might have considered it. Now, after I've had time to process everything? Nope." Even now, a tiny piece of her still second-guessed her conviction in that decision.

"You guys dated for over two years."

"Thank God it was only dating. No legally binding documents involved. Just a lot of deposits on services for the wedding."

"He reimbursed those fees, didn't he?"

Twisting a curl, she blew out a long breath. "Exactly half of them. I finally paid my half off a month ago."

"What a mess."

Sometimes the time and place to tell the story would pop up. At least that was what Reagan's therapist had said. A good chunk of the label was free of the sweating bottle and she pulled the rest of the paper off. She took a deep breath. "Things went downhill in a hurry when he wanted a prenup."

"I remember." She glanced over Reagan's shoulder. "Makes me want to be careful with my own future plans."

"The funny part? For all Clayton knew, I had nothing to 'nup'. He thought he was only protecting himself." Her smile felt wrong—tight and forced. "Get it? He figured I was the poor outdoor education instructor marrying an up-and-coming financial analyst. There has been money from Brady's and Mom's life insurance policies, but I didn't want to touch it. One day, I will. But money shouldn't be the deciding factor for anyone's love life."

"Makes sense." Kate hesitated. "Mum's the word." She played with the condensation on the glass. "Hey, Trissa's going for another spin with Tex out there."

"Good for her jumping right in. I have to warm up to that level of crowd interaction."

"I hear you." Another sip. "You never told us what all Clayton tried to put in the prenup. Only that you were pissed."

The remembered stab of pain from the first time she read the terms of the agreement made her head ache, and she winced. "He put in way more than he should have. That was the problem. Oh, he listed the standard financial stuff, where I'm not entitled to his pre-existing property and savings. But he tried to sneak in clauses about how he wanted me to look and act a certain way."

Kate gasped and peeked around again before her mouth gaped. "He did *not*. You never mentioned that." She shifted in her seat. Her face went pale.

"Not something I cared to share. Yes, he did add those extra conditions."

"How you looked…" Her eyes went wide and her jaw dropped. "Oh, God, you mean the birthmark? He wanted you to get rid of it?"

"He tried."

"No way."

A sad laugh escaped her lips. "The judge told him she'd never accept a prenup with a clause saying that I had to 'resolve cosmetically objectionable features'. By then, the damage was done. I knew how he felt. That was the last straw." Actually, the part where he tried to force her to sign the prenup was the last straw. The *way* that he forced her was even worse. She rubbed her lower back.

"Wow. I had no idea." The corner of her perfect, red mouth lifted. "Well. Onward and upward, as they say."

"Um, sure." Reagan indicated for the circulating waiter to bring her another beer.

Kate repeated her drink order as well. "So, tell me. Are you ready to see anyone?"

"Why the inquisition?"

Her friend shot her a mischievous smile. "Because Mr. Tall, Buff, and Handsome over at the bar hasn't quit staring at you for a solid fifteen minutes." She grabbed Reagan's forearm. "Don't look!"

"What?" Of course, Reagan pivoted around.

As she locked eyes with Pele, a virtual boxer's punch of connection knocked the wind out of her. The crowd sounds receded into a dull rumble.

Every inch of Pele's considerable frame and the

entirety of his dark gaze lasered in on Reagan. His dark pants and gray t-shirt with an untucked lightly patterned unbuttoned black shirt over it worked for him. Worked so well. She hadn't really appreciated his arms in those flannel shirts at camp, but the short sleeves bulged with the cords of muscle peeking out beneath the fabric.

Why was he here? A wave of irritation battled with a rush of pure feminine interest. He lifted a Michelob and gave her a half smile, dimple visible.

Reagan swiveled back around, knocking her knee on the center post of the table. She ignored the prickling sensation on the back of her neck. "Whatever."

Stalker? Funny, he didn't strike her as the type. Of course, he did have a habit of ending up wherever she was. No way was that a coincidence.

Kate's brows rose. "What the hell is wrong with you? That man is good enough to eat." She darted her tongue over her mouth. "Delicious."

Reagan groaned. She knew. *Yum* was the correct assessment, damn it all. He tasted like coconut cream and powerful male and felt like iron covered with warm velvet. *Oh, God. Please let that be the beer talking.*

He'd followed her here. The gall.

"Holy cow, Reagan. Check it out. That woman with an ah-mazing figure for days and a super short skirt walked up to him, and he totally ignored her," Kate whispered behind a hand. "Gay?"

Evidence would suggest not.

Pele leaned against the bar, chest muscles straining against the t-shirt. The casual pose was offset by his sharp observation of everything around him. Like he was memorizing his surroundings and everyone.

Including Reagan.

The air stuck in her throat.

Breathless and beaming, Trissa returned from the

dance floor and slid back into her chair. She blew a kiss to her dance partner as he swaggered back over to his friends. "Well, that was a good way to kick off the evening. Did I miss anything?"

"No—" Reagan shouted.

Trissa reared back, lifting her hands. "Whoa, girl."

"You missed everything while you were doing the Git Up over there!" Kate grinned. "Tris, check out the hunk over there. Your eight o'clock."

After she tilted her head to the side, Trissa's eyes narrowed and then widened. She slowly rotated back to face the table. Her hand went to her chest, and she fanned herself. "Baby Jesus dipped in chocolate, that is one hot slab of man."

Reagan and Kate burst out laughing.

"You're an atheist!" Kate said.

"What? I'd turn religious for a guy like that." Trissa raised her chin.

"No one doubts your spiritual, uh, commitment." Reagan coughed.

"Wow." Kate took a sip and leaned forward. "Okay, ladies, lean in. We need to caucus."

Oh, no. A weight dropped deep into Reagan's gut. Whenever she and her friends had a group meeting, something embarrassing often occurred—usually to Reagan.

Kate set down her drink with a deliberate *clunk* and shot them both a dead-serious expression. "You want my opinion? I'd get with a guy like that eight ways to Sunday. And that's coming from a gal who is in a long-term, committed relationship."

"I second that motion, minus the committed relationship part. Though I'd be happy to be long-term committed to that guy," Trissa offered. "Can I at least have sloppy seconds? He's … like a Manwich. Sauce and all." She mimicked holding a hamburger to her mouth. "One little bite and you can call me Sloppy Joe."

"You're also vegetarian!" Reagan giggled. Her friends were talking about Pele like he was something to be tasted. Oh, my. She knew how his lips tasted. Her cheeks heated.

Trissa gave a Cheshire cat smile. "I'd convert religion *and* sacrifice my core values to spend time with a man like that. Dibs."

Holding up a hand, Kate interrupted. "Tris, wait. What about Reagan? Our girl needs to get back on the proverbial horse. What better guy than Chocolate Jesus Manwich?"

Uh-oh. Reagan held up her hands and reared back. "No, guys. No. Come on now. No chocolate or meat analogies. No religion. No riding horses or whatever other metaphor you're throwing in there."

"Oooh, riding! That's a good one." Trissa's lashes fluttered. "Lordie, can you imagine how good—"

"Yes, fine, Trissa. We know you think he's hot. And usually you get the pick of the litter." Kate lifted her chin. "But he's making dirty eyes at our Reagan—" She stopped any further arguments with the lift of a manicured finger. "I think he'd be a wonderful rebound ride. Don't you think, Trissa?"

Trissa lifted a shoulder. "Saddle up, girlfriend. Be safe. Don't forget to wear spurs."

A belly laugh erupted from Reagan as she raised her hands. "No, ladies. Thanks, but no."

"How about we ro-sham-bo for him?" Trissa held a fist in her palm, ready to go. "Because one of us needs to find out if those shoulders are as massive as they look. Research. It's for the good of humanity."

"Like doing our duty!" Kate said.

Trissa solemnly nodded. "The sacrifices we make for scientific inquiry."

Reagan knew firsthand how broad Pele's shoulders felt. She could formulate a hypothesis on other areas of his anatomy.

"No, we are not playing rock, paper, scissors to see who gets to say hi to him," Reagan protested. "Besides, what if he's nearsighted and we're misinterpreting what he's doing? He could be staring at someone else nearby."

"Really? Were you born that stupid or did you work extra hard to become that way?" Trissa scowled. "You're beautiful, sweets. Inside and out."

"Don't look now, girls. He's heading this way." Kate's eyes widened.

No! Pele couldn't come over here with her friends. If they realized she worked with him, the heckling would be relentless.

Reagan pushed away from the table. "Fine."

"Go get 'em, cowgirl," Trissa hooted.

With burning cheeks, Reagan slung her purse over a shoulder and hurried to intercept Pele before he reached her table. She stopped a foot away from him. Up close, his dark patterned unbuttoned shirt had a fine linen thread pattern to it. Every movement of his chest shifted and stretched t-shirt material beneath. Dark hair gleamed in waves off his forehead. Somehow, he had gotten bigger, taller, more muscled.

Every inch of his big frame appeared rigid, locked and ready for action. She pressed her thighs together.

The warm air moved around them, and she caught a whiff of his spicy aftershave. That meant that he had shaved. She glanced up. Ah, yes, his strong jaw was nice and smooth. Reagan couldn't stop licking her lips.

His dark gaze narrowed and raked her up and down. When he completely focused on her like that, the perusal felt sexy, not lewd. Her body tingled. In another place and time, she would love to be the recipient of that attention.

Another time. Not this week, after their lip-lock sessions on disastrous replay.

She needed to get him out of this club so she could return to her nice evening with her friends.

"What are you doing here?" She managed to form a sentence.

"Your birthmark is hidden." It wasn't quite a growl. Not a comment, but not a compliment, either.

"What?" She pulled her hair over a shoulder. "Oh, sure. Fewer questions to deal with."

"No one should ever question you," he said so quietly, she had to lean forward to hear him over the din of the club. "You're beautiful tonight. You're beautiful every day."

The intensity of his simple statements made her shiver. Wow, he was extra serious tonight. Maybe he'd been drinking? She sniffed. Didn't smell of alcohol. Sure appeared stone-cold sober to Reagan.

He touched a curl of her long hair, then dropped his hand back to his side. "I've never seen you with anything but your hair pulled back."

"Well, I—"

"I like it." In the crowded bar, his low tone cut through all the other voices. She rubbed her bare arms.

"Thanks." Drinking in the image of his big shoulders, she tried not to think about other areas that might be big. Damn her friends, planting images in her brain. "Mind if we go over there for a minute?" She lifted her chin toward the less-crowded back corner of the club.

"Sure. Why?"

"My friends are having way too much fun watching us."

A hint of a dimple winked on his cheek. "Got it." He preceded her through the crowds while tugging her by the hand. He wasn't aggressive, but his presence had people giving him plenty of room. When someone jostled her, he pulled her to his side and kept an arm secured around her. Warmth flooded through her upper back and shoulder as the band of his muscled arm tightened up.

He stopped at the end of the bar where the crowd thinned out, away from her friends' line of sight.

She spun around. Even with her boots, she had to tilt her head up to look him square in the eye. "Why are you here?"

He pressed his lips into a firm line. "I wanted to unwind after work. I had the evening free."

Crossing her arms, she glared at him. "Try again."

He shifted his weight from foot to foot and glanced at her with as earnest a set of eyes as she'd ever seen. "Linda said you were going out here. I didn't know any places to go. I don't know anyone local—besides you and the people at camp. It sounded a little like one of the bars from military training." He continued. "I thought it might be nice to try it out. Meet some people. You know, socialize."

"Still not sure I'm buying that. You don't strike me as a country-bar kind of guy."

He lifted a dark brow. "Is that a stereotype?"

"No," she huffed. "Yes." Her spine unstiffened. "Damn it. I'm sorry. I'm making assumptions, and it's not okay."

"So. Do I have your permission to hang out at the bar?"

"Yes." She shifted her purse strap up higher. "You can be anywhere you want to be."

"But?"

"Can you stay over here and let me have a nice night out with my friends?" As soon as she said the words, she regretted them. Petty. Unkind. That wasn't Reagan's M.O., and she slapped a hand over her mouth. "Forget I said that. That came out mean, and that's also not okay."

"There are a lot of 'not okay' things lately."

"Look, Pele. We've had a rough start to our ... friendship." Did he snort at that statement? "After last night and everything, seeing you here kind of threw me. Do you understand?"

"Think so." He took three slow breaths and glanced over her shoulder. He trailed a finger over her arm, and she shuddered. "You look nice tonight."

Irritation bubbled up, and she moved away from him. "Seriously, what's your angle, Pele? What's the game?"

"Game?" He dropped his hand to his side.

"It's all a little weird. You shove me away last night. Then all of a sudden you're interested again. You show up here—"

"Reagan?" a too-familiar voice cut into the conversation.

No. Holy shit. Not possible.

"Reagan?" someone repeated.

Did all of her karma decide to collect tonight? Damn it.

If she ignored the voice behind her, maybe he would go away. She could still escape before the public humiliation began. She searched for an exit route. None. She was in a corner. With a large Pele—

"Is that you, honey? Hi."

—and an asshole.

She closed her eyes and prayed she was having a hallucination. Turning, she spied Clayton wearing a designer cowboy shirt. Pearl buttons gleamed. Snug Levi's with a shiny belt buckle emphasized the total package, so to speak. When he smiled, sure, he was handsome in a meticulously put-together kind of way. Brown hair gelled to slightly mussed perfection. The image of a well-dressed, typical "gentleman."

To Reagan, his too-friendly smile felt like a condescending smirk.

When he reached toward her face, she flinched. Flashes of memories. His slaps and kicks. Then he grabbed her chin and kissed her left cheek. Before she could react, Pele took a big step forward and inserted a shoulder between Reagan and her ex, forcing Clayton to break contact.

Oh, no.

She gulped, patted Pele on the back, and shot him a weak smile when he glanced back at her. With a frown, Pele shifted so that he stood to the side, but he maintained a position halfway between Reagan and her ex.

"Clayton," she said, her voice coming out flat, detached. She would stay calm if it killed her. He didn't get the privilege of an emotional response. Not anymore.

Pele watched her with his eyebrows raised, then his stare narrowed.

Her ex-fiancé shot her an overly concerned expression, innocent, with wide eyes and a lean forward. "Reagan, I was super worried about you when you didn't return my messages the other day. You've always called me right back." He flicked a glare at Pele, then back to placid innocence. "We need to talk."

Crossing her arms over her chest, she muttered,

"There is nothing to discuss."

"Of course, there is. Our future, for one."

Seriously, what planet was this guy living on? "No. We have no future. That was made clear."

Rage curdled his features for a split second, and she caught her breath. Then his face calmed to a placid pool again. Amazing how he could flip back and forth.

She knew all about his changing states.

"Why not?" Clayton scowled at Pele, who, for his part, maintained an unhappy, vigilant stance.

Pele looked to be balanced on the balls of his feet. If he was truly military, then the guy could likely go zero to sixty in the blink of an eye.

"Oh, are you with *him* now?" Clayton spoke the words as if *him* denoted some kind of downgrade. Someone less worthy.

Pele might be fighting some personal demons and dealing with PTSD, but he was ten times the man Clayton ever could hope to be. It was so clear, with both of them standing in front of her.

"Well?" Clayton said, so polite. "Who is your *friend*?"

How she wanted to melt into the floor or slap Clayton. Fine. She would do the introductions. She stepped up, in front and to the side of Pele, completing the sick triangle of dysfunction. "Clayton, this is Pele. We work together at camp. Pele, this is my ex, Clayton."

Neither man shook hands.

Her ex turned to her, ignoring the massive guy glaring at him. "Looking good, Reagan." He studied the right side of her face and frowned. "Hey, congrats. Looks like you got it fixed."

She paused. "What?" Her heart tattooed her ribs. Sweat broke out over her lower back.

"The bad spot." He reached for her cheek and

neck, and she flinched again.

She almost didn't detect the movement, but Pele blocked Clayton's hand, pulled Reagan back a socially-acceptable half step, and ended up standing closer to her, not quite touching, but within mere inches of her. Heat poured off of him. Every inch of his frame vibrated with anger. He remained stony and silent.

Clayton rubbed his wrist then made a nasty face and backed away. "About time, huh? The doctors did a great job." He gave her a thumbs-up hand motion from a safer distance.

She wanted to break his fingers.

Pele's eyes cut to Reagan and then back to Clayton. He said nothing, but the press of his strong mouth worried her. Somehow, Pele had managed to get bigger, from the wide set of his legs to his partially flexed arms at his sides. He reeked of barely contained competent aggression, all without moving a muscle. *Oh, God.*

It took her a full five seconds to formulate an answer without saying something shameful. "No, Clayton, this is makeup." Damn it how her voice quavered. She swallowed her emotions. "Thank you for the concern."

He lifted his hands and smiled. But his eyes remained angry. "My bad. I just figured you surely would have, after..." In a fake private voice that anyone in a ten-foot radius could hear, he said, "Does your friend know about what's wrong with your face?"

Asshole, asshole, asshole.

He was going out of his way to be a jerk. Did he know she would be here tonight?

"What do you want, Clayton?" Each word was squeezed out between her clenched teeth. Every cell in her body screamed at her to run and hide. Curl into a ball. But Pele's silent strength next to her helped to stiffen her spine and stare down Clayton.

He sniffed and hooked a thumb in a belt loop. The action looked unnaturally casual. "It would be nice if you told your friends to quit talking trash about me," he said.

Ah, now she had the reason why he went to the trouble of harassing her tonight. "I don't control my friends. They can say whatever they want to. Free speech and all."

"Whatever. Tell them to shut up. My boss heard all about our breakup from lots of people, and it's not helping my ten-year plan at the company. The breakup ruined my reputation. People are saying I dumped the 'disfigured' woman." He made air quotation marks.

She sucked in air. Talk about saying the quiet part out loud.

Clayton continued. "They're trying to make me out to be the bad guy. Hey, I was going to do you a favor. All you had to do was learn some respect."

Would anyone notice if she punched him? She'd show him disfigurement and learning some respect. Sweat rolled between her breasts as she trembled with the effort to remain impassive. On the one hand, she hated to give him the satisfaction of getting under her skin. On the other hand, popping him in that cleft chin would feel so good.

A low rumble began next to her shoulder.

Before she could move, Pele closed the distance to Clayton in a smooth blur. He grabbed her ex's upper arm in a white-knuckled grip where all the muscles and tendons in Pele's hand and forearm bulged. A muscle jumped in his hard jaw, seen in sharp profile. *Oh, man, not good.* Her trembles had turned into full-body shakes.

Then Pele bent his head next to Clayton's ear.

Reagan had to strain to hear his low voice over the sounds of the club.

"… nothing wrong with Reagan. But there's a ton that's wrong with you. You were too stupid to realize how amazing she is. You lose. You're a loser. I don't like how you look at her. I don't like how she wants to get away from you." He glanced around. "If I find out *why* she wants to get away from you, there is a good chance I will commit a felony. Now, you *will* leave her the fuck alone or I will make it so you can only eat through a straw. Got it?" A smirk came and went. "Cowboy?"

Then, like he was hanging out with a friend, Pele clapped his other hand on Clayton's back and shot him a tight smile.

And shoved him back a foot.

Oh, no. Wow.

Clayton pushed his brown hair back off his sweaty forehead. With a cruel twist of his mouth, he spat, "You're nothing without me, baby. You had a chance to be rich with me, but you screwed up. We could have had such an awesome life together. All you had to do was learn some respect for your future husband. Not so hard." A corner of his mouth curled. "Obviously too difficult for you to understand."

The air got stuck in her throat.

He pointed at her but didn't approach. "Do you think this meathead will stick around once he sees what you really look like? No way. I was willing to make the sacrifice and pay to fix it so you could become the beautiful wife of a successful financial analyst who is heading to the top of his company." He barked out a nasty laugh. "Call me when you want a good life. If you're lucky, I'll answer."

He spun on his heel and stomped through the

crowd, careening off other patrons as he left.

Pele took two heavy steps after him, then checked himself and pivoted back toward her. She'd never seen rage like what burned in his eyes right now. Like he could rip someone apart with his bare hands. With a few deep breaths and the clenching and unclenching of his huge fists, he scanned the crowd and mumbled to himself. The word *friend* floated over to her. After a few minutes, his deadly expression settled into something resembling controlled anger.

Or disappointment. That made more sense.

Her ears rang, and fury blurred the edges of her vision. She couldn't move. Couldn't speak.

"Reagan?" The sudden concern in Pele's voice came damned close to launching her into tears. "Reagan."

Crying would be unacceptable on so many levels.

When he reached out, she stumbled back. "Please don't touch me." She clapped her hand over her mouth, like she was trying to erase the humiliation.

"You want me to go out there and take care of him?" he asked, crossing his arms.

Holy mackerel, he was dead serious. The last thing she wanted was for Pele to leave her here right now. Ironic, since not five minutes ago she had accused him of encroaching on her girls' night out. Damn this whole messed-up situation.

Hot air sawed in and out of her throat a few times. Pain lanced through her stomach. It took her another minute before she could speak a full sentence. "Actually, Pele, no. I don't want you to take care of him, tempting as that might be. He doesn't deserve you wasting your time." She lifted a hand toward her purse strap. The damned hand shook. "I need to step into the ladies' room. Would you pardon me, please?"

His dark gaze flashed. "Are you sure you don't need help?"

"In the ladies' room?" Her voice cracked, on edge, manic. She couldn't laugh without fear of crying.

"You know what I mean."

"I'm just fine. Perfectly fine. Super-duper."

She turned on her heel and tried her damnedest to keep her head up while she could feel his stare boring into her back.

Chapter Eighteen

Pele had come dangerously close to removing that asshole's spleen, right here in the middle of the club. After that disgusting conversation, nothing would have given him more pleasure. It took every ounce of control to hold on to the virus, which lunged against its imaginary chain. How amazing would it be to let the Morpheus Virus take over all control while Pele used his augmented strength to go medieval on that *puaaelo*.

Pele performing efficient disemboweling with military precision would attract all the wrong attention.

The desire to hurt that guy continued to simmer.

He scanned the club for the fiftieth time. Friend or enemy? Air in. Friend or enemy? Air out. Clench fists. Unclench fists. Repeat. He kept going until the virus receded into a disgruntled background rumble.

How could anyone say things like that to Reagan? She was a lovely person. Anyone with half a brain could tell.

Her responses to her ex-fiancé didn't suggest a mutually broken engagement.

He saw the fear and pain. *Ti'o*. What had that guy done?

He fought another viral wave urging him to find Clayton and beat some respect into him. When had he come this close to losing control? Never. He needed an antidote shot soon. With a massive effort, Pele shook out his fists and checked his watch.

Reagan had been in the restroom for quite a while. Maybe she needed … what? Help? Support? Was she going to pieces in there after what her ex said? Anger had him fantasizing about how he could create some fresh birthmarks on Pretty Boy's face.

That guy had some balls to disrespect her. When it came to Reagan's fiancé, *o le tau o le maile oe*. That man had the value of a dog. Less than a dog.

The club had gotten more crowded in the past half hour. Bodies moved in time to the loud music. The scents of beer, sweat, and perfume combined in the air. Several patrons sauntered up to him, but he shook his head each time.

He only wanted one person.

He paced in front of the ladies' room, drawing glares and interested glances from the women entering and exiting. Still no Reagan. He'd give her another five minutes, then he was going in after her, and damn anyone's offense.

Three minutes later, Reagan emerged with her long, curly hair pushed back over her shoulders, chin up, mouth set in a determined line. Her skin glowed. She'd removed every trace of makeup.

The only hint as to her true feelings could be seen in the glitter in her eyes and the quiver in her lower lip.

Ti'o, he wanted so badly to wrap his arms around her, insulate and protect her, and convince her that that jerk was wrong. He wanted to prove that she was beautiful.

But she didn't need Pele's help.

She proved the fact of her beauty to herself. As well she should.

"Reagan?"

She lifted a hand. "I'm sorry you got involved in that exchange." Her level, cold voice scared him. Like she was a tight piece of crystal.

One tap on the glass and she'd shatter.

Shaking his head, he said, "I should have stepped in sooner." Although he needed to touch her, he paused when she stiffened her posture.

"Wasn't your job." Her neck muscles moved as she swallowed. "Hopefully this won't ruin your evening."

"Hanging out with you? Not at all."

"No, I meant later, here. You wanted to get away from work, and dealing with stupid drama involving my ex isn't exactly relaxing."

"This is right where I want to be." Too bad she didn't know the accuracy of his words. He had to keep track of her for her own safety. Little did he know that in the process of doing his Morpheus Squad mission, he'd also get to step in to knock a pissant down to size.

Now he wanted to be near her for his own selfish needs.

"Yeah, okay then." She looked at the floor.

"Reagan?" He couldn't resist touching her. He prayed he could keep the contact gentle and smoothed his hand from her hair to her jaw. Guiding her chin up with one fingertip, he studied her carefully controlled expression.

The moment when she swallowed while looking right at him hit him like a kick to his solar plexus, and the damned virus jumped into a new gear, wanting to kill anyone who dared hurt her. Hell, it wanted Pele to kill anyone who so much as looked at her the wrong way. With herculean effort, he locked down the destructive urges. Stared at her. *Friend versus enemy.* Breathe in. Breathe out. He knew which one Reagan represented, and his anger-blurred vision latched on to her beautiful face and calmed. The hungry, furious virus had no place here tonight.

She pressed her lips together.

Easing away from his finger, she sighed.

He dropped his hand to his side.

"Normally … it doesn't bother me. The

appearance. How it looks." Her mouth twisted as she bit the inside of her cheek. "Thank you for standing up for me tonight. You didn't have to do that."

"Yes, I did, because—"

"Please." Her hoarse voice ramped up his need to protect her. Surround her with his body, his entire being. "Pele, don't complete that sentence."

"Okay." He rubbed his thigh. "What can I do for you?"

A man in a cowboy hat passed by and gave a double-take and a frown when he noticed her birthmark. Pele fought the urge to punch the guy—any person—for thinking anything negative about her.

"Walk me out to my truck?"

Ti'o. He'd do anything she asked right now. Especially if it meant he could be close to her. "Sure. Do you need to let your friends know you're leaving?"

"Already texted them." She patted her small purse and ducked her head when a woman passed by and stared. "Let's go."

"Of course." He tugged her into his side opposite his hidden Sig. As they moved toward the door, he put his arm around her shoulders. No one would bump into her or touch her without her say-so. He would be her armor.

They slowly made their way to the door and out into the cool, clear night. He kept his arm around her as they wove through the parking lot. He didn't want to break contact. Not yet.

Some men a few rows over laughed and upended bottles as they leaned against a bumper. One glanced up, then checked his phone. Strolling through the parking lot, a young couple held hands and headed toward the front door of the club. Two patrons waved as they got out of their vehicles. Normal activities. Normal patterns.

A breeze moved pieces of her curly hair around to brush against his arm. The whisper of movement sent bolts of desire down deep into his gut. What would her hair feel like drifting all over his naked body as she moved over him?

The skirt hem, which stopped above her knee, shifted as well. A wave of hunger served up an image of him pushing her against her truck and plunging his hands in her thick hair while he kissed her. He wanted to explore the skin underneath that skirt, lifting that lace with his hand, tracing the skin up to her core. Before he could follow that thought any further, he whipped his head around.

His steps faltered.

Then he stopped, all senses focused on his environment. Patterns.

Patterns. They were wrong.

Even though they were sixty feet from where she had parked, his enhanced skill to detect patterns picked up unnatural, shadowy movement near her truck. The group of men drinking toward the front of the lot had disappeared. His attention twisted into sharp focus. Visual patterns didn't fit. The gravel was disturbed around the truck. He slowed his pace and surveyed the area.

Behind the truck was an overgrown ditch filled with shrubs. Ample space to hide. He knew that because he'd surveyed the entire lot before entering the club.

Normal sounds—trucks on I-40, thumping bass beats filtering out of the club, the tinkling of glass bottles—all faded into the background. An abnormal sound and shadow pattern emerged. Someone was in that ditch. How many?

Couldn't tell.

Cold sweat broke out on his forehead. Fear. The

virus didn't let him experience that emotion.

Fear lanced through him. The virus rushed through his veins to counteract the emotion.

Ti'o. If Pele could track her here, then what was to say Lequire's men couldn't do the same? Or worse. The switch flipped, and he went into full security mode, scanning the area, senses open, listening and watching.

With instincts honed from several tours of duty where he had to enter dangerous and unsecured locations, from dealing with IEDs and roadside bombs, and from his virally charged ability to pick up on abnormal patterns, there was no doubt: she should not get back in the truck.

"Reagan, could I drive you back? It's late."

She paused. "What about my truck?"

"We can pick it up tomorrow or this weekend."

Out of the corner of his eye, he spied someone ducking behind the vehicle. *Ti'o,* and his gun hand was around her shoulder. His second gun was in his left boot, out of reach.

He slid his left hand to his lower back and curled his fingers around the knife hilt in the holster there. *Wait.*

Wait.

The best weapon was one he never had to use.

He took a deep breath. It might look like he was relaxed, but instead, Pele was centering himself to prepare for every angle of attack and any means of protecting Reagan. "You're tired. It was a long week for both of us, and a stressful night. I'd feel better if we went back together."

An abnormal reflection in a car window down the back row of the parking lot had his instincts screaming. Another figure approached her truck from the other side of the tailgate. If she didn't agree to leave with him, he'd have to pick her up, throw her in his car, and take off.

Yeah, all caveman like that. He didn't care if he made a scene or if she hated him afterward. At least she would be alive.

She bit her lip.

His heart stopped. *Please agree.*

"Well. I could use a return trip to get some supplies at Turkey Creek shopping center." She shivered, and he tucked her even closer to his side, rubbing her bare arm. "Does your car have heat?" she asked.

"As much as you want."

The expression she shot him had such a mixture of sadness, interest, and hunger, it made his stomach tighten. *Focus.* He could not afford to lose concentration.

"Over this way." Trying not to hurry, but needing to get her away from potential danger, he guided her to where he'd parked, on the opposite end of the lot and far away from her truck. With several quick checks over his shoulder, he made sure no one followed them. If he'd been lucky, he had detected the people around her vehicle well before they saw him.

If he was lucky.

Regardless, now he had to deal with a compromised truck. He'd sweep it for bugs or tracking devices and assess for sabotage later. One step at a time. For now, he had to get her back to camp safely, where he had security measures in place, additional stashed weapons, and a modicum of control over the situation.

Step two. Stick close to her.

Step three. Figure out how to stick very close—without hurting her this time.

Chapter Nineteen

Reagan woke up when the growl of Pele's late-model Dodge Charger on asphalt changed to a rumble under the wheels as they turned onto the camp's gravel road. The toasty interior of the muscle car and the heated leather seat had lulled her to sleep as they left Knoxville. She smiled at his profile as he maneuvered up the road. His cell phone glowed in his hand with several black and white videos and pictures. He clicked off the screen and tucked the device in his pocket.

"Awake?" His low voice in the confined space sent a quiver through her heart. He glanced over and licked his lips.

She followed his gaze to her thighs, which peeked out from the hem of her skirt. Warmth flooded her upper chest.

"Yes." She rolled her shoulders, smoothing the skirt down. "Sorry to be terrible company for the ride back."

"That's okay. I'm glad you rested. It was a stressful evening."

They passed the camp buildings. All the lights were out.

"No one in camp tonight?" he asked.

"Chad and Jamila are out, and Linda went to visit her parents in Nashville. No groups of kids to yank fish out of the stream, no night hikes, no loud dining hall until Monday." She blew out a breath. "Don't get me wrong, I love all of those things, but it's nice to have a break every now and then."

"I can see why. Those school groups take a lot of energy."

After another few minutes of the car gently

bumping toward the end of the road, he pulled up in front of her cabin and parked, hurrying around to open her door. His warm hand steadied her as she exited.

"Do you need a flashlight?" he asked.

"No. I know the path well."

He kept hold of her hand until they reached the front door and she opened it.

At a flutter in her chest, she tamped the response down hard. He'd made his feelings clear last night when he left. She knew the score. And she knew that her emotional state wasn't the most stable right now.

He cleared his throat. "Reagan, are you okay from … everything at the club?"

"Fine," she said too quickly. "Thanks for your help."

When she tried to enter the cabin, he didn't let go of her hand. "He's an idiot, you know. Your ex."

"Yes, I know. Thank you again—"

"That's not why I said it." Pele followed her into the cabin and flipped on the overhead light. They both flinched at the sudden brightness.

He kicked the door closed with his booted foot and turned to her. "I meant what I said. You're beautiful."

"I, um— Okay, thanks."

"No, Reagan. You don't understand." When he framed her face in his hands, a strange emotion, something sad but hopeful, sparked deep down inside her walled-off heart.

Almost reverently, he brushed his lips over her forehead, her eyebrows, and both cheeks. Shivers shot through her body after each light kiss, and she leaned into his touch.

As much as she wanted him to transport her on a cloud of happiness, they'd been here already. Twice. She didn't trust either of them in this situation.

"Pele, stop for a minute." Tugging on his wrists, she pulled his hands away, hating the lack of connection. She needed a little distance to breathe. To think. "See this here? You and me in the cabin? Doing this?"

"Yes."

She stepped back, breaking contact. "We've rehearsed this scenario before. Spoiler alert: It ends with you making an excuse and then running out that door."

"I had to go before."

"Sure you did." She waved off his retort. "Look, you're a great guy, like, really great." She swallowed. "But I don't have it in me to go through another repeat of how we've done this before." Damn it, when her voice cracked. "I can't handle another rejection. Not after this week, and not after tonight."

"I didn't reject you," he protested.

"That's not how it appeared from where I stand." She crossed her arms. "Why are you here, now, Pele?" she said, not caring if she made him uncomfortable. It was time for stark truth. "What do you want?"

His jaw worked for a full minute. Cords tightened in his neck and shoulders. Damn. She might not want his answer if it took that long.

The words came out raw, like he'd yanked them from his chest. "I want you, Reagan. All of you."

She sucked in a breath. "You have a funny way of showing it."

"Like, I said … chalk the last two nights up to really bad timing and some personal issues on my part."

"Huh. Go on." Was that sweat on his brow? Good.

"I would only want to … be with you, if you want the same exact thing."

"Be more specific."

"*Ti'o*, you aren't making this easy."

"It hasn't been an easy week for me."

"That's fair." He rubbed his thigh and glanced over her shoulder toward the window. Then the full weight of his deep, dark eyes fell on her. "You want specific?"

"Yes?" Her voice cracked.

"If it was up to me, we would go downstairs to your room. I would strip you naked and taste every inch of your body before we have what I pray to any god out there is a night of amazing sex where you are totally satisfied. Multiple times."

"Oh," she exhaled, a liquid heat pooling between her legs where a throbbing sensation began.

"You asked for specifics." Was his chest rising and falling faster? "Let me know if you want more details."

"Tell me you're not playing me," she whispered.

The edge in his voice made her jump. "No. Way. Absolutely not. Not with this, Reagan." He rolled his lips together, and she wanted to lick him there. "But I will walk away if that's what you decide. It'll be damned hard, but I will do it if you say so."

Her heart pounded double time. Decision time.

She knew what her body wanted. Pele.

What about her heart?

Her future. They hadn't talked future. Was it necessary? No. For once, she didn't need to plan her life beyond this one evening.

"Reagan?" The harshness of his low voice strafed her raw nerves. "Should I leave?"

She rubbed her arms. "That's not what I want."

"Okay." His pupils dilated until there was nothing but black in his intense gaze. "Then you tell me how you want this evening to end. You choose. You are in control.

I will do everything in my power to make what you say happen."

Damn, he didn't tiptoe around things. She rubbed her cheek, then made a conscious effort to bring her hand back down to her side. No more hiding. God help her, but could she take the chance that he was sincere? She drowned in his dark stare.

Utterly sincere. Stark honesty. Wow.

Swallowing, she answered, "I want us to be … together. Completely. Yes. Um, but at the end of the evening, I want you to still be here. With me. No running."

He stepped forward in a broad, open stance, cupped her face, and kissed her until her knees wobbled. Breaking the contact for a moment, he growled. "Done. But I do need to take care of something first. Restroom?"

Reeling back a step, she pointed across the cabin. "There."

He was in and out in a few minutes, this time carrying his button-down shirt in a wadded-up, bulky bundle which he set on the floor near the door to her apartment. Weird. Not that she was complaining at all. The ridges of muscles shifted under the tight t-shirt as he stalked back toward her.

Snaking an arm behind her back, he pulled her into his hard torso. She put her hands up and met ridges of muscle that flexed beneath her fingertips. As he kissed her again, she matched his mouth, pressure for pressure. Every angle and quick breath. Faster and harder, the kisses rained down on her, and she kept up, returning each one. Somehow, she ended up against a wall, with his hands planted on either side of her head, bracketing her. No escape. Not that she wanted to leave. No way.

When he leaned into her, his pants-covered erection hit her at the perfect spot, grinding against her.

She met him with a thrust of her hips, sending delicious sensations deep into her tingling core.

He nipped his way down one side of her neck and up the other side while skimming her arms with the rough pads of his fingers. Between her overheated body and his warm torso, she might burst into flames. Spontaneous combustion. What a way to go. She closed her eyes, stopped competing with him, and accepted the feathered kisses over her eyelids.

When he untucked her denim shirt and trailed his fingers over the skin of her back, she shuddered.

"Your room?" His voice, so close to her ear, sent another quiver through her body.

"Through that door." She managed to motion in the general direction.

He locked the front door, turned off the light, glanced out the window, picked up the shirt bundle, and guided her down the dark stairs and into her small apartment. Almost like he'd been there before. Maybe he had good night vision.

She flipped on her bedside lamp. He dwarfed everything in the room. The double bed would barely hold his frame, much less both of theirs.

Problems that could be solved later.

Turning, she pulled him down for another kiss and darted her tongue to meet his, pleased to hear a deep groan of response. God, the tone vibrated through her ribs, making her breasts tighten.

"Different light?" he asked.

She frowned. "You want less light?" Her face burned. Her heart pounded, and not from the kisses. No. She would not return to how things had been with Clayton.

He shook his head and turned on the fluorescent overhead lights. "Please," he said. "I want to see you.

And I want you to see all of me."

An odd request, but she could live with it, especially if it meant watching his muscles ripple every time he moved. Heck, she'd take a front-row seat and get a bucket of popcorn if he wanted to put on a show.

When he kissed her, he stroked the sensitive skin under the hem of her denim top, raising more goose bumps.

With eager fingers, she pulled his t-shirt up and off. Her breath caught. He was all smooth, golden-brown skin layered over hard muscle. When she trailed her fingers over the planes of his belly to the low-slung waistband of his pants, he shuddered and gripped her upper arms.

Lower, over his hips, the skin itself formed ridges. She leaned back and peered at him.

An intricate, black geometric pattern began about six inches above his hipbones, curved down and disappeared below his waistband. Even his navel had dark marks next to it. Tracing the top of the design above his hips, she followed the raised skin in a horizontal line around his back. He hissed.

"What is this?" she asked.

He hesitated, his brows drawn down, wary, watching her. Like her reaction mattered.

"It's a *pe'a*. It's generally known as the *tatau*, or what you call a tattoo." He sucked in a breath as she swept her fingers over a black square that included his navel. "The *pe'a* can be … surprising … if you haven't seen one before. Um, some women don't like it."

What wasn't to like? This was Pele. She felt the skin over his hipbones again. "Why is the skin raised?"

Studying her, he answered slowly. "In the Samoan technique, the *pe'a* is a full-thickness skin-marking process. When they do it the traditional way with sharpened bone instruments, the ink is driven down much further into the skin than with a typical tattoo."

"Was it painful?" She traced the geometric pattern visible above his waistband and glanced up at him.

His brows drew together. "Yes." He took her wrists and eased her away. "This is part of why I wanted the lights on." He touched the button of his pants. "Can I show the rest of it to you?"

Who the heck would say no? She wanted to see what lay below his waist. All of it. With a jerk of her head, she nodded.

A muscle jumped in his jaw as he kept his gaze locked on hers. He unbuttoned his pants, let them drop to the floor, and stepped out of the pants, shoes, and socks, leaving him only in black briefs.

Her mouth went dry.

He stood before her, all glowing skin and thick muscle. The black pattern continued in thick horizontal bands of triangles, leaves, and arrows in a design down his legs that stopped an inch below the knees. His erection strained against the dark fabric of his briefs. His chest and abdomen moved with his harsh breaths as he watched her.

"How much did they tattoo?" she asked, then flushed. "Um."

Smiling, he turned around. She swallowed hard. His lower back and legs were heavily muscled, and the markings gave him an even more powerful appearance.

Glancing over his shoulder, he winked. "Just about everything."

She swallowed.

"Wow. This is so intricate." She traced more of the patterns down to the waistband of his briefs, then the backs of his thighs.

He shuddered again. "You have to stop that."

She froze and snatched her hand away. "Oh, gosh. Does it hurt?"

"Not at all. But if you continue to touch me like that, I won't be able to control what happens next." The low, hungry growl of his voice made her nipples tighten.

She moved around to face him, slid a finger under the elastic band, and drew the garment down and away. "Is loss of control the worst thing ever?" His thick erection reached almost to his navel. The ink stopped above the base of his penis.

Stroking the hot, velvety skin covering his hard erection, she smiled when his breath rasped in and out of his open mouth. Then she slid her hand down to cup his heavy scrotum. The ink stopped at the crease of his groin.

Her internal thermostat shot up twenty degrees.

He gripped her upper arms. "You have far too much clothing on."

"Do you have a solution?"

"I have an idea." With a wolfish grin, he leaned down to kiss and lick her collarbones, then slowly unbuttoned the shirt until it rested in a pile on the floor. He drew her bra down and away. "*Ti'o*. You're beautiful."

When he put his mouth on her skin, it was on the top of her right shoulder, where the port-wine stain started. He lifted her hair and kissed along the birthmark to her cheek and back down again.

"You have a *tatau* from God." Avid hunger lit his liquid brown eyes. He spun around, sat on the bed, and snagged her around the waist until she stood in front of him, her hands resting on his shoulders. "I've wanted to see you like this since the first night in the cabin."

Leaning forward, he licked her hard, aching

breast. Her knees nearly buckled, but he held her steady. His mouth worked patterns over one breast while his hand caressed the other.

She groaned and slid her hands up his neck to grab the short hair at the nape. Anything to remain standing, which became hard to do when he pinched a nipple. Her knees went weak, and she moaned. Then he sucked the nipple into his mouth, held it between his teeth, and laved the tip with his rough tongue.

"Oh, God," she whispered. Damp warmth blossomed between her thighs.

"We're just getting started." His voice against her breast made her sensitive skin quiver.

He reached around and unzipped her skirt, pushing it down and away. Helping her to balance, he supported her as she removed her boots. Now she stood in front of him wearing nothing but her panties.

Leaning forward from the edge of the bed, he kissed her belly, and she shuddered.

"I need to see more," he said, slipping the panties off. He eased her legs apart.

The urge to cover up hit her out of the blue, but his intense expression stopped her. Watching the way his chest hauled air in and out as he moved from one breast to the other made her shake. When he stared at her, his smile appeared possessive, hungry, appreciative. With a growl, he dropped his face back on her breasts and nipped and licked her into a frenzy.

Sliding a finger down her stomach, he moved lower and separated her folds. Sparks of pleasure entered her vision. He dipped a finger into her liquid heat.

Reagan dug her fingers into his broad shoulders. "Pele, oh my God." She groaned as he worked his rough palm and fingers against her sensitive skin for several blissful minutes. When he pulled away, the loss of sensation had her grinding her teeth and arching her pelvis toward him. More. She wanted so much more.

Standing, he cupped the back of her head and kissed her, thrusting his tongue deep into her mouth. He turned them until her legs hit the bed, and he guided her down onto the mattress, kneeling over her. The bed creaked. His massive frame took up all of her field of vision. Overhead light streamed around him.

Pele occupied every thought in her mind, every sensation in her body.

With his touches that alternated between soft and hard pressure, she bucked against his hand. He repositioned himself to kneel between her legs. Then he slid her legs wide, opening her. She shivered.

When he slipped two fingers inside, her whole body tensed. With a frown, he held still, and with his other hand, he stroked her sensitive skin until she melted, legs falling to the sides. More curling sweeps of his fingers brought her higher and higher until her whole body tensed and released, shaking all around him. Gripping his arms, she held on as she rode his fingers and the waves ebbed away.

He withdrew his fingers and licked them, staring at her like she was a feast to consume. "You're amazing."

A shiver ran through her tingling body.

He leaned over the bed and opened a foil packet on the bedside table, sheathing himself.

A new bolt of excitement hit her. Wow. His pulsing erection jutted out hard and massive. When he nudged her legs apart again, she trembled.

On all fours, he knelt over her, not touching her, but so close that the heat pouring off of him seeped into her skin. As she'd seen with him before, his frame seemed to grow, took up more space. Every muscle bulged in his big body.

His erection teased her wet entrance as he trailed his fingertips over her chest. "I have to be careful," he gritted out. "I want you more than I've wanted anyone in my entire life." Sweat glistened on his brow. "Reagan, I don't want to hurt you. But I'm on the edge here."

She dug her fingers into the hard muscles of his lower back, guiding him down toward her. "Screw going slow, Pele. I need you inside me." She lifted her hips. "Now."

At his achingly slow first thrust to enter her, Reagan's heart almost stopped as she stretched to accept him. He held still for a few seconds, cords of tight muscles popping out on his neck. Then he withdrew and thrust again, deeper this time. The rhythm sped up, and she rocked her hips with him. Gasps and moans filled the room until, with a guttural groan, he had seated himself completely in her.

Then he really started to move.

Oh, God, that had only been a warm-up?

The muscles on his arms bunched as he pushed out a faster pace.

Meeting his hard thrusts, she panted with the growing pressure and need for another climax.

He was muttering in between groans. "Control it. Control it. *Kefe.*" Cords stood out stark on his thick neck.

"Are you okay?" she managed to ask.

He sat back on his heels, shaking. They were still connected. God, she wanted him to move.

Framing her face in his hands, he panted. "Are *you* all right? *Ti'o.* Please tell me I'm not hurting you. I swear I'm trying to be careful." Sweat glistened on his brow.

"Not at all. I—" She swallowed, needing all of him without his restraint, without any hesitation.

"What?"

"Please, Pele. I don't want you to hold back. I want all of you. Please. Give me everything."

His jaw hardened.

He blinked, like flipping an internal switch.

Then his eyes bored into her soul. He snarled, feral and teetering on a threshold that she couldn't fathom. With a guttural roar, he drove in even deeper, over and over, until she whimpered with pleasure. All the nerve endings ignited. Her head spun. He snaked his arms under her back and grabbed her shoulders, locking her in place. His movements had become wild, fierce, and he groaned with each stroke deep into her core.

She hooked a heel around his hip, and the change in angle activated nerves she didn't even know existed. Under her hands, his muscles bunched and released as he thrust faster than she could match, so she hung on for the ride.

With another harsh growl, he panted, "Reagan, you … I'm going to come."

Sparks of pleasure combined into a firestorm of need as the sensations converged until she couldn't tell where his heated body stopped and hers started.

Their cries and moans blended with the sound of skin slapping together until stars burst in her vision and she tightened in a quick rhythm around his pulsing erection as they peaked at the same time. She lost all ability to control her body for how long—minutes, hours?—as she drowned in a tidal wave of ecstasy.

When she came back down to Earth, Pele was there, holding her shuddering body, stroking her sweaty skin. The hunger in his dark gaze shook her to the core.

Tenderness and stark need. All focused on her.

Chapter Twenty

Reagan's flesh quivered as Pele swept his fingers, starting at her hand and then moving up her arm and over her chest. Over and over again, trying to convince himself this experience was real. Lying on his side, he traced invisible patterns over her breasts and belly. He'd left the lights on. Her curly orange-blonde hair had tangled around her shoulders, and her lips were swollen and damp, tempting him to kiss them over and over.

He might not have a normal life expectancy, or the expectation of a normal life. But if every day on this earth that he had remaining came with a vision like the one before him, he would be the luckiest man in the universe. The simple act of watching her sleep kept the beast inside of him vigilant, possessive, but calm. As long as he could see her, touch her, and hear her breathing, he would be okay.

He had checked his security measures on his phone as she slept. After they had connected on such a primal level, his viral urge to protect her had shot off the charts. Every moment she slept, he listened for anything abnormal outside the cabin. Any change in normal sound patterns. Anything that could harm her, he would stop it before it could reach Reagan.

Or die trying.

The virus rumbled agreement through his veins.

When her eyelids fluttered open, the intensity of her sky-blue irises stopped his breathing.

"Hi," he said, cupping one breast. It fit in his palm perfectly, like everything else about her.

"Hi, yourself."

With a sweet yawn, she stretched like a cat, despite the fact that their limbs were still tangled together. Then she touched his hip. The simple act of her hand skimming over the *pe'a* ridges set his skin on sensual fire and made him want her to touch him everywhere else.

When she frowned, he rubbed a finger over the furrow between her brows. "What?"

"How long did it take to get it?" She traced a triangle pattern.

"The *pe'a*? Six hours a day for three weeks."

"You're kidding."

"No, it was a rite of passage, I went back to Samoa to complete it. There was extended family present, singing, resting their hands on me. That all helped me connect with my home and my culture."

"That's a hell of a way to connect." Her smile emerged like the subtropical sun rising over the Pacific Ocean.

Careful not to exert too much pressure, he stroked her cheek with a knuckle. "Not all men will do it. Some can't complete the process. The symbols represent our individual journey and our family. The pain is meant for the men. Women bear children, men bear the *pe'a*." At her raised eyebrows, he laughed. "That's not to say some Samoan women don't get a version as well, but it doesn't cover as much skin. The *malu* is more … delicate … might be the accurate term."

"Did you feel more connected, um, to your culture?" An odd flicker of sadness changed her expression for a moment, and then it was gone.

"For a time, yes. But that wasn't all that I wanted out of my life. It's an important piece of who I am, but it's not everything." It had taken some time and distance to figure it out, but his path lay in a different direction.

"Thank you for showing me this." She traced the design down to his outer thigh.

"Not many people get to see it. It stays covered up. Too many questions. Too much attention."

"I understand."

He let a finger drift over her birthmark until she shivered. "I know you do." Smoothing the pad of his thumb over her lips, he then dipped down and kissed her until they were both breathless. After only a few kisses, he was hard and ready again.

"Anything else you feel I should understand about who you are?" She raked her fingers through his hair, making his scalp tingle.

When he sat back on his heels, something was obvious. His erection wanted one thing: Reagan.

"Well. I believe that I might have above-average … stamina."

When she wrapped her hand around him, he lost the ability to speak.

With a wink, she licked her lip and did a clever twist with her hand. "Do you think it's true?"

When he could form words, they came out hoarse. "You would be a better judge. We should probably test the theory." His virus raged to life, ready for the challenge.

He grabbed her bent knees and scooted her to him. Her yelp of surprise changed into a breathy moan when he licked the sensitive spot between her legs.

Thank God he'd packed extra condoms. If he had any say in it, he would test his stamina for the rest of the night.

****

Reagan groaned as she pulled on her light hiking boots. Her hips ached in the best possible way after the amazing night with Pele. The mere thought of his mouth on her body, his heavy thrusts inside of her made her throb for him all over again.

He'd left this morning, saying he needed to make some calls, but not after throwing her legs over his broad shoulders and going for round … God knew how many.

She strolled down the path toward the gravel road. Camp Foxfire remained silent and peaceful. Probably good it was deserted with as much noise as they made last night. If there had been campers around, most of them would have needed counseling if they'd listened in on Reagan and Pele.

Well. For a gal who had sworn off men, that was a hell of a rebound. He'd supported her with Clayton and had taken care of her. He'd stayed the entire night and held her in his arms, mostly because the bed was tiny and that was the only way they'd fit. She could still feel the imprint of his big frame wrapped around her from behind, keeping her warm and safe. It would be hard to compare any other guys to Pele in the future.

Did she want to compare more?

Not going to answer that question. Not her decision.

If he decided he needed someone steeped in the tradition of his home, she would never fit the bill. However, she had made peace with that realization. No more than she wanted to be changed to fit someone else's idea of an ideal mate, Pele shouldn't have to compromise either. He had as much right as anyone to choose the shape of the rest of his life.

Still didn't lessen the sting of loss that would come if he decided his life didn't have space for her in it.

At the end of the day, she would be okay. Her heart lifted.

She would be okay. Wasn't that a wonderful realization?

A whippoorwill in the nearby trees called its own name from the high branches but had no useful answers for Reagan in the cool air.

Picturing Pele's face in her memory, she stumbled on the gravel underfoot at another brief flash of déjà vu.

Why did she still have that lingering sense that she'd seen Pele before? Seemed like she'd figure it out by now. He had a military background, so it could be due to some passing familiarity to her brother Brady.

Reaching the deserted camp office, she flipped on the computer and checked emails. She groaned. The internet ran slowly today. They still had to connect via satellite link, which didn't play well with dense tree cover. She was surprised when any data made it this far out here.

Gmail loaded, and she clicked on the inbox.

Nothing from Kiera.

Dad sent her a funny cartoon about the mailman and a dog, along with fifteen other humorous emails. It always made her giggle, her father recently discovering the full use of email. Now he spammed her with jokes. Which suited her fine except for the part where it took forever to download the files.

An email from Britt caught her attention. Damn it, how had Reagan forgotten about the big fashion show next week? It was an invitation to Britt's final project from college—the fashion show. Reagan smiled. Her final, *final* project. Of the major she had finally decided on. Finally.

Of course, with her flighty sister, a month left of school meant there was still room to change her mind. Reagan chuckled to herself. No way would she miss her sister's senior project. It was happening in a week. She'd figure out how to get time off.

With a quick reply, Reagan RSVP'd and hit *send*.

When Pele finished making his calls this

morning, he and Reagan would head back to Knoxville to pick up her truck at the club. Good grief, was that nasty confrontation only last night? Her stomach clenched. Stupid Clayton.

In other email news, the apologies rolled in from Kate. Turned out, Clayton had gotten her to spill that Reagan was meeting her girlfriends and when and where. He said he was eager to talk to Reagan and apologize. Wanted to try to get back together. Kate never knew about the abusive background and thought she was helping.

Clayton, apologizing? He'd been eager to insult her.

As a grown woman, Reagan could deal with a jerk. She could stand up for herself. But how nice had it felt to have Pele's calmly dangerous presence next to her? She could almost believe that Pele saw the real Reagan, inside and out.

He bolstered her confidence. With Pele around, she felt stronger, more capable of dealing with life.

With a sigh, she patted her pocket where her truck keys resided. The small thumb drive of pictures swung from the chain, and she stared at it for a minute, debating.

She could do this today.

She had dealt with Clayton. She had gotten to a good place with her own hang-ups. Now it was time to start dealing with the memories of her brother.

Then she did something she'd been unable to do yet. She plugged in the drive and opened the folder.

His Fallen Comrades photo came up first. The official picture Brady had taken before he died. His reddish-brown hair had grown out enough to cover the scar on his forehead from his head injury. A thickness formed in her throat as she studied the sincere expression on his handsome face. She ran a fingertip over the screen, skimming his cheek in the picture. God, she missed Brady.

All of his online pictures had been saved to a few personal thumb drives after her family scrubbed his social media squeaky clean for his job at Fallen Comrades. Having this reminder of Brady with her at all times reassured her. Unsettled her.

Such a shame that her brother had died. So many questions hadn't been answered.

No, Brady didn't die. He was killed. At least according to Kiera's theory, and maybe that was part of why her sister had been incognito for the past year. Reagan had heard enough whispered conversations last summer between Kiera and Mateo, Brady's Army buddy, to get the gist of what they believed and why.

Reagan wanted to help, but with the insane and terrible year she had experienced, there was neither time nor emotional energy to investigate.

Had she neglected the memory of her brother because of her own selfish pain? A twisty sensation in her chest told the truth: possibly.

Reagan didn't know what to believe. She had tried not to think about Brady for the past year.

So, why now? Why today?

Perhaps it was the first time in a long time that she had dumped her other baggage enough to deal. Or it was simply time.

Or something about being around Pele had cracked open the hard shell protecting and insulating her. Regardless, she wanted to know more about her brother's life and death.

With half of her attention focused on the computer, she clicked on Brady's photos and scrolled through them. The most recent ones showed him in physical therapy and occupational therapy—at the VA—and no thanks to the corrupt Fallen Comrades, despite the organization's promises of support and treatment. Long-suppressed anger rose in a hot wave. The so-called veteran's charity had used her brother's story about his injuries received in service to the country to persuade people to donate. She pulled up a press photo of Brady shaking the hand of the Fallen Comrades' slick CFO, Beau Lequire. That guy had said all the right things but followed through on none of the promises to find out the real cause of Brady's death.

Clicking through the images, her vision blurred as she blinked back tears. Brady had been her big brother, her protector, and her friend. The injury in Afghanistan while he had been on a mission with his Special Forces squad had earned him an honorable discharge. Even after treatment, he never was the same Brady again, thanks to the brain damage. Yet, he never talked about any of his teammates or their missions. Ever.

No squad members visited him after he returned stateside. Only Mateo and Jake came to the funeral.

Why didn't the team show up when Reagan and her family laid her brother to rest? Brady was a great guy. A good teammate.

Anger bubbled up again. Why did Brady have to die? What had truly happened to her brother? None of the police reports of a gang shooting in Atlanta made any sense. Beau Lequire, who acted like Brady was his best friend in front of the media, never returned emails or calls from the McNeill family.

Click, click. She tapped the mouse. The content of photos changed from recent backgrounds of lush green trees in Atlanta and east Tennessee back to dusty blue skies, gray-brown hillsides, and tan-colored vehicles as she viewed the older pictures from Afghanistan. In a group photo, Brady had his arms around two other men. Each squad member had black rectangles over their eyes and nose for security purposes, or they wore sunglasses.

Reagan checked the date. One week before he'd been injured.

She clicked again, flipping back further. Groups of men in desert camouflage uniforms. Soldiers wearing Special Forces stripes and green berets. Most sported beards and hard, grim lines of their mouths. She squinted. A man next to Brady faced the camera. Intense expression, even with sunglasses. Was the man's tan from being in the sun during his tour of duty?

The set of his shoulders. Familiar.

Deep in her gut, a sick twist began.

She clicked again and found a photo of the same man without the Kevlar jacket over the uniform. No name on the uniform. Eyes blacked out in the picture.

Scrolling back further, she studied more photos. Green trees again. Special Forces training. Must be near Fort Bragg in North Carolina. A small group of men that she assumed were his squad teammates.

His arm was slung around the big shoulders of two teammates clad in sweaty t-shirts and shorts, like they'd just finished a PT run. The man next to Brady must have worn black compression tights that came below the knees.

Wait. No.

Her hand shook as she clicked the mouse.

After centering the magnifying glass over the man's knees, she enlarged the image.

Not compression tights.

A dense, black geometric pattern.

Pe'a.

Chapter Twenty-One

In the empty gravel parking pad above the dining hall, Pele set up his computer and satellite phone and waited for Hunt to pick up. He scrolled through the security cameras for the millionth time and visually scanned the surrounding woods and building, looking for any pattern that didn't fit.

Thank God Pele had secured Reagan's cabin and set up the perimeter alarms before he tracked her to the club in Knoxville and then returned with her. He couldn't have handled leaving midway through that incredible night.

If it meant keeping her safe, yes, he would have left, but it would've killed him to hurt her once again. He never could have come back from one more betrayal of her.

Speaking of safe, he patted the foil packets remaining in his pocket. He always made sure sex occurred with a condom, but since receiving the Morpheus Virus several years ago in the Army, he'd become even more aware of the importance of protecting his partner. From the best information available, it was believed that the virus couldn't be transmitted during sex, but Pele refused to take any chances with Reagan.

Walking out of her room this morning, after untangling her sexy limbs from around him and kissing her until the taste of her lips imprinted on his senses, took a massive force of will.

He hated leaving her, but he had to call in an update to Hunt and then get his antidote dose. He had gotten twitchy the past twenty-four hours, and his ability to control the viral urges had slipped. Hypervigilance and fatigue shortened the time between doses.

At least Reagan had promised to go straight to the office and wait for him there so they could return to Knoxville in an hour. He'd deal with her vehicle when they reached the club parking lot. He felt somewhat confident that he had the area from her cabin to the office locked down as tightly as possible.

If she went elsewhere, all bets were off as to his ability to keep her safe.

Pele had made a decision. After seeing the suspicious activity around her truck last night, either he needed more help right now, or he had to explain the security situation to Reagan so she could participate in her own safety. Besides, he hated keeping the truth of his mission from her. It was her life—she deserved to be better protected or at least know what was going on so she could help him in the mission.

His CO picked up after three rings. "Hunt."

Before Pele could answer the barked greeting, the trail cam alarm buzzed. Every sense focused on the blinking screen.

"Hang on, sir," he mumbled, putting the phone down.

Pictures downloaded. He squinted.

The image of a man, this time straight to camera, flashed on the screen. Same hard eyes, same scowl as the guy he'd seen on the cam previously.

Pele didn't breathe.

With a sinking weight in his gut, he identified the camera. There was a time lapse, a delay due to signal strength and tree cover. Fifteen minutes ago. The signal came from a perimeter camera in the woods above her cabin. The guy was headed down the mountain toward the main camp.

Next image, five minutes ago, crafts cabin camera: Reagan, her eyes wide, looking back toward the trail cam over her shoulder.

His heart stopped.

The alarm buzzed again. He refreshed the screen and uploaded the last image. Current time.

The man again, now moved past the cam in the same direction as Reagan.

He spoke into the phone. "Gotta go. Shit's going down. May need help. Update soon." He hung up on his CO's response.

Throwing equipment in a backpack, he sprinted back to the room where he'd stashed his supplies. He deposited the backpack on the floor.

He shoved the night-vision scope into a pocket, checked the guns in his underarm holster and in his boot. He confirmed that the knives rested in their separate sheaths on his lower back, ankle, and thigh. A compact GPS and water filter straw rounded out his rapid collection of gear. Before running out the door, he paused and rifled through the bag again, pulling out a reflective Mylar square and a few protein bars and stuffing them in pockets.

Instincts and one pissed-off virus screamed at him to run directly after Reagan and destroy anyone following her. No. Think. He needed a plan. He had to stop and consider who else might be out here. The camera had picked up one pursuer. No idea how many more were out there. If he couldn't stay hidden himself, then Reagan was as good as dead.

Maybe Lequire wanted her alive for leverage. Or not. Didn't matter. Lequire or his cronies would not get their hands on Reagan. Simple as that.

Approaching the camera by cutting through the woods, he slunk down to the area he'd seen in the pictures. Two new sets of footprints indented the damp ground: a large deep print with lug soles and a smaller shallow boot impression. A ringing in his ears accompanied a wild wave of rage. He couldn't think. He couldn't see or hear while the fury tore through every cell in his body. He pressed a fist to his chest and fought to contain the virus's urges.

Searching the surrounding woods, he strained to pick up visual cues and sounds. *Friend versus enemy?* He sucked in air and blew it out slowly. His fisted hands shook. He had to gain control over his responses. *Friend versus enemy?*

Neither. No pattern. Damn it.

Regain control. The sound of a thousand buzzing hornets filled his ears. He swiped at his head. *Stop.*

He was due for his next virus antidote, but he hadn't stopped to take it before he left. Might be a good thing that he skipped it. If he had taken the antidote, he could think more clearly, but his strength and enhanced abilities would suffer.

So, instead, he teetered, a hair's breadth away from losing all sanity. The virus strained against imaginary bonds deep inside of Pele. If he let it take over, there was no guarantee as to what would happen. No one knew. No one dared to perform that experiment.

More importantly, if he lost control, Reagan could be hurt. Or worse. He refused to think about the *worse*. With a desperate groan, he clamped down on the eager virus.

Maybe later, he'd get a chance to let his beast out to play with some new friends. A growling laugh briefly escaped him.

If those men so much as touched Reagan, Pele would unleash every ounce of viral rage to destroy the bastards. Didn't care if he lost his mind or his life in the process. He licked his lips and rolled his neck.

As much as it killed him to take the time to do the

job correctly, he got low and moved in a slow, silent stalk.

****

Damn her stupid déjà vu. Reagan's chest ached like her heart had been ripped out of it. She stubbed her booted foot on a root as she walked toward the craft cabin, headed to the ridge for a brain-clearing hike.

Pele had been in Brady's Special Forces squad.

PTSD reactions, her ass.

Okay, fair enough, he probably *did* have PTSD, what with all the team went through in the Middle East.

He had said nothing to her about the connection to Brady. Why the heck was he here at Camp Foxfire? No way was this a coincidence.

All the things she'd said about Brady and her family? He knew everyone involved.

A wave of nausea stopped her in her tracks. Pele had pulled off an intricate operation to play her.

He'd lied to her. Actually, no. He hadn't lied, but he'd withheld a boatload of key information that she should have known before he made multiple passes at her or engaged in mind-blowing sex.

Her trust. Betrayed again. Damn it. Hadn't she learned her lesson from Clayton's lies? Rinse and repeat with Pele.

Her gut churned. What else didn't she know about him?

The brisk hike over the noon hour had seemed like a great way to blow off steam until a strange feeling crawled up the back of her neck. Something was wrong in the woods. Things didn't sound or feel right.

A chill rippled through her spine. What if Pele's vigilant behavior had been legitimate?

She shook her head. Seriously, why would there be anything weird going on at Camp Foxfire? This was the safest place she could imagine.

Stopping dead still, she tilted her head to the side and listened. There. A steady, dull crunch of decaying leaves being stepped on.

Anyone knew if you wanted to sneak through the woods, you never walked at a regular pace. Forest Craft 101.

Her mind spun. If she was in danger, then Pele might be as well.

As a fancy-schmancy Special Forces soldier, he could damn well take care of himself.

As a liar and a jerk who had used her? He could go to hell.

Man. She had fallen for his line of bull, too. She had freaking made him Samoan food. Let her heart go pitter-patter. Fell for the hidden *pe'a* crap. What an idiot she was.

Fool me three times. Damn, damn, damn.

Behind the familiar background noise of birds chirping and animals scurrying in the trees and underbrush, she heard it again. Regular crunching footsteps became louder. Her heart raced.

Why would someone be out in the woods, following her? Was it Pele? She shook her head. The steps didn't sound heavy enough, and besides, as a Special Forces operator, he should remain noiseless.

So, whoever walked through the woods toward her wasn't Pele and didn't know how to truly hide their presence. She thought back to the blue truck that followed her into Maryville. Was there a connection?

It could be a lost hiker, though this section of the National Park didn't get much foot traffic. So for now, she had to assume the person out there did not have innocent intent.

She glanced left and right. Nothing but trees and

undergrowth to the sides and a steep ridge in front of her.

What advantage did she have? Speed and strength—probably not.

Reagan knew this property and this section of the Smokies like the back of her hand. She had the forest survival skills to disappear. Okay, her skills might not be as good as, say, a trained Green Beret.

Pulse pounding in her head, she hurried up the main trail, taking time she didn't have to roll her footsteps soundlessly. Reagan then veered off on a faint deer path that took her up a gorge and toward the saddle. From the ridge, she could gain a vantage point and better decide which direction to go.

Her breaths rasped as she scrambled over muddy rocks and up a knoll. Her quads burned with the relentless uphill climb and extra foot placement to stay silent.

Once at the top, she had a better view down the mountain on both sides. Cupping her hands behind her ears, she turned slowly and listened for anything out of place. There—now several sets of too-regular footfalls and rustling in the brush. A cough.

A dark shape worked its way up the gorge below her, and another human-sounding set of crunches could be heard over a hill to her right. And a third gravel-crunching pattern came from her left on the ridgeline trail, getting closer. That third person would see her when they came around the last curve in the trail. She paused. Was there a fourth sound? Couldn't tell for certain. No time to figure it out.

Hot air sawed in and out of her throat.

People converged on her location. Why? Somehow, it had to do with Pele suddenly showing up at camp and all that jumpy you're-not-safe crap he was pulling. He thought she was in danger.

Might not have been wrong. The blue truck. Who would want to hurt her?

Didn't matter. For whatever reason, she was either being herded or hunted, and she hated both ideas. Glancing over her shoulder at the vast forest of the southern end of the National Park, she made her choice.

Not only was she familiar with all the well-established trails in this area, she knew the terrain if she needed to go off-trail.

If those guys wanted to track her, then Reagan would give them something to track.

Time for those jerks to fear her outdoor education skills.

Chapter Twenty-Two

Pele crept up the mountainside, inch by painstaking inch. The ambient temperature was cool enough that the scope still detected heat signatures. He spotted three human-sized targets spread out in a loose arc, converging toward a lone target at the top of a ridge.

Reagan.

Fighting the instinct to hurry, he continued his maddeningly silent progress. When he rechecked the view through the instrument, she had disappeared. Quelling the urge to charge the hill, he forced his muscles to relax and focus on the stalk, as he'd been trained. The virus disapproved of standard operating procedure.

Once he rounded a small rock outcropping below the ridge, men's voices drifted down to him. He inched up until he could hear what they were saying.

"… she was up here a minute ago. Couldn't have gone far."

"Which way did she go?"

"Don't know. But if we don't find her in the next few hours, we'll call in the drone for tonight. Then we can spot her."

"Damn, I wish she'd gotten in her truck last night. We wouldn't be slogging through the wilderness. Would have finished our job once and for all. *Kaboom*!"

Pele froze. *Ti'o.*

He had the answer as to whether Lequire wanted her dead or alive.

"Why didn't she get in?" one of the men said.

"That overgrown Boy Scout."

Pele stopped breathing.

"Think he'll be a problem?"

"No." A click echoed through the woods. "And if he does become a problem, we've got the goodies to take care of that asshole, too."

Ice clogged Pele's veins. His big, slow breath-and-relaxation techniques did little to calm him down.

Friends versus enemies? He clenched and released his fists as he forced the mental exercise.

Enemies.

"As far as the woman." One man laughed. "You know what Lequire said. If we take her alive, we can have some fun before we kill her."

"Hell, yeah. I can think of some frolicking we could do here in the woods."

"No one would hear any screams."

No. Absolutely not going to happen.

The men's low laughs sparked a volcanic rumble of rage in Pele's gut, building up pressure. One crack, and he'd erupt, break cover, and attack them all. He gripped a rock and crushed it, ignoring the blood stinging from his torn palm. If he didn't kill them all, then her life would be at risk.

No way would they ever put their hands on her.

Kefe. Her life had no value to them.

One man urged, "Check your equipment again. Maybe you missed her."

"For a second, I thought I saw something near that creek down there, but now the image is gone. Probably an animal. Makes more sense that she went down this ridge trail. It leads to the road."

"Fine. I want to be done fucking around in these godforsaken woods and get back to Atlanta. We had our chance to finish her two days ago going into Maryville, but that was a bust. Now the miss from last night. I'm getting sick of it. Let's check along the ridge and be done with this. I want my warm bed."

The three men trudged away.

After waiting several excruciating minutes, Pele crept to the area where the men had been standing. Footprints disrupted mud and leaves, then appeared on the trail that led along the ridge and presumably down toward the two-lane road. Before heading off to track the men, he knelt and examined the ground again, using his ability to see patterns.

What didn't fit?

Large prints. Large prints. Large prints.

Ah.

A smaller indentation had disturbed some leaves on the edge of the trail. He frowned. Another indentation a few feet away, and another. But spaced in an irregular pattern. The pattern of disrupted rotting leaves headed downhill, into the forest. At the bottom of the steep hill was a rushing creek, swollen with early spring runoff.

He whipped the scope out and scanned. There, he spied a large signal near the edge of the creek. Frowning, he rechecked his readings. Not as bright of a signal as the humans he'd seen earlier. What the hell did that mean?

Zigzagging down the steep slope, he tried to obscure his own path as much as possible, in case the men returned. About twenty feet from the spring-fed creek, he spied movement.

Creeping the rest of the way down, he advanced on the target, pulling his Ka-Bar knife from the holster. What would cause a human-sized target to have a reduced heat signature on thermal imaging?

A pale foot entered his field of vision, then retracted below the edge of the bank.

He dropped down another five feet, knife raised, and froze.

What could cause a reduced heat signature in a human target?

The pulse pounded in his ears.
A hypothermic human.

Chapter Twenty-Three

Pele spied Reagan, huddled in a ball against the bank, naked and soaking wet. Her lips were blue and her teeth chattered, even over the rushing creek.

Staring up the hill, he said a prayer that the men wouldn't come back for a while longer. He holstered the knife and grabbed her arms.

"Reagan? What happened?" He searched her for trauma. *Ti'o.* Had she been raped? Injured? Any broken bones?

"C-cold."

He pulled her quaking body into his chest. His own skin cooled through his shirt, her skin was so frigid. "Where are your clothes?"

"Over th-there." A mountain laurel bush hid a pile of clothing.

Quickly, Pele got her back in her underwear, jeans, and shirt as she stood there, shaking. Once she put on the long-sleeved top, her color improved. Marginally.

He helped her to sit and dried her blue-tinged feet on his pants as best he could. Then he put her socks and shoes back on. Whipping off his fleece vest, he tugged that on her and zipped it up. Fear had him hauling her up into his arms again and chafing her back until the shivers improved.

"What the hell?" he said. He'd found her. Alive. He couldn't make his arms loosen their grip on her.

Her voice came out muffled, with her face buried in his chest. "Halfway down this hill, I heard those men say something about infrared detection. I wanted to get as far away from them as possible and came down here. But when I saw them at the edge of that ridge, I stripped and jumped in the creek. Figured that would hide from the infrared." She leaned back, her lips a pinker shade of blue. "Water's a little brisk today."

"Are you kidding me? You could have died."

"It's not like I had a lot of options."

He wrung out her dripping hair. "Damned smart move if you ask me."

"What? You think Special Forces folks are the only ones with stealth and evasion abilities? I have skills." She stepped up, crossed her arms, and glared at him, still shivering.

He stopped breathing. *How did she know?*

"Damn you." She jammed a finger into his chest. "All this time, you knew who I was, knew about Brady. You played me. That was the whole point: the game. You lied to me. And last night—" She took a shuddering breath. "Last night was just for fun, wasn't it? Fun built on top of lies."

The hurt in those blue eyes made him want to hide. Or beg.

"That's not exactly true." He kept his voice down to prevent detection but really wanted to shout the words.

"At any time, you could have told me who you really were. Any time. Lots of opportunities." She shoved her wet hair back with a shaking hand. "I'm so stupid. Damn it."

"Please, Reagan." When he reached out, she flinched away. He cursed. "It's a long story, but I had to keep what I was doing here secret."

"A secret? Okay, fine. At what point would you have told me? Before or after the dudes caught me? Because apparently honesty wasn't a prerequisite for sex."

"*Kefe*. This mission has been a nightmare from the get-go."

"Your. Mission?" At least the blood flow had

returned, judging by the furious red flush tinting her neck and cheeks. "I'm a 'mission' for you?"

He backed away from the palpable waves of fury. "No, not a mission. Okay, technically yes, but not like you think."

"All that bull about hanging around me and then when we, last night—" She clamped down so hard her jaw muscle moved. "Did your mission involve seducing me? Was last night also a 'nightmare' for you or just part of the operation?" She half-turned away from him. "God damn it!"

"Please don't shout." He couldn't hear much above the rushing creek next to them.

"What?"

"The men might come back. And no, you don't understand the situation."

"Um, yes. I believe I've got the gist of what occurred etched pretty clear in my mind, thanks." She rubbed her neck. "Gah. I'm such an idiot. The stupid coconut eel story, the Samoan dinner you had to cook and clean up. Maybe you made that part up, too, along with all of that cultural identity crap."

He shoved his hands in his pockets. "Hard to fake my *pe'a*. What with the pain and ink and all."

"See this face?" She scowled as she drew a circle. "No sympathy. Save your line of bull for another sucker."

"Reagan?"

"What."

A movement at the top of the hill made him glance up. His skin crawled with imagined laser sights dancing over him. "We really have to get out of here before those men return."

"And go where? To do what activity? For what purpose?"

"I can't—"

"If you say one more time how you can't tell me, so help me I will punch you in your lousy jaw. There are men who want to track me down. Who does that? So, I believe you should spill whatever information you know so that I can stay alive."

Would it be too much to ask her to keep her voice down while she handed him his ass? They were in danger here.

Ti'o. He'd never seen a woman this mad before. Ever. Not that he didn't deserve it, but she was incandescent. Vibrating. Terrifying.

"Can we get going?" he said. "It's not safe here."

When she crossed her arms again and planted her feet, he felt all the air leaving his lungs in a *whoosh*. Even his damned virus waved a white flag, curled in a virtual ball, and whimpered. Big help there, buddy.

"Nope. Explain it all or I'm not going anywhere with you."

"Short version for now. I'll get to details later, okay?"

"Depends on how good your short version is."

"Fair."

"Are you going to tell me to trust you? Because I promise that will not go well for you."

He held his hands up. "No. I swear."

"You swearing doesn't mean much right about now."

Grinding his molars together, he gritted out, "I get that."

"Spill, then."

There was a mission to complete and killers to outrun, yet they were standing around talking like two villagers on a market day. Ridiculous. "Okay. Those men want to kidnap you."

"To do bad things? Or kill me?"

He glanced up the hill. No shadows up there. Yet. "Looks like both."

"So, my future is bright. Great. Why do random guys I don't know want to hurt me?"

They were wasting precious time. If he wanted her to go with him, he had to explain everything. Well, not everything, but enough to get her to leave with him. He grimaced. "Okay, so you know how Brady worked for Fallen Comrades a while back, then he died suddenly?"

"Yes. Still suspicious about how he died."

"Your sister, Kiera, was suspicious, too. So she went undercover for the past nine months at Fallen Comrades."

"What? How?" Her eyebrows rose. "Why didn't she tell me?"

"I'm part of a covert ex-Special Forces group called Morpheus Squad. It's made up of most of the guys from Brady's Special Forces team."

"Not following."

He lifted his palms and glanced up the hill again. "Hang on, I'll explain. When Kiera uncovered information to expose Fallen Comrades' illegal activities, the company's CFO, Beau Lequire, came after her. With guys like that." He pointed toward the ridge.

Her face paled. "Is she okay?"

"She is now."

"How do you and I figure into this mess?"

He swallowed. "Lequire can't get to Kiera. But he can get to her family and use you all as leverage to silence her."

"My family? Dad and Britt, too?" Her mouth gaped.

If he didn't believe she would hate him or kick

him in the balls, he would've hauled her into his arms until her fear drained away. "They're under protection, like you."

"Is their protection better than mine?"

With that sarcastic statement, Pele's desire to wrap his arms around her quickly fled. Comforting her would be like hugging a pissed-off porcupine.

"Really?" he asked.

She popped her fists on her hips and leaned forward. At least her lips weren't blue anymore. "What? That's a legitimate assessment. It's not like their security detail could be worse than this. As it stands, I had to come up with a plan to rescue myself a few minutes ago."

"In my defense, this assignment was thrown together at the last minute. Most of my planning was done on the fly."

"Your training is in unconventional operations?"

Those verbal jabs irritated the hell out of him, like mosquito bites where he couldn't quite reach the bug. "Yes."

"So, you're an expert in security and covert activities in highly irregular situations?"

"Uh, yes."

"Subterfuge is, like, your entire job."

"Well, most of it…"

"I rest my case." She rolled her eyes.

It wasn't irritation that he felt. It was the fact that she had so little faith in his ability to keep her safe that made him feel like half a man. Judging by his track record thus far, she had a right to be skeptical. He needed to prove himself.

"Reagan—"

A chop of her hand stopped him. "So, what's the next move, or should I take on planning duties on as well?"

He sucked in a deep breath as prickles of wounded pride dissipated. "Well, part of the assignment involved the need to keep Morpheus Squad secret, but that's out the window."

She snorted.

"Next step is to get you extracted safely."

"Extracted? As in, what I was already doing?"

"Reagan," he growled. "Look, you're going on a vacation for a week. Family emergency and all."

"Now you're making this decision?"

Ti'o, her jutted chin did not promise cooperation.

"It's either that or you may die."

"Well, that's pretty clear. How exactly do you plan to get me 'extracted'? Because if that plan is as good as my security detail, then we might as well send up a flare for the bad guys to find us and get this over with," she spat.

His skin prickled at her assessment. "Good question." He paused. "You're familiar with this area. We need to get to a place where my team can pick us up, undetected. What do you recommend?"

Chapter Twenty-Four

The litany of bad words and threats she wanted to hurl at Pele rolled through her mind at a breakneck pace. Unfortunately, Reagan didn't have the energy to say them, since she was trying not to trip as they jogged the trails on their trek toward Parson Branch Road, her recommended pickup location on the other side of the Smokies.

Mr. Energizer Bunny, on the other hand, acted like he was out for a pleasant stroll. The big, lying jerk hadn't even broken a sweat, and that pissed her off even more.

She stubbed her toe on a rock and nearly face-planted. *Concentrate.*

It was four o'clock. They had another hour to travel as far as possible, and then they needed to bed down for the night and pray they could avoid detection from heat-seeking drones. Drones. Who the hell sent drones after a person who worked at a kids' camp? She didn't even have an exciting life.

Well, not until meeting Pele, enjoying the best sex of her life, discovering his ulterior motives and hidden identity, and then finding out that a bunch of dudes wanted to kill her.

A cool breeze off the rushing creek brushed over her. The temperature was dropping. Would be close to freezing and damp in the humid mountains tonight. Damn it, they needed a good shelter before night fell. With luck, Pele could find a safe location where the satellite phone worked and call in the coordinates for the team to meet them tomorrow.

If not, she and Pele would have to evade capture tomorrow and hide out again the following night. Each additional hour they stayed in the forest, the chance of Lequire's men finding them increased.

They traveled up and over a mountain and then turned south on Hatcher Mountain Trail. Familiar territory for Reagan. Abrams Creek faded in the distance as they kept jogging on the less-traveled trail. More roots threatened to trip up her tired legs.

The goal for tonight was to get as close as possible to the exit point on Parson Branch Road, a dirt road that led out of Cades Cove onto the highway south of the Smokies. Tomorrow, they'd have to go off-trail and bushwhack to the exit location. Parson Branch Road wasn't open for public access this time of year, but Pele assured her that wouldn't stop his team from reaching them.

Stopping to drink from the filter straw a few times, she stayed hydrated. At some point, though, lack of food was going to play a bigger role in slowing their progress. Not a lot of edible forage available at this time of year, and anything she found—like fiddleheads— would need to be boiled. He didn't have a pot in one of his pockets, and they couldn't start a fire.

Her stomach rumbled.

Seemed like Commando Joe could have brought more than two long-gone protein bars to this adventure, but no. Prepared security expert indeed.

No time to get mad at him. There were people out in these woods who wanted her dead. She would get mad at them first. Then she'd unload on Pele. For now, she'd keep going as long as she had to if it meant surviving this mess.

When Pele called a stop to their jog, Reagan pegged them as being a mile or so onto the eight-mile section of Hatcher Mountain Trail. They'd covered a good distance today. No established backcountry campsite for them tonight. Too obvious. Too exposed. So they traveled into woods a hundred feet off the trail and into the thick underbrush.

"Okay, here's the problem. We need to stay warm but also avoid infrared detection tonight," he said.

"I'm still not happy with you," Reagan reminded him.

He looked to the sky, then back to her, mouth moving like he counted to ten. Then he took a massive breath. "Yes, I know," he said. "Why don't you blow up after we get out of here alive?"

She crossed her arms over her chest. Damn his handsome face and her growling stomach, but she couldn't stay mad at him for long. That wasn't to say she trusted him. "Gladly."

"No fire."

"Not if they're searching for heat," she agreed.

"Shelter?"

"I can make a small survival hut, if you'll help me. We won't be super warm, but it will keep us alive. Not sure how we can avoid detection altogether."

He pulled a shiny square of fabric out of his pocket. "Mylar blanket."

"Won't it be bright and reflective?" Damned if she didn't get a little flutter when he gazed at her with a thoughtful expression. Like what she said mattered.

At least one of them had a plan. *Two thumbs, right here. Good ol' Reagan, getting survival stuff done.*

He smiled. "Not if it's under the shelter roof. Also, it reflects heat downward, so it should help with warmth."

"That'll do. I'll get to work." Despite feeling weak and hungry, fear pushed Reagan to hurry as she dragged branches over. Pele followed suit. She kept glancing over her head, expecting to see a small drone homing in on their location.

A long branch wedged in the crook of a fallen tree provided the naturally-appearing angled spine of the structure that tapered from the crook a few feet high down to the ground where their feet would rest. More branches leaning against the spine finished the frame. Then they piled leaf litter and hemlock boughs against the roof beams until there was a foot or so of debris on top of the roof and it appeared to be a downed clump of shrubbery instead of a constructed hut. In the last bit of light, more hemlock boughs on the floor of the structure provided a semi-insulated place to rest.

She took one more hemlock bough and disturbed their footprints and broken twig patterns so the ground appeared more natural.

Over her shoulder, she heard a rustling sound, and she whipped around, heart thudding.

Squirrel. Damn her nerves.

Hey, this was a massive National Park with thousands of draws, ridges, hells, and hollers. Unlimited places to hide. They might pull off this escape.

Pele unrolled the emergency blanket and crawled into the small shelter. Once he had everything arranged, he motioned for Reagan to join him.

"No funny business. You're on my bad list," she warned him.

His dark expression still managed to curl her exhausted toes. "While I would love to engage in so-called 'funny business' with you, I need to save my energy for tomorrow's push to the extraction site."

"Have I mentioned that I'm not happy with you?" God, a night in close proximity to Pele after he'd lied to her and used her? This roller coaster of crazy kept going faster and faster.

"Yes. Now please get in here before the eye in the

sky finds you."

She crawled into the shelter, which had already warmed from Pele's considerable body heat. There was no space to spare, which was the whole point of an emergency shelter. But how would she endure the night with Pele right there? With a high-pitched crinkle, he pulled the blanket over her and tucked it in around her.

"What are you using for heat?" she asked.

"I'm fine."

"Is being stubborn a Samoan trait or military trait? Or your own special-ness?"

He paused. "All three." Damn how his voice rumbled through her bones.

"Figures." She lifted the side of the blanket closest to him, turned on her side, and inched over until he spooned against her backside. "Put this over you and don't complain."

"Yes, ma'am." He rested his arm over her upper chest, pulling her firmly against him. The blanket covered the top of their spooned bodies.

"Last warning," she gritted out between her teeth. It sucked how perfectly they fit together.

"Too tired to try anything if I wanted to." His mouth was way too close to her ear, making areas of her anatomy wake up. "And yes, I would like to try."

"Hmm."

"Reagan?"

She dreaded what he had to say. Her exhausted, beaten-up heart couldn't take much more. "Yes?"

"I really am sorry for all that I've put you through."

"I know." She yawned. "Go to sleep. We have a long hike tomorrow."

****

The high-pitched hum woke Reagan up from a

dead sleep. When she shifted, Pele's arm tightened around her.

"Don't move," he whispered. Slowly, he eased the blanket up over their heads. "Drone. They've been circling our location for a half hour. They might have detected our heat signature, even with the blanket."

"What time is it?"

"Midnight."

"We have to wait another six hours before it's safe to move?"

"At least."

Voices filtered through the woods. More crunches of footsteps.

Next to her, Pele went rigid.

"Thought there was a signal coming from over here," one male voice called.

A fainter voice called back, "Check it out." It sounded like a second man was on the main trail, a mere hundred feet away.

The heavy thud of footsteps transmitted through the ground. Reagan gasped.

Pele curved his hand over her mouth and then inched his other hand behind her back and then across his chest into what felt like his armpit. He kept moving his hand until she heard a dull snap. Then he eased his arm up over her head.

She shifted until he stilled her with a firm squeeze.

"Gun," he whispered.

She froze. Then a wave of cold panic swamped her.

He slowly rolled a quarter turn, limiting the crinkling noise of the Mylar, until he lay on top of her. Heat poured off of him and melted into her backside. He quietly adjusted the blanket until they were cocooned in the Mylar, with a small air hole at the top. From where he took aim.

The footsteps crunched louder.

Until they scuffed to a stop at what sounded like a yard from their location.

Reagan trembled. No way could Pele get a shot off and exit the shelter fast enough to avoid getting hurt, if not by the first guy, then the second one who would come running.

What if Pele did get hurt? He had already told her if they got separated that she was to stay hidden, then try to go directly to the ranger station in Cades Cove and get them to help her. It wasn't the neatest plan, and it would possibly blow Morpheus Squad's cover. The plan hinged on Lequire's men not trying anything in a public area.

No guarantees.

It didn't take a genius to realize that the longer it took the men to bring her in, the more desperate Lequire would become.

Another footstep.

Her breathing came in shallow gasps, partly due to Pele's massive weight on top of her.

The other part? Well, unlike her Special Forces buddy here, she had a healthy appreciation for staying alive and avoiding armed conflict. Fear played a big role in that motivation.

"Anything?" The voice from the trail drifted over to them.

"Not sure."

She jumped. The man's voice was so loud. He had to be standing right in front of the hut. Pele gave her shoulder a firm squeeze.

"Weird readings around here, man. Wait a sec—"

Her heart hammered like a deranged drummer, her rasping gasps coming too quick and erratic. She clamped her lips together.

Pele's breathing, on the other hand, remained slow and steady. Like this was another day at work for him.

Damn him, it *was* another day at work for him.

The man outside took another step. This time the sound was way too close. She angled her face toward the small opening in the Mylar. Damn it. One more movement and he'd kick the wall of the survival hut.

Pele shifted, every muscle in his frame tensed. Somehow, he'd grown larger, taking up all of the space in the shelter.

Oh, God, if he goes out there...

"Hold on, guys. There's something here," the man said. "Hmmm, let's see."

The click of what sounded like a gun safety being released came from about five feet above her head. Sweat rolled down her forehead, but she didn't dare move to wipe it.

Pele had partially drawn his legs up into a crouch, like a sprinter about to leave the blocks, leg muscles bunched and rock-hard.

"What the—" A harsh barking growl came from above them. The man shrieked, "Bear!"

Reagan gave a yelp, luckily hidden within the man's scream.

A quick shuffle of leaves, then a heavy thud like the man had fallen was followed by pounding footsteps receding into the night. Leaf rustles and huffing bear noises receded as well.

Neither she nor Pele moved until there was total silence for what had to be thirty minutes. Her ears rang as she strained to hear anything abnormal outside of the shelter.

Finally, he rolled off of her, stowed the gun, and

yanked her into his arms, surrounding her with his massive frame. He kissed her sweaty temple and rested his chin on the top of her head.

"*Ti'o*. I thought we were done," he whispered. "Reagan, you're shivering. Are you cold?"

"Nope. Terrified. Not too proud to admit it." She was thankful he couldn't see the tears burning her eyes.

He got his muscled arms all the way around her and held her so tight it almost hurt. But she didn't care. Not right now.

"I've got you," he said. "I will keep you safe. Promise."

After a few shaky breaths, she had a grip on herself again.

Wow, his breathing was really harsh. And low and loud.

She froze.

That wasn't Pele.

A huffing, growling sound outside their shelter got her attention. She'd heard that sound in the woods before. Something nudged her head, followed by a rotting fish and glop scent.

Bear.

Chapter Twenty-Five

Pele looked up.

A dark snout filled his field of vision, blocking out the sliver of moonlight. Deep, chuffing accompanied the worst breath imaginable.

A black paw with long, lethal claws dug at the dirt right outside the hut.

Kefe.

When the massive, smelly head nosed Reagan's hair, she whimpered. At that tiny sound coming from her quaking body beneath him, Pele's virus went from dormant to *kill* in a split second.

He slid his hand around to cup the top of her head.

If the damned bear wanted her, it would have to go through a virally enhanced, angry Special Forces soldier first. Deep down inside, the virus raged, wanting a piece of the bear. Now.

Stay calm. Try. Try to think. His head spun with blood lust, spurred on by that relentless virus boiling inside.

How far had those men run? He couldn't risk discovery. Couldn't risk injury or death, either. Was the drone gone? He couldn't hear any low buzzes in the sky over the raging hum in his brain.

Friend versus enemy. Focus. He sucked air in and out, calming the virus.

Which was worse: inside or outside the shelter?

Hot, fetid breath and a deep, rumbling growl raised the hairs on the back of Pele's neck. Tremors raced over Reagan's frame tucked beneath him. Like puzzle pieces falling into place, chunks of his existence took stark clarity.

Screw this entire bad situation.

What about this life that wasn't truly his own?

Yeah, screw that, too. All of it. The danger and the hiding. The fear of becoming a prisoner of the U.S. military once again.

He had hurt Reagan to do his job.

Enough.

Enough.

An answering growl grew in Pele's chest and expanded out in all directions. Like a dog gnashing its teeth and straining against chains, the virus wanted out.

His ability to see and hear grew. Every nerve quivered as he focused on the massive beast that nosed far too close to the woman Pele would die to protect.

In one explosive motion, he launched himself at the animal, knocking a few branches off the front of the shelter and slamming his shoulder into the beast. A combination of a grunt and howl telegraphed the animal's surly mood. In the moonlight, the bear swiped him with a heavy paw, drawing long lines of hot, red rage across Pele's chest.

The virus loved it when Pele bled. Drank up the pain and feasted on fury. Wanted more. So much more. It had waited so long to come out and play. Tonight.

Release.

An inhuman roar rose from the depths of Pele's soul and projected directly onto the angry animal. He vibrated as the virus pushed his body to a new, larger level. Rage fed his muscles. With every passing second, he became more like the bear and less like a human. His last coherent thought: do whatever it took to protect Reagan.

The virus within him agreed.

When the large black bear rose on his haunches, Pele lifted his arms, challenging the beast, hoping the animal would attack. *Come on. Do it.* Any excuse to rip the creature from limb to limb. He could almost taste the blood.

Froth formed at the black bear's mouth. Lips curled back from big incisors as the male bear popped its jaw and growled.

Yes.

Reagan lay vulnerable, mere feet from this animal.

Pele's world tunneled in on eliminating the threat.

The bear lunged and slapped the ground with a low clack of its teeth.

Pele leaned in, fists curled and ready. He projected all his frustration, passion, fear, and anger into an answering growl.

The bear stopped its forward movement with a howl.

Every inch of Pele's frame quivered with virally fueled adrenaline. Every muscle fiber tightened, primed and ready to strike.

With a chuff of submission, the bear hunkered down on all fours.

Pele took one step forward, then two. Each cell in his body was prepared to rocket him after the animal.

Pursue. Kill.

A small cry behind him penetrated his fogged brain. He paused.

Another bear?

No. The sound was familiar. A magnetic pull swiveled his body around. He desired the source of the sound. Wanted it a fraction more than he wanted to eliminate the threat that cowered away from him. After a jerky wave of Pele's arms and another growl, the animal lumbered away into the woods.

Empty, unfulfilled, the virus drove him to attack

something. Now.

"Pele?"

He whipped around in a crouch, ready to destroy whatever lurked there. His vision had clouded. If it was daylight, it would be tinted red, thanks to the virus running unchecked in his system. Dim moonlight dappled everything in patterns that confused him.

"Hey. We're good now. Let's go back in." The muffled words reached him as if filtering through multiple layers of cloth.

That voice, a light in his darkness, sounded so familiar. What was it?

The virus still drove him, whipped the muscles to act. Destroy.

That voice—should he kill it?

"Pele?" she asked again.

Reagan's shaky voice acted like a homing beacon for every one of his base desires.

She emerged from the shelter and stood.

He struck, grabbing her and wrapping her in his arms, lifting her from the ground. Squeezing tight. Unable to let go, he glared around at the forest, daring anything else to try to hurt the woman in his arms. He squeezed harder, needing to surround her with his entire body.

"Pele?" A desperate wheeze reached his ears. "Stop. You're hurting me!"

Chapter Twenty-Six

"Please, Pele." Reagan started to shake again, but this time because this massive man was acting like a human boa constrictor. As her ribs creaked, her vision went gray. "I can't breathe," she whispered.

If he kept going, something was going to break. As if in answer, a pop of the bones in her back ricocheted in the quiet darkness. A chiropractor would be jealous of Pele's skills.

What little moonlight she could see receded along with the air from her lungs.

His tight muscles bunched even tighter. Her back and arms burned.

"Pele," she wheezed. "Stop."

Another few seconds of the solid squeeze, then he stammered, "R-Reagan?" His voice sounded hollow, desperate, like a man who had lost his soul. "Reagan." The word struggled out of his mouth. He'd become a wild animal himself.

"Let. Go." She managed to gasp.

When he released her, she staggered and her knees buckled. She would have hit the ground if he didn't drop to his knees and cradle her against his chest. His pounding heart thudded against her ringing ear.

"*Ti'o*. Are you okay?" His rasped whispers abraded her senses like sandpaper. "Please. Talk to me." He brushed hair back with hard, jerking movements of his hands. Like every movement was manually regulated. "I couldn't stop. I couldn't stop—" he muttered. Pele crouched over her in a living cage.

No need for a cage. She couldn't have gotten away from him if she tried. Against a sore back and ribs, she pulled in a deep lungful of cool mountain air.

His head, so close to her, blocked out the faint light from the stars and crescent moon. "Reagan, I'm sor—"

"Wait." She gripped his iron-hard upper arms. A high-pitched buzzing noise came from above them, growing louder. "What's that?"

He glanced toward the sky and stiffened. "Get back inside. Now."

Before she could get up, he lifted her, lurched, and shoved both of them back into the now too-small shelter. In the cramped space, he used the few inches of overhead space to crouch over her, running rough fingers over her face, neck, and body.

"Are you hurt? Please talk to me," he said. "I can't believe I almost—"

Coughing, she grabbed his thick wrist and stopped his frantic movement. "I'm here. Pele, It's okay. The drone."

Keeping his arms braced on either side of her head, he dropped his sweaty forehead to hers and gave out a gut-wrenching groan. "I'm so sorry."

"Blanket. Heat signature," she gasped.

With a crinkle and a shrug, and way too much of their bodies rubbing together, he maneuvered the foil sheet over them. After several tight minutes of not moving, the only sound that remained was their harsh breathing. The drone must have moved away.

"What happened out there?" she whispered. "What were you doing?" She swallowed, her mouth dry. "What are you?"

"It's…"

"Complicated? You're like a song on repeat." She shifted, creaking a rib. "Yeah, I gathered as much. You attacked that bear like it was no big deal. That's not normal. How about you tell me what's going on?"

He didn't move for a full minute but took several slow, deep pulls of air. Strange, he seemed to get smaller again. Well, not exactly small—no one could accuse him of that. He took up less space, somehow. He was less intense, if that made sense.

Nothing about this situation made sense.

He moved to lie on his side, still far too close for comfort in the confined space, the blanket above them.

Clearing his throat, he started again. "So. Things happened to me before. In the Army."

"Not following."

"*Ti'o*. You weren't supposed to know." His words barely registered above a whisper. "Secrecy was part of the mission."

Irritation poked holes in her sympathetic nature. "We're literal miles past keeping secrets about this mission, Pele."

Seconds passed. "You have no idea what you're asking me to tell you."

Licking her lips she said, "Do you trust me?"

Another pause. "Yes." He blew out one more lungful of air. "You know the Morpheus Squad I mentioned?"

"Yes."

"I didn't tell you everything about us."

"Here's my not-surprised face you can't see in the dark. What a shocker. You, withholding information from me."

"I'm sorry, Reagan. It's—"

"Don't say *complicated*. So help me, I will knee you in the granolas."

"Got it." He moved his groin back a few inches and rearranged the Mylar, the high-pitched crinkle too loud in the confined space. Tucking it over his back and her, he continued. "Each Morpheus Squad member was selected based on our self-discipline, the ability to follow orders but also improvise, and our willingness to undergo a top-secret military experiment."

"What?" She peered at him as if she could tell whether he lied or not, but in the pitch-black shelter, he was a mere hint of a shadow.

"We were each given a dose of what they called the Morpheus Virus. It was meant to create super-warriors for the Army. But…"

She sensed the bob of his Adam's apple as he swallowed. "It backfired?"

"Worse."

"What's worse than that?" Out there, with the bear, losing his mind. That was worse.

"We turned into ultimate warriors, killing machines, rarely needing rest. We could overwhelm any enemy force, even with a portion of the team deployed."

Here she sat, lying next to this infected killer. Great. Pushing the words past a lump in her throat, she said, "Sounds like that's what the military was going for, right?"

"Yes." His low voice drilled into her soul. "Until the virus started to change us."

"What?" She froze. Here she sat right below Pele's puma perch. One wrong move might trigger him again.

"We became less predictable, more aggressive. The military couldn't control us. Once the virus took over, we didn't always follow orders. We preferred to kill instead."

"That sounds terrible."

The harsh growl strafed her like rough nails against her skin. "You have no idea. Our lives, our purpose, all got consumed by how the virus drove us to destroy the enemy."

"And?"

"The government loved it and hated it."

"What did they do?"

"We were given an antidote."

Maybe this story had a happy ending. "So you were cured?"

His chest flexed and shifted, moving the Mylar. "No, the antidote only contains the virus for a period of time, but we are never completely cured. It never lasts. We always need another dose of antidote to keep from losing our minds."

"Oh, God. Wait. Brady?"

"Your brother was injured and got discharged before we took the virus. Actually, his injury motivated us to become better soldiers and volunteer for the experiment." He took another breath, and Reagan felt her shoulder lift along with him. "If he'd had the virus on board, he might have recovered."

"He would have been a monster."

His whole body tensed. "Like me?"

"No, not—"

"Yes. A monster. He would be a slave to the virus."

"And to the military."

"Yes."

"So what happened out there? What was that with the bear?" She lifted her chin, but of course he wouldn't see it in the darkness.

"When we're exposed to extreme situations or prolonged stress, the virus kind of makes us go crazy. Focuses us right down to the bare bones of our mission, which usually involves a need to destroy anyone and everything that is perceived as a threat. We kind of lose our minds to the virus."

She shivered. "I can tell."

"If we don't take an antidote dose to stop it, we will go past the point of no return. Lose our minds permanently."

"How often do you take a dose?"

A growl. "Every ten days."

Licking her lips, she said, "How long has it been since your last dose?"

Quiet. Too quiet. Finally, he murmured, "Eleven days ago."

Her gut clenched. "God."

"I'm okay, Reagan. I can function. I'll control it."

"You call challenging a black bear 'functioning'? Still in control, but for how long?" Her brittle laugh scared even herself. "Hate to see what lack of control looks like."

The night sounds of critters rustling in the brush and a distant owl hoot filtered into the scant space between them.

When he spoke, the words were ripped out of his throat. "I'm so sorry you had to witness that, Reagan. *Ti'o*. I can't believe I hurt you when I... For a second, I didn't know it was—"

"Me?"

"Yes. That's the problem." He groaned. "I could have ripped you to pieces."

"That's not comforting."

"I know."

"I can't leave."

"I know."

Their breathing and the occasional crinkle of Mylar filled the tiny space for several minutes.

Reagan finally said, "Well, I'm here now and in one piece."

"You were never supposed to see that part of me."

"Yet here we are—" Air stopped halfway down her throat. Speaking of seeing parts of him. "Wait a minute." Her stomach knotted up. "You have an active virus in your body, and last night we had sex… Oh, my God. Did you give it to me?" She would have scooted away, if there was room. As if she could escape. If he was determined to keep her close, he would succeed, no matter what.

"No! You can't get it." He paused. "At least I don't think so."

Irritation flared again. "You don't think?"

"I did use a condom."

"Several."

"Yeah."

The brush of his finger against her cheek was feather-light. Damn her, but she responded, warmth bursting to flame where their skin connected.

He lifted his head. "The condom was to protect you."

"Against the virus or pregnancy?"

"Virus." He sniffed. "Uncle Sam offered to take care of our ability to reproduce."

"Wait. Your whole team?"

"Whoever wanted a vasectomy, got one, free of charge, courtesy of the US military."

"So you…"

"Yeah." The broken, mirthless laugh coming from such a big man made her want to cry. "How's that for a future?"

Her heart flopped in her chest. "That's not what I meant, Pele." Tentatively, she patted his corded arm that propped him on his side. "You didn't have any say in your future."

"Technically, I had the choice. It was just made clear what the right decision was. Not all of us took the offer. Most. But not all. Now, we have to be careful."

"I can't imagine how you made a decision that impacts the entire rest of your life and family."

"It wasn't a hard choice, once I saw what the virus did to me. You saw what I can become. A terror. A monster. So now I can't pass down my messed-up genetics to any offspring." His chest rose and fell again, slower now. "Our doctor doesn't believe it can be transmitted from person to person. So this is our own personal nasty little devil hiding inside. The virus activity ramps up or down, depending on the situation and the time since the last antidote."

"Wow." Damn the quaver in her voice. "What if you couldn't control the virus … um, with me?"

He briefly rested his hand on the top of her head. "I don't know for sure. But I would hope I could maintain control where you were concerned."

This information. She was being handed a dirt sandwich and told to eat up. The truth kept getting worse and worse. "You would hope?"

The words tumbled out of him. "You want the real info? I have no idea. It's terrible. I don't know what I might do to you if the virus truly went out of control, and that knowledge destroys me inside."

She had an idea of his potential, if her sore ribs were any indication of what he looked like while still in some control. God.

Wasn't that a big kick in the butt? Even bigger than finding out he betrayed her trust by withholding his connection to Brady and the mission.

She had fallen for a rage-a-holic mutant with an unstable, unpredictable disease. Who could kill her with his pinkie finger.

So, yeah, her relationship radar obviously sucked.

"Pele?"

"Yes, Reagan," came his hoarse reply.

"If I'm out in the woods on my own with those guys hunting me, I'm as good as dead, right?"

"Yes."

It hurt to say the words. "Can you keep from your virus killing me tonight?"

"Oh, God, yes. Reagan, I would die before I hurt you. I'd do anything to avoid causing you pain. I swear, you'll be safe. Whatever it takes." The fervor in his tone made the ground rumble. He hadn't actually answered the question.

"Promises coming from the guy who has stalked me, almost killed a bear single-handedly, and has exposed me to a military-grade STD?"

"Well. *Ti'o*." He mumbled against his arm. "It's not an STD. Never had one of those, and I test regularly."

"Details."

"Okay. Yes, all of that is true, sort of. But—"

"Pele, shut up. Just keep me from dying, either by your hand or someone else's."

"I wouldn't—"

"Look, I can't take any more right now. I can't process all of this. We're stuck together for now. Good night." In her physically and emotionally drained state, the last conscious thought was of Pele tucking an arm around her.

Chapter Twenty-Seven

Pele had been in foxholes while bombs exploded nearby. He had seen mangled humans on roadsides. He'd dragged his injured teammates to safety. He'd watched the entire world burn down around him.

Last night had been one of the worst nights of Pele's life.

He spent last night fighting the urge to hunt down Lequire's men and then destroy that bear, but fear for Reagan's life kept him pinned in the dark shelter, arms wrapped around her. Fear, a foreign emotion, rattled him. He remained wide awake and vigilant, listening to her soft murmurs in her sleep.

He clung to Reagan like she was a safe island of rock in a stormy sea.

At what point had she become more than a mission? At the point where he had decided to lay down his life for her and risk exposing his entire team. When did he crave her, not as his assignment, but because she was simply Reagan?

At what point had he lost control and almost ended her life?

All night long, he wrestled with the answer to those questions and still came up with a big goose egg.

To make matters worse, when he held her, that sweet body curved perfectly into his and woke up far more than a protective instinct. *Ti'o*, could a man die from six hours of partial erection? No, but Pele could have done without having to find out the answer to that question firsthand.

How was sexual interest even possible, with all the energy and adrenaline burned over the past twenty-four hours?

Apparently, if the answer involved Reagan, then it was very possible to be interested.

6:00 AM. The sun brightened the sky but wouldn't fully reach this shadowed area for hours.

They had survived the night.

He listened. No distant buzz of a drone. Lequire's people couldn't run one in the daytime over the national park without risking detection.

However, those men could still be out there, waiting.

Easing away from Reagan's toasty body, he pressed a quick kiss to her parted lips. Her hair had gone wild and tangled from the creek, the run, and last night's close call. In the soft-pink morning light, she looked adorable and sexy with the tousled curls framing her face.

He deserved none of this view.

"Stay here," he whispered. "I'll make sure we're clear."

Her eyes widened, but she nodded and remained silent as he slid and scooted out of the shelter. He looked back, chest swelling with pride at the way the shelter seemed to blend into the thick undergrowth and downed trees. She'd done a great job, setting the structure up in record time last night. Saved both of their butts.

He surveyed the surrounding area with his scope. No big heat signatures, including that damned bear. Stupid animal might have saved their lives by scaring off the guy hunting Reagan, so he'd take the small victory where he could.

Carefully walking to the main trail, he continued to scan the area in case the men waited across the creek or on the surrounding hillsides. He paused, listened, and looked.

Nothing. No abnormal patterns.

Yet.

Time was limited.

Today, he needed to contact his CO, meet at the planned location, and get Reagan to safety. Alive.

Simple enough.

After climbing up a knoll to send a text out via satellite, he returned to the survival hut.

"You're good to come out." He extended his hand and helped her from the shelter.

Her stifled groans matched how he felt inside. Nothing like running for miles on empty stomachs, sleeping on the hard ground, and then getting up to run some more. He carefully folded the Mylar blanket and stowed it in a pocket. His goal was not to have to use it again.

There were no guarantees out here.

No guarantee that both of them would survive.

Reagan grumbled as she finger-combed twigs and leaves out of her wild hair and twisted it into a loose braid. Fatigue drew dark circles under her eyes, and a flicker of fear clouded her perfect blue gaze. A smudge of dirt at her temple was bisected by a clear sideways track from … dried tears?

His fault. His chest ached. Damned virus. Damned loss of control.

Reality stiffened his spine. He didn't deserve this brave, beautiful woman. His eyes burned as he took in her tousled appearance. Pele made the only decision he could, under these circumstances.

After this mission, he'd cut her loose. Had to. A future with Pele promised her fear and pain.

Pele's future without Reagan promised him pain and regret.

Too bad every time he got near her, his life became bearable, if only for a second. She was a salve on his tortured existence. But he'd take a life of hell on earth if it meant she would not be harmed.

"Pele, you're hurt!" The sharp tone of her voice yanked him from his thoughts.

He followed her shaking finger to his shirt. Blood stained the edges of the shredded t-shirt fabric over his chest. Blood-crusted skin showed through the tears. When he stretched his pectorals, yeah, that movement stung. Damned bear. Rubbing the back of his neck, he pushed away a residual viral urge to track and kill the beast.

"I'm fine."

She pulled up his shirt and gasped. "Obviously not. Don't you need to clean this out or take antibiotics or something?"

Wrapping his hand around her wrist in as gentle of a hold as he could manage, to stop the wonderful sensation of her touching his chest, he said, "I've had worse."

Her chin jutted. "Whatever, macho man. When you die of gangrene or rabies, I get dibs on saying 'I told you so.'"

"What?"

"I'm still mad at you," she said, with a strange smile on her face.

The virus must be slowing down his mental faculties. "I don't understand."

Scowling at him, she said, "We might not have a future, you know."

"I—yes, I get it. We're not out of danger." His jaw tightened.

"There might not be tomorrow."

"Yes, I know. But—"

"But what?" She planted her hands on her hips.

He was in big trouble. "Nothing," he muttered.

Grabbing the shredded shirt, she pulled him close and kissed him hard.

He forced his hands not to squeeze her upper arms. When she paused, he said, "What was that for? After the things I've done."

"And? The day isn't done."

A strange floating sensation bloomed in his chest. Was that what hope felt like? He grinned. "Added to the fact that I'm going to ask you to run and hike for another several hours on zero food?"

"Then you'll have to give me a little more energy." She pulled him back to her mouth for another kiss.

Stunned, he stood there and let it happen.

Somehow, the terrible day appeared brighter.

Chapter Twenty-Eight

Reagan stumbled again on the uneven ground, going down hard on a knee. The palm of her hand jammed against a partially buried root. Pushing back to her feet, she stopped and looked around at the dense, green forest all around. A bucolic scene, if it weren't for the pain happening right about now. Her legs had gone to Jell-O a few hours ago, calves and quads cramping, her stomach growled, and the trunks and leaves spun in her field of vision.

Terror and determination kept her going. No way would she stop.

Once they'd turned south, leaving Hatcher Mountain Trail, they began bushwhacking toward Parson Branch Road. She thought that cross-country hiking would be easier than trail running.

Nope.

There was a reason the settlers called the overgrown brush thickets "hells."

He turned and asked, "You okay?" Because he had no problem plowing through the undergrowth with his stupid muscles and stupid endurance from his stupid virus.

He also didn't appear to have a problem with his stupid lack of snacks.

"I'm fine," she snapped. "You sure your friends will be there?" She pitched her voice low, as he had requested. Made sense. No idea where the guys were who had found them last night. She and Pele both figured that leaving the trail and going overland, instead of taking the trail straight to the road and then traveling down the road, would decrease the chance of detection.

Their plan came at a price. She sucked a finger

that had been pricked by an early spring briar.

"My colleagues are on their way." He stopped and checked the GPS. "One more ridge up ahead, then we travel down one, maybe two draws to the road."

She refused to ask how those directions translated into distance or time because she didn't want to hear the answer.

He pulled the filter straw from his cargo pants. "Water? We'll be leaving the stream for a while to go up and over there." He motioned to the wooded hilltop several hundred feet above them.

Her empty stomach had become a sucking black hole of unhappiness. Stars danced at the edge of her vision.

Come on, now. Would it be too much to ask that he packed a Snickers Bar in his pants? Bag of chips? God knew, he had enough pockets.

Some Special Forces planning and preparation. Didn't those guys have rules? Like, bring extra snacks to a covert op? Not a difficult concept to grasp.

"Sure," she grumbled. At least water would take up space in her gut.

Snickers. Bar.

He held the straw out to her first and she drank her fill and pretended it was more than water. Then she sat on a fallen log and passed the straw to him.

"At least we haven't seen any signs of Lequire's guys since last night." Leaning forward, she rested her elbows on her knees and dropped her head into her hands.

"Yeah, that is good—"

When he paused, she lifted her head. "What?"

He straightened, held up his hand, and scanned the terrain around them visually and with his monocular instrument.

She didn't move. Peering into the thick forest, she tried to see what he saw. Hear what he heard. Nothing seemed unusual to her senses.

"No sign of them." He put away his imaging equipment in one of his many pockets that did not contain food.

"No sign. Yay, us."

"That might not be good."

"What?" Was he delirious? Escape was escape. The sooner, the better.

He pinned her with his dark gaze, setting off flutters in her chest, which probably had to do more with her hypoglycemia right about now. "Reagan, why haven't we seen or heard any sign of them? They were all over the place last night."

Her empty stomach twisted into a nasty knot. "Lucky? Outsmarted them?" That wasn't the right answer and she knew it. "I mean, we are in a section of the Smokies that sees almost zero human activity. No trails, no campsites, no roads."

"No." He rubbed his thigh. A muscle jumped on his hard jaw. "We're not lucky."

Oh, crap. "They gave up?"

"Unlikely."

"Then what—" A chill raised goosebumps on her arms. "What?" His worried grimace did not give her confidence. She stared up at the woods all around them, feeling the prickle of invisible eyes on her. She and Pele were surrounded by acres and acres of nothingness.

No help. No escape.

"What would you do if you guessed the direction someone was going? Out here, in the big, wide mountains. Would you track them directly, or do something else?"

She thought. The sweat on her neck and chest

cooled. Oh, no. "I would go to the areas where I believed they would cross a trail or road and … wait for them."

"Right." He scrubbed at his face, then methodically pulled out a gun from his under-arm hiding spot and another one from his boot. He checked both. Loaded. "I don't like this situation."

"You're the expert on subterfuge. I haven't liked this situation from the moment when I dunked myself in the freezing creek because random dudes were trying to kill me."

He snorted and nodded. "If Lequire's people have predicted our extraction site"—his brief smile changed into a frown—"then that means our team is also driving into a trap. Come on. We need to hit that high point and pray we can get a signal out to Hunt. We have to warn the team."

"Sure." She put her hands on her knees and pushed to stand up. A wave of dizziness came and went. She swallowed, her mouth already dry again. More hiking was exactly what she didn't want to do.

They were quickly running out of options.

Thirty long minutes later, they reached the relative high point. Pele pulled out the satellite phone. He cursed.

"What?"

He dropped it back in his pocket. "It's dead."

"You don't have a solar charger in there or something?" She clicked her tongue. "Here I thought you planned for everything."

He rubbed his thigh. "Apparently it takes a beautiful woman to make me very sloppy. All my training and discipline have gone to hell since meeting you." He winked.

"You're welcome?"

He shook his head. "I have to stay sharp."

"I'm here to help."

With a brush of his knuckle against her cheek, he gave a half smile. "I know you are. I—we have to make the plan work."

"What does that entail besides what we're doing?"

"Reach the extraction point first and position ourselves in strategic hides. With the sun up, the infrared detection is less helpful, for both parties. That's good and bad news. It means we have more places where we can disappear. We are also less likely to detect the enemy."

One by one, their options were vanishing. Chances of success were dropping. None of what he told her sounded positive. A wave of panic rushed up, and she swallowed hard. "If you say so."

He tilted her chin up with a finger and brushed a kiss across her lips. "I'm going to get you out of here alive and in one piece. That's a promise."

****

How the hell was Pele going to get her out of here alive and in one piece?

Only an idiot would make that promise.

Or a desperate man.

Pele's brain spun while they bushwhacked down the last draw toward Parson Branch Road. By the GPS, they had over a mile to go. Depending on the terrain and undergrowth, and at their current pace, two hours. Damn it, they were moving slowly. Reagan was having more trouble stepping over tangles of downed trees and getting through the thick mountain laurel clumps.

He rolled his tired shoulders. They were both in trouble.

He needed to save some energy to fight or to run with Reagan in his arms. Too many resources needed and not enough of Pele available.

He checked his watch. 10:00 AM. They'd pushed hard for almost four hours. How Reagan kept going with no food and little rest, he had no idea. She continued to slog through the thick undergrowth.

Extraction time was noon.

They had to hurry. He pushed another snarl of hemlock branches back.

He kept scanning the hillsides, but his enhanced senses didn't pick up any pattern changes. The scope wasn't detecting much now that the sun warmed the south and eastern-facing hillsides. He kept them in the sunlight, using that factor to their advantage. If his scope didn't work in sunlight, neither did the enemy's.

Ninety minutes later, they emerged onto flatter terrain and the obstacles thinned out. In another few hundred feet, he could make out the brighter cut where the dirt road passed through the forest. They approached the road several hundred feet downstream from where the creek crossed the road. Hopefully it was the correct crossing Reagan had aimed them toward.

Because that was where the team would look for them.

Picking a warm, sunny patch of thick woods, he turned to Reagan. Abrasions from the multitudes of branches marred her soft cheek. A blast of anger shot through him.

"Can you climb?" he managed to ask.

"Sure, I guess…"

"Get up there." He pointed at a large white pine tree with a thick, sturdy trunk. "Stay on the sunny side of the tree. Hug the trunk. Once you get situated, don't move. They shouldn't be able to see you with standard detection, only if they're looking straight up at you."

He ground his teeth at the idea of having her out of his sight, not being able to maintain physical contact with her, but he had run out of options. Until his teammates arrived, he and Reagan had to wait in as safe a place as possible and avoid exposure.

The sun dappled her face and made her hair glitter like a brass casing. All he wanted to do was drink in the view of her for another few minutes. Hours. Weeks.

He didn't have the luxury of time.

She peered up at him. "What are you going to do?"

"Try to hide where I can guard your position. I'll run interference if I have to."

She swallowed. "Okay."

"*Ti'o*." He hauled her against him and kissed her until he had the taste of her imprinted on his lips. He wanted to taste her more, later. After they got out of here alive.

That meant he had to do his job better than he'd ever carried out an op.

"You want me to climb after that kiss?" Her cheeks shone red.

He smiled in response, then got a stranglehold on his libido. "Boost?" He bent down and cupped his hands. The bottom tree branches were broken from age, but eight feet up, solid footholds began. If she could stay next to the trunk, the evergreen's branches should conceal her. Hopefully.

He tossed her up to the sturdier limbs. Losing contact with her felt like one of his arms had been ripped off. "If you see the team vehicle, I want you to get down here and run straight to it. Got it?"

"Yes."

He pitched his voice just enough to carry. "When you run for the team, you do not stop for anything, understand?"

The midsection of the tree branches swayed. "Yes," came her muffled response.

Good. Now to get in the best guard dog position.

Her life depended on how well he did his job.

Failure was not an option.

Chapter Twenty-Nine

Reagan had reached the end of her energy reserves. Actually, hours ago when they started trekking through the laurel hells on no food—that was when she reached the end of her energy reserves.

Now she functioned on adrenaline and fear.

Climbing forty feet up a tree while exhausted and lightheaded didn't sound like a smart decision, but she was too numb to offer up any alternatives. Her arms and legs shook as she heaved herself up the last branch. Her grip slipped, and she re-planted her hand on the next limb, grimacing when she came away with a palm full of sticky sap.

This activity would be so much easier if she were, say, a virally enhanced super soldier. Who had brought snacks.

The tree swayed as she got into position on the top third of the tree. The sun warmed her backside as she hugged the trunk and laced her fingers together. She could barely see the sun-dappled ground far below.

What a mess. She had entrusted her safety and now her life to a man who had lied to her. He was a man who didn't meet any criteria for being normal, not with that weird virus inside of him that drove him to the brink of insanity.

Seriously, her radar for men needed rewiring. Time to take a break and go be a hermit for, say, ten or twenty years, until she could make better choices.

A flash of Pele challenging the bear made her legs shake. Hard to tell what had frozen her in place more: the realization of Pele's true nature or the growling, jaw-popping, pissed-off bear that wanted to attack.

Pele did try to help her and keep her safe. Except for the part where he attempted to squeeze the life out of her, but that was the virus talking, right? Not his fault.

Damn it, she was making excuses for a man. Again.

What about his behavior at the club, standing next to her and helping to put Clayton in his place?

One right did not make up for a whole lot of wrong. She should have learned that lesson by now.

She leaned her forehead on her arm. This was a heck of a time to analyze her hang-ups and long string of relationship disasters. So here Reagan sat, alone except for a strange, virally enhanced stalker dude somewhere nearby. She was perched high up in a tree in the middle of a deserted area of the Smokies, waiting for bad guys to kill her or the less-bad guys to somehow get her out of here.

Terrific.

She reset her boot placement on the branch beneath her, shaking out a cramp in the quivering calf muscle. Squinting through the branches, all she could see was more greenery below and high above, blue sky and surrounding mountaintops.

Okay, hiding in this tree was a decent idea. Credit where due. Sunshine streamed down over the tree, obscuring her location in a crazy quilt pattern of light and shadow. As long as no one knew that she was up here, this was the safest place to be.

Unless bad guys spotted her, and then they'd shoot her out of the tree like a clump of mistletoe.

All right, then. Options. Plan B.

Look at her, thinking like a Special Forces operative. She grimaced.

Studying what terrain she could see from up high, she noted that her hiding tree was on the edge of a relatively flat area, about twenty feet away from a steep dirt embankment that stopped at a ditch trickling spring runoff from the nearby creek that flowed across the unmaintained rough gravel single-lane road—Parson Branch Road.

Twenty feet to safety. Not too far.

Unless someone was trying to actively kill her, then it was a country mile away.

Where was Pele? He'd faded into the scenery after she'd climbed a few feet up. Her heart thudded. Of course, he'd be fine. He could take care of himself. The guy was a muscle-bound super-soldier, after all.

She touched her cheek and got rewarded with another glob of sap. Wiping it off with her sleeve, she rubbed her fingers across the bark to remove the tacky goo.

And looked down.

A man crept through the woods, directly below her. A few faint crackles drifted up to her.

She clutched at the trunk, resetting her sweating grip.

The noise of her hands scrabbling on the bark sent that man's head on a swivel.

She pressed her lips together. *Make no noise. None.*

He walked in a circle around the tree while she remained frozen, wobbly legs locked in place, fingers digging into the trunk.

In the distance, the growl of a vehicle echoed off the mountainsides.

Oh, no.

The man spun around and stared down the road.

If you see the team vehicle, I want you to get down here and run straight to it.

How was she supposed to do that with the man in

her way? Pele hadn't offered a contingency for this wrinkle. She couldn't breathe. Her heart thudded so hard, she could feel the pulse in her cramped fingers.

A black SUV, now visible, wound slowly up the road, the crunch of gravel beneath the tires ricocheting loudly in the silent, dense forest. The car would be in a perfect position to receive a ton of bullets in about thirty seconds.

Even worse news. According to Pele, if they didn't rendezvous on time, the vehicle would turn around and go back down the road to a second meeting location. Then they would leave and await further instructions.

She eased down one branch, then another as her quad muscles cramped with each step.

When her shaky leg slipped off a branch, she stifled a cry and hugged the trunk with every last bit of her strength. Her toes tingled. She peeked down at the ground.

The man's head tilted up. His brown hair was arranged too perfectly for someone out hiking in the woods. Even at this distance, she could see his massive shoulders with ridges of muscles visible beneath a nice-looking thermal shirt.

The vehicle was now about a hundred yards from her position. She was still stuck in a tree.

"Well, hello there." The man laughed, his southern voice both smooth and slimy at the same time. She shivered. "Want to come on down and play?"

She didn't move. This might be Lequire. Hard to tell at this distance and comparing him to Brady's pictures.

She squinted again. Her breath caught. It was him.

The man who tried to kill her sister. The man likely responsible for her brother's death. Reagan's head swam.

"Let's help you decide what to do." He pointed his gun and fired. The bullet whizzed through nearby branches, and she nearly lost her grip. "You see, it wasn't a request. Get down here. Now. I want to, um, talk with you, darlin'."

By *talk*, he likely meant *hurt* or *kill*.

What other choices did she have? Stay in the tree and become his target practice or reach the ground and have a few more options. Maybe she could attract the attention of the team in the vehicle. Did they have a signal? Secret bird call? A good ol' Tennessee *yee haw*? Pele had left out key details of the plan.

Every inch of her body quaked as she descended on weak legs until she was twenty feet off the ground. A few more branches to go, then a drop to the leaf litter.

"Keep on coming." He cocked the gun and widened his stance.

The SUV had pulled nearly even with her position. They weren't slowing down. They didn't see her.

The man's gaze darted toward the road. One tiny lapse in concentration.

Like a shadow shot from a cannon, Pele rocketed out of nowhere and smashed into the man as the gun went off. Grunts and shouts filled the air as they rolled on the ground.

Another yell preceded two more men crashing through undergrowth down a nearby hillside several hundred feet away. A fourth voice came from up the road, in front of the vehicle.

Pele exchanged well-matched, vicious, bone-deep blows with Lequire. Grunts and thuds filled the clearing. With a decent punch followed by a crouched pivot kick that happened almost too fast to see, the guy dropped to his knees where he lay on his side, wheezing.

Pele ran back under the tree. "Reagan, get down. Come on! Hurry."

The vehicle passed by.

Three of Lequire's men, probably with guns, were headed this way.

Pele, his handsome face upturned, opened his arms.

A few yards away, Lequire, heaved back up to his feet.

With a glare of pure evil, he stared at Pele and Reagan and pulled out a gun. A fist of ice formed in her chest.

"Jump, Reagan!" Pele held up his arms. "Please."

She lowered herself to the next branch and let herself drop, expecting to land in his firm grip.

A gunshot went off as she fell.

Pele crumpled as she impacted his slack body, flew off his shoulder, and hit the ground.

A crack and blinding pain lanced up her arm.

Then she sucked in air and screamed as the bones midway down her forearm shifted.

Pele grunted, holding his leg as he crawled toward her, about ten feet away.

"Go," he yelled, voice hoarse as he panted for breath, veins bulging on his neck. His forehead and cheek were swollen and red.

Lequire took one slow step then another, a nasty leer plastered on his mug. He wore hiking clothes, but they appeared brand new. Even his nails were perfectly trimmed.

No way was that guy going to hurt Pele. "Come with me," she gasped, creeping over damp leaves toward him. A poker of pain burned through her arm with every movement.

"Damn it, Reagan, go! The plan!" Pele gritted the words out.

More footsteps and shouts came through the underbrush. The men converged where the trees met the open flat area.

The well-dressed jerk was now a few feet from her.

The vehicle stopped. Two men in black vests jumped out and crouched behind a door, guns pointed up toward them. Their angles were all wrong.

A pulse pounded in her head.

Lequire plucked a leaf from his otherwise perfect hair and gave a media-ready smile as he walked to Reagan.

The lower part of Pele's pants leg was soaked and his eyes had become glazed. Oh, God.

With a chuckle, Lequire knelt down next to her. Fiery pain burst from her scalp when he grabbed a fistful of her hair and jerked her head up, the movement shaking her injured arm. She half yelped, half whimpered as she clutched the arm to her body.

"Stop it, Lequire!" Pele yelled, his voice hoarse and tight, laced with anguish. He tried to stand up, but the leg buckled and his massive frame crashed back to the ground.

Beau Lequire. The man would kill or capture anyone in the McNeill family to accomplish his goal of securing all his secrets.

Lequire laughed. "You're not in any position to argue."

"Why are you doing this?" she gasped, stars popping in her field of vision when the man closed his fist, yanking hair at the roots and wrenching her neck back.

"Why? Because you are my next best option."

Kneeling down, Beau Lequire placed his lips next to her earlobe. His hot breath made her skin crawl. She didn't move. Then he bit down on her ear hard enough to make her cry out. "Yum." He chuckled. "You might be as fun as your sister."

"What?" she whispered. Kiera? What had he done to her? Britt?

"Stop it!" Pele shouted.

Nausea churned deep in her gut.

At Lequire's hand gesture, his men approached.

What about the guys getting out of the vehicle? She dared to peek over her shoulder. Too far away. Too late.

"Pele!" she screamed as Lequire loomed over her, cocked his gun, and pointed it at her head.

"No!" Pele launched himself at Lequire, knocking him away from her.

She scrambled away, crawling on two knees and one good arm.

She glanced back. Pele and Beau traded more punches than she could follow. Lequire's men circled the fight, headed toward her. With a desperate-sounding grunt, Pele stopped trying to stand and fought from his knees. Still, he leveled the man with a fast series of blows.

Then Pele crumpled to his own hands and knees.

As hard as he had pounded Lequire, that man should have stayed down. Forever.

Instead, Lequire planted his palms on the ground. Shook his head.

How was he still conscious?

He staggered to one knee, bloodshot eyes pinned on Reagan.

He spat a mouthful of blood. "You're mine."

Pushing into a wide stance, he took one step, then

two, growing larger with each passing second. His men stood in a loose semi-circle, apparently waiting for some signal from their boss.

She opened her mouth to scream but no sound came out.

Lequire reached out a hand for her.

"Pele!" Keeping her injured arm close to her chest, she used her good arm and two legs to push away, leaves skidding out from under her. The drop-off to the ditch grew closer.

Lequire kept coming, step by step. He reached for his gun and froze. Empty pocket.

With a strange smile, Lequire shrugged, planted his feet, and cocked a massive fist back.

"No!" With an awkward limp and a dive, Pele blasted into motion.

Instead of going after Lequire, Pele grabbed her, wrapped her up in his arms, and rolled. Gunshots rang out.

They tumbled over the edge of the embankment and then came to a bone-jarring halt in the wet ditch.

She couldn't breathe. Pele's weight was fully on top of her. Continuing to roar, he tightened his arms around her until pain and fear braided into white-hot agony.

A cold trickle of water seeped into her clothes. Rocks jabbed her backside.

Hands grabbed her away from him.

"No!" When she reached out with the wrong arm, pain stopped her movement. She gave a gurgling yelp.

Gunfire erupted from the top of the embankment. She curled into a ball.

"Get in. Now." A man with an unforgiving, square jaw and a businesslike scowl gripped under her armpit and shielded her with his big frame as he pushed her toward the SUV. "It's okay. Doc's got Pele." When she hesitated, he added, "Ma'am, I'm Commander Hunt. We're here to help. Get in."

Bullets pinged off the vehicle as she dove into the back seat, cradling her arm.

The man in the front seat with short black hair glanced over his shoulder and grinned. "I'm your chauffeur, Gonzo. Nice to meet you, ma'am." Like this was a Sunday drive out in the country.

A tall man with straight black hair cut short, presumably Doc, along with the commander, shoved Pele into the vehicle as Reagan scooted as far over as possible. Doors slammed. Pele's warm body sagged against hers.

"Turn around! Now!" the commander yelled as he dove into the front seat.

Lequire jumped down the embankment in one giant leap.

No one could do that.

She gasped. Pele probably could do that.

"No can do. How about reverse?" Gonzo said.

The SUV jolted and skidded as Gonzo maneuvered down the narrow gravel road at high speed. Backward.

After running a few steps to follow the car, Lequire stopped and fired several shots. She flinched at the dull thuds as the bullets impacted what she hoped was reinforced metal and bulletproof glass. She stared at his wide, wild eyes until his figure disappeared around a corner.

The vehicle barely made it around a tight turn with a steep drop-off, and her heart stopped until all four wheels firmly gripped the road again.

Pele groaned and grabbed his chest. His huge frame took up so much space that she was pinned against the door. When he roared and flailed in pain, his knuckles smacked her cheek.

She yelped. Pain bloomed where he'd hit her.

Doc held Pele's arms in place while Pele huffed, like the bear last night. Incoherent sounds came from his mouth.

"Boss, we need to pull over and let me fix our guy," Doc said. "I'm not performing another emergency medical procedure in the backseat this month."

"Flip it, Gonzo," the boss called.

Gonzo picked a marginally wide spot and performed a nauseatingly fast k-turn using what felt like brake and accelerator at the same time, with one wheel dipping over the road edge. Then the vehicle sped down the washboard-marred dirt road at an ungodly rate of speed, gravel clattering against the undercarriage as they flew over a section of rutted road.

They rocketed onto Highway 129 and swerved around hairpin curves that had her gulping back stomach acid. She made the mistake of clutching the door handle with the wrong hand and she shrieked.

Pele's head lolled in her direction, his eyes glassy. His aggressive sounds had faded to harsh breaths. He'd turned gray, which she didn't think was possible with his skin coloring. The tight lines forming at the corners of his mouth and his tightly clamped jaw told her he needed help and fast.

He inhaled like he wanted to say something, but it cut off on an animal-sounding yowl. He clawed at his thigh.

"Find a pull out, Gonzo," Doc said, leaning over to cut open Pele's pants. He pressed a large piece of gauze to his bleeding leg. "We've got issues back here."

Reagan froze. She wanted to help but didn't know what to do.

Gonzo yelled over his shoulder, "This road has nothing, man. No overlooks, no side roads. Not even shoulders. Shit." He pointed. "Boss, find something."

Hunt tapped a mobile phone. "No signals down here."

"Use the goddamn paper map." Gonzo added, "Sir!" He gripped the wheel as they careened around another corner, wheels screeching as they traveled well across the solid line. "We can't stop on the highway or we'll be found. Or we'll get run over."

Reagan leaned her forehead to the window and immediately regretted doing so. The view of a wooded drop-off didn't reassure her. If they flew over the edge, at least a few trees would slow them down before they got totally pulverized. Wouldn't that be a kick in the pants? Surviving hypothermia, a bear encounter, an attack by Lequire, only to die on The Dragon's Tail, Highway 129?

Pele groaned, and Reagan held his slack hand with her good one and squeezed. The weak answering press sent a wave of cold terror through her. The powerful man was losing strength quickly. Anxiety had wrapped a set of talons around her throat, and she couldn't swallow. Would he survive?

Hunt unfolded paper, muttered to himself, then called out, "Forest access road coming up on the left in two hundred feet, one hundred feet, fifty, twenty. Turn."

Gonzo squealed wheels across two highway lanes as he punched through a locked National Park service gate, pulling up the rough dirt road far enough so that no one on the highway could see them.

All three men burst out of the vehicle. Hunt opened her door and helped Reagan out. "Sit down for a second, ma'am," he said.

She shook her head and, cradling her aching arm,

staggered to where the other two men struggled to lift Pele out of the back seat.

"Freaking *gordito* here's been eating extra healthy again. Ask me how I can tell," Gonzo said through gritted teeth. "Thought he only ate fruit and fish and tropical cuisine like that."

Hunt jumped in to assist, and the men laid Pele on the gravel in front of the SUV. Pele didn't move.

The thudding of her heart stopped.

Reagan swallowed and fought to stay upright, planting her feet as she focused on the man who had saved her life.

That act might have cost him his own life.

Doc rushed to the back of the SUV and retrieved a big nylon bag that he opened to reveal pockets of medical supplies. He cut the remainder of Pele's pants leg. A nasty bullet hole puckered the skin about six inches below the knee and another hole marred his big thigh. The thigh injury bled briskly. Lashing a tourniquet above the upper wound, Doc then cut open the front of Pele's shirt and felt along the ribs, then listened with a stethoscope.

"Broken ribs, decent breath sounds, no rubs. Hasn't dropped a lung. No tamponade," he muttered. "Hand me that pulse ox, would you?" He hooked up the equipment and a quick pulse beeped, the electronic tone out of place in the middle of nature. "Gonzo, help me roll him over. Let's make sure nothing else is going on."

As they checked his back, Pele lashed out at the men with a gut-wrenching groan that scared the hell out of Reagan. Her legs no longer held her weight.

As her vision blurred around the edges, she heard voices.

"Hold him, Gonzo."

Doc called out, "Shit. Hunt, grab her, she's going

over…"

Chapter Thirty

"Hi, sis." That voice sounded so familiar. Light, friendly. Reminded Reagan of pillow fights and dancing to Rihanna tunes and giggling over boys. Reminded her of home.

Reagan tried to open her eyes and failed. Slow beeps continued.

"Hey, Reagan? Are you awake?" A shake on her shoulder had her squinting against the light.

Familiar hazel eyes and a pretty face entered her field of vision. Kiera's skin glowed.

Wait. Kiera?

Reagan opened her dry mouth. No sound came out. Then her vision blurred. She worked hard to blink a bunch of times. Kiera? Damp warmth flowed over the cheek closest to her sister.

"Oh, honey," her younger sister said as she blotted away Reagan's tears with her sleeve. Kiera's hair was a deep brunette instead of her natural bright auburn.

When Reagan tried to sit up, Doc appeared. "Do not get up." He shook his head. "You McNeill women are two peas in a pod, aren't you? Take it easy. No more procedures for either of you, understand? That's an order." He smoothed back his hair and grumbled, "I'm not on call anymore."

"Pele?"

"He's fine. Now quit wiggling." He glared at her, his mouth twisting into a frown before he ducked behind the curtain.

"He's awful grumpy," Reagan grumbled as her sister giggled.

"Doc's had kind of a long week."

"What day is it?"

"It's Sunday. You arrived yesterday afternoon and slept until now."

She almost sat straight up again. "Pele?"

"He's safe."

Reagan blinked. "What are you doing here, Kiera?" She peered around the small, sterile medical room. A curtain was drawn next to her. "Where's *here*? Your hair color—"

Kiera gave a half smile. "We're at the Morpheus Squad compound. You're safe." She pulled at her dark brown, shoulder-length hair. "This was … necessary."

"I don't understand."

"It's complicated."

"I really wish people would stop saying that," she muttered. "You didn't talk to me for over a year!" A wave of anger and sadness crashed over her.

Kiera's eyes shimmered and her chin quivered. "I wanted to. But Mateo and I were undercover. No direct contact with friends or family, no visits, no possibility of blowing our cover. We did it all to avenge Brady."

"Brady." A tightness in Reagan's chest finally released. She sniffed. "Did it work like you'd hoped?"

"Not exactly as planned." She frowned and bit her lip. Her face seemed fuller than it had been the last time Reagan had seen her. "We still don't have all the pieces in place to take down Beau Lequire and Fallen Comrades yet, but we're close. It's important to make sure you, Dad, and Britt are safe before the team acts on the intelligence I gathered. The corruption in Fallen Comrades goes way deeper than anyone had ever thought. They were defrauding disabled vets and the people who donated to support the vets. Now we've discovered deeper government ties and possibly Russian drug trafficking."

"That all sounds awful."

"It's not good. Cost a lot to get the information." Her eyes glistened. "Cost Brady's life. He found out about the company but never had a chance to tell anyone. Mateo and I went undercover. Then Mateo died when he bought me time to escape and reach this team."

"Oh, man. Mateo was one of Brady's best friends."

"Yes."

"So, you really were doing something this past year. I thought you were just avoiding all of us."

Kiera leaned down and pressed her cheek to Reagan's. The connection filled a huge hole Reagan hadn't realized existed.

"No way." Her sister sighed. "The hardest part of the past year was not having any in-person contact with you and Britt and Dad."

Tears pricked again as a wave of emotion swamped her. "I miss Brady. And Mom."

"Me too." She gently squeezed Reagan's fingers.

"The last year was rough." Glancing over her body and cataloging her injuries, Reagan snorted. "This year is shaping up to be even worse."

A wistful, soft expression floated over Kiera's face. "Maybe not all of it was bad."

Huh. After a moment, Reagan said, "So you know about the team. Do you know about the, um, virus thing?"

Kiera tucked her hair behind her ears. "Yeah, I'm aware of it."

Seconds passed in thoughtful silence.

Reagan studied her casted right arm and a bag of IV fluids dripping into her left arm. "So, what exactly happened? I feel awful."

"Doc?" Kiera said, turning to the team member who reappeared as if by magic from behind the curtain.

His calm face gave nothing away. "I heard that you ran for more than fifteen miles in the mountains with no food and little water. Then you fell out of a tree and broke your arm. Then my teammate rolled on top of you."

Explained the hit-by-a-truck sensation. *Oh, no.* She tried to sit up. "Pele?" she asked again.

"Lie back down, or I won't show you anything," Doc warned.

She obeyed. She had to see Pele.

Doc pulled back the partition and pointed.

Over on the far side of the room, Pele's big body was covered with a sheet to his upper chest. He had IV fluids running, and a heart monitor displayed pulse, blood pressure, and oxygen levels. His chest rose and fell in a regular rhythm.

"Is he okay?"

Doc smiled. "We had to give him a powerful sedative so he would stop trying to get off the bed in an effort to get closer to you. Kept opening up his wounds." He raised a brow. "Anyway. It was helpful to knock him out while I fixed the gunshot injuries. No way would I attempt to sew that guy up while he was conscious."

Reagan eyed the still form. "Is he going to be all right? Did he get his antidote?"

"Yes. I gave it to him. He's calm now. He'll heal quickly. His body is pretty banged up, too, but he's tough." Doc smiled. "So are you."

A lungful of air whooshed out and she relaxed, despite her sore back and ribs. "So, is this like a hospital?"

"A very basic clinic space, or field hospital, depending on the day of the week," Doc said. "We have it set up for matters relating to Morpheus Squad." He slid a wry glance toward Kiera. "It's gotten too much use in the short time we've been here."

"Why do I feel so strange?" Reagan asked, shaking her head.

"You're waking up from a sedative, too. I had to set your arm before casting it. Most folks prefer not to be awake for that experience."

"Thanks."

"It's part of the all-inclusive package when you hang out with the team. Escape bad guys, enjoy medical procedures, get free anesthesia. It's like a BOGO deal." Was that a smile? His brows rose, then his face reset to neutral.

"What about Britt and Dad?" Reagan asked her sister.

"Still safe. The guys are watching them," Kiera said. She paused. "I have some other news." She nodded at Doc again, and he left the room.

A minute later, another man returned with a small bundle. Reagan frowned. He looked different than she recalled from last year at Brady's funeral.

"Jake?"

The man smiled. "Yup."

"What are you doing here?" she asked, taking in his multi-pocketed military pants and vigilant stance.

"I work here." There was an odd lift to the corner of his mouth. "At least, now I do." The bundle in his arms made a cooing noise, and Jake's gaze softened.

Reagan frowned. "What's this?"

Kiera took the baby clad in a pink outfit with pink flowers printed on it. The baby had a pink headband, too. The adoring expression on her sister's face stunned Reagan. "This is your new niece. Mattie."

"Are you kidding me?" Reagan said. "You disappeared, completed a covert operation, went and got pregnant, *and* had a baby—all without telling me? When did this happen? She's so cute."

Doc piped up, "Did I mention that the last week has been pretty busy?"

"I'll say." Jake shook his head and stroked the baby's cheek. Then when he gazed at Kiera, his rapt devotion shocked Reagan.

"What the heck?" Reagan examined the baby girl's shock of strawberry-blonde hair sticking straight up from her perfect head. "No way. You and Jake? But you were on the mission with Mateo."

"It's complicated, sis. Mateo and I are—were—friends. I wouldn't have escaped if it wasn't for him. He died so I could make it to the team and so Mattie would survive."

"But…"

She leaned back into Jake's chest and his arms came around her. "Yes, this beautiful baby is Jake's. It's…"

"Complicated?" Reagan finished for her.

"You have no idea."

"Um, I get the picture." She frowned as she took in her sister's glowing visage and Jake's protective stance. "Well, okay, then. Congratulations, you two. She's beautiful."

"I agree," Jake said. "Just like her mother."

The baby fussed, and Kiera bounced her in her arms. "Fine, I got it. You're starving again." She glared at Doc, who hadn't said a word. "I know, I know. Feed the baby. Doctor's orders or something like that."

With a tiny smile, Doc shrugged one shoulder.

Kiera moved Mattie to the crook of one arm. "We'll catch up later, sis. You get some rest, okay?"

Reagan accepted the awkward neck plus baby hug and watched her sister and Jake leave.

"Wow," she breathed.

When she turned her head, Pele was watching her with a clear, serious expression. He didn't move. Bruises and scratches dotted his forehead and cheeks. Bandages covered half of one eyebrow and his chin.

"Many things have changed, haven't they?" Doc glanced between the two of them. Like he wasn't talking about Kiera and Jake at all. He stood and cracked his back. "Well. I'm going to take a well-deserved break after spending the past day duct taping you two adventurers back together. Why don't I scoot your bed over to make more room in the clinic?" He glared at Pele. "You better not screw up any of my hard work, got it?"

Pele nodded as Doc unlocked Reagan's bed wheels and lowered the side railing. He pushed her gurney right next to Pele's and locked the wheels again.

Reagan fastened her gaze on Pele. She was close enough to touch him with her good arm. As they linked hands, she heard a door close quietly as Doc exited.

"How are you?" Pele's hoarse voice made her flinch.

"I should ask you that question."

"I'm much better now that I can see you're alive."

Beneath the intensity of his searching stare, she asked, "Are you in pain?"

"I've had worse." His Adam's apple bobbed. "You know what really hurts?"

"What?" She looked over at the door. "I can get Doc."

"No." He shook his head. "What really hurts is the fact that I wasn't honest with you. Couldn't be." Careful of her IV, he squeezed her fingers. "I am sorry. It's no excuse, but my hands were tied. I couldn't tell you why I was at the camp. It would have put everyone else in danger. I should have never—"

He should have never … yeah.

That was the bomb he needed to drop. Their night together. He thought it had been a mistake. Okay, then.

The vacuum of air escaping her lips caved in her aching chest. "So, what parts of the past week were true, Pele?"

"The part where I think you're beautiful. The part where I wanted all of you for my own selfish reasons that had nothing to do with any mission. I wanted to protect you. Badly. Keep you from any harm." He made a fist with the hand that didn't have an IV in it. "I didn't do a great job of that one."

A hard lump formed in her throat. "I think you did okay, given the circumstances."

When he sat up, she protested, but he held up a hand. "I need to be upright for this conversation." He pressed his hand to his ribs and grimaced, pushing their beds apart. He swung thick legs over the side of the hospital bed and stood in front of her. He tucked the sheet under his arms and wrapped it around him.

"We both should be vertical for this."

Gently, he helped her to sit and face him. It took a few seconds for her head to stop swimming when she sat up. Pele held her lightly at the waist, hands branding her through the hospital gown.

Lifting his chin toward her arm, he frowned. "Sorry about that."

"You got shot and couldn't catch me when I fell out of a tree. Degree of difficulty extremely high. Not exactly your fault."

"I should have hung in there." Darkness glinted in his narrowed eyes. "I really would have loved to kill Lequire. He deserved to die for hurting you."

"But?"

"Your life was more important than my need for revenge."

She could drown in that liquid-brown gaze. Wow. "Okay."

"But yeah, I should have protected you better."

"Hey, macho guy? You did a good job." She pointed at him. "I'm surprised you were even alive after that guy shot you. How are you even standing?"

"Superior healing ability?"

"Huh. How did you manage to get us off that hill and next to the SUV?"

"It might have been hard to run and harder to scoot, but rolling was easy." A line formed between his brows. "Why didn't you listen to me when I told you to leave?"

"You don't have the corner on the hero market, you know. I wanted to protect you, too." She would have crossed her arms, but the less movement of her broken arm, the better.

His sad smile made her heart flop. "Reagan?" He held the hand of her non-broken arm. "Can you forgive me? Do you think that one day…"

"What?"

"Never mind."

She slid her hand out of his and touched the uninjured side of his jaw. "Please. Tell me."

The muscles of his neck worked. "Could you one day see past the monster I've become?"

"I never said you—"

He pressed a finger to her lips. "I'm aware of what I am. If the answer is no, I will respect your decision one hundred percent. I will leave you alone."

The thought of a life without Pele in it created a bone-deep ache in her heart.

With a heave of his big shoulders, he said, "I

have no right to ask."

"But."

"Do you think there's ever a chance that you would be willing to try again? With me? Us."

"Um—"

"I wish a lot of things could have been different." The words tumbled out like water rushing down a mountain stream. "Secrets and all. Uh, we got off to a rough start."

"Not all of it was rough." She ducked her head on a smile.

"So true."

The sexy harshness of his voice sent shivers down her back.

He licked his lips. "*Ti'o*, how I would like to make love to you again."

A coil of pleasure swirled in her belly as she met his avid stare. "Really?"

"That part was never a lie. Or the part about how smart and resourceful and beautiful you are, inside and out. You have to know that."

With a blink to break the thick tension and to clear the burning beneath her eyelids, she eased her hand away. "Pele, after what you told me, I may not be what you want. Or need. You know, I'm not Samoan and I'll fully know your culture."

"You did explode the *umu*."

"Well, yeah, that, too"

With a hearty groan, he shifted from one leg to another in front of her. A grimace of pain contracted his brows.

"Should you really be on your feet?" she asked.

The dimple winked on his scratched cheek. "Does it allow me to be closer to you?

"Yes."

"Then that's exactly what I should be doing." He leaned in between her knees and rested his hands on her upper arms as he pressed his forehead to hers. "Reagan, I am falling in love with you. If there's a chance that one day you might feel the same way, I'd like to try again. Slowly. At your pace. Without any lies. Give us a chance to create some kind of real future together."

"I need to be clear about this, Pele. I know what it is to have to bend too much for a partner. To become someone I'm not. I won't do that again. And you shouldn't have to compromise what you want in the person you…" She couldn't finish the sentence.

His low voice rumbled through her. "Where I come from will always be a part of who I am. It will influence the rest of my life. But I need to create a new path." He sighed, his big shoulders rising and falling. "I'd like for that life to have you in it. With me."

"There's a 'but' coming."

"Your life will change, too." He leaned back. "For starters, you have to stay here at this compound for the foreseeable future."

"No."

"Yes. It's for your safety. It's even more important for the safety of your family. Until we've got the Lequire situation sorted out." He stared into her eyes. "I'm sorry. I know that's not what you wanted to hear."

"Wow. My job?"

"On hold indefinitely. Knowing the guys, they've already taken care of the paperwork and the appropriate phone calls."

An off-balance feeling flowed through her, and only his anchoring hands on her upper arms kept her stable. "So…"

"I wish this situation could be normal. I wish I was normal. That we could have a normal relationship.

That's why I will understand if you don't want—"

She swallowed. "Pele—"

"Yes." He trailed his fingers up her back and over her shoulders until he rubbed his thumbs over her collarbones. When he touched her, the connection felt so right. He barked a dry laugh, but the wary expression remained. "I mean, you're stuck here anyway. We can use the time to work on our relationship. Like regular couples."

"Who are trapped in a compound. Surrounded by virally enhanced super soldiers."

Clearing his throat again, he continued, "You don't have to answer right away. My timing is awful." He looked around the room that appeared to have been carved from solid stone. "In the med bay of a secret compound." He groaned. "It's not super romantic." With a grimace, he finished, "You with a broken arm and everything. Me with the military-grade virus inside. *Ti'o.*" Raking a hand through his hair, he studied the floor. "Damn it. I shouldn't even be asking you— Forget I said anything, okay?"

Reagan took stock of everything. She didn't need white lace and promises. Her heart simply wanted what it wanted. "Yes."

"Huh?"

"Well, as you say, I'm stuck here for a while."

"Sorry."

"Might as well be stuck here with you."

"Reagan."

Squeezing his forearm, she said, "You know what? I don't know at what point I fell in love with you, Pele, but I'm there, too. Damned crazy virus, bizarre situation, and all." She put her good hand on his corded forearm. "I'm still working through some of my own issues, too, you know. It's going to take time. Are you willing to deal with the extra baggage?"

"Is it your baggage?"

Her stomach clenched. "Yes."

"Then I will help you carry it."

Her head came forward until she nestled against his bare chest above the sheet. Perfect fit. "Let's try," she said.

"Really?"

Leaning back, she smiled. "I can't imagine anyone I'd rather be with."

"That's my line." He lifted her chin with a thick finger and kissed her so tenderly it brought tears to her eyes.

Beneath the soft press of his mouth and his heated skin under her palms, she felt his muscles tense up. Raw power and passion held in check. In control. For now. How long would be a topic to deal with later.

She sighed and angled her mouth.

After a series of breath-stealing kisses, punctuated by a gentle nip to her lower lip, he whispered, "I'm guessing Doc will object if I climb up and have wild sex with you right now?"

"Pretty sure he'd sedate you again if you tried." She laughed. The room *had* gotten a little too warm.

"Hopefully we won't have to wait too long to get the all-clear," he murmured next to her ear. "When you're ready. If you want to. Again. Sometime. As many times as you want."

His voice sent shivers down her back, and she groaned. "Don't you have to heal up the rib fractures and bullet wounds first?"

Widening his stance, he pressed into her. "Did I ever tell you about the stamina that virally enhanced Special Forces guys have?" He guided her good hand to his groin to prove how much stamina he had available.

She gulped. Then she gave him a tiny stroke over the hardness separated from her only by the sheet.

With a hiss, he manacled her wrist in the gentlest of prisons and lifted it away, then tucked her forehead into his chest and kissed the top of her head.

A laugh bubbled up from the depths of her soul, clearing out sadness and regrets. Replacing them with happiness. Pele.

Reagan slid her hand out of his grip and looped her good arm around his back, leaning into his strong embrace.

Injured, homeless, and with a future in doubt, she found what she needed. Pele accepted her and loved her for being her. She accepted him for what he was: the man she wanted. Whether he was a super warrior or not, whether he was damaged or not, she loved him for being Pele.

No question, he would love her and keep her safe, and she would continue exploding fire-baked stones for him. For as much time as they had together.

The End

ACKNOWLEDGEMENTS

Thanks for three amazing beta readers Mickey, Carmen P., and Lisa C. who provided valuable feedback very early on in this book's development. Big thank you to Diane Wiggs, whose feedback and eagle eyes have made all the difference!

Wonderful agent Jana Hansen, I could not have done this without you.

Research notes/background on the novel:

Those night hike tales are both actual stories! The one that Reagan told was "King Arthur and the Riddle: The Wedding of Sir Gawain and Lady Ragnell." The story is either attributed to Chaucer or in the tradition of Chaucer, depending on the scholar. Interestingly, this tale has been around for literal centuries and the core lesson is applicable today. Personally, I think someone should marry because they like the person, not because some rando chick in the woods helped a dude cheat on a quiz and then aforementioned rando chick blackmails the dude into letting her marry a hunky knight. But all's well that ends well in Arthurian times, I suppose. Interestingly, it is a story that gets told at a Smoky Mountain summer camp! (Among their many other wonderful stories.)

The night hike itself is also something I've experienced and led as part of a job in the Smokies I once had many years ago. The night hike is transformational in that we have to overcome our ingrained fear of the dark and the unknown. There are quite a few life lessons we can draw from this activity, like going through the darkness and trusting that we can find our way out. Media and horror films play a big role in our discomfort with the dark. There is literally no additional light brought to the night hike, but once our eyes become accustomed to the darkness, we realize that with enough ambient moonlight and starlight and using other senses like hearing and the touch of our feet on rooted paths, we can navigate surprisingly well. Of note, if you are doing a night hike, be sure to view the path, people, or objects from the corners of your eyes and you will be able to see better. Fun fact: on our retinas, the cones that pick up color reside in the center of the retina and are basically useless at nighttime. The rods, on the lateral areas of the retina, have everything to do with seeing in dim light and give us black and white (shades of gray) images. By looking "sideways" at something in the nighttime, you can discern it better!

Can black bears attack? Yup. Ever been to any major tourist area, picnic spot, or campground in the Smokies? Never *ever* get between a mother bear and her cubs. Unfortunately, tourists in the Smokies have habituated black bears to humans by feeding them and interacting far too closely with them. The bears have learned to become more demanding when it comes to things like peanut butter sandwiches, trail mix, and toothpaste. Yes, I said toothpaste. If you're backcountry camping in the Smokies, you'll find metal poles or two trees close by where you can loop ropes and hoist the backpack off the ground for the night, suspending the pack between the two tall objects. Never forget to put the toothpaste in the pack. Ask me how I learned this lesson... Unfortunately, when a bear becomes aggressive, the park service often tries to relocate it—or for repeat offenders, euthanize it. All because of human behavior changing the bear's habits.

Parson Branch Road is a one-lane, one-way dirt road that exits Cades Cove southeast into North Carolina. For several years, it was closed altogether but recently opened again seasonally for vehicles. Even when it's open, the road is considered "primitive," meaning you might not get over certain hills or through creek crossings in a sedan. Parson Branch Road ends at Highway 129, otherwise known as the Tail of the Dragon, which boasts over 300 curves in eleven miles. I've burned out sets of brakes on this stretch of road, and yes, I've gotten sick with someone else driving it. Motorcyclists love The Tail of the Dragon and will often "lean in" over the center line when traveling at high rates of speed. Crashes off the side of the mountains (there are no guardrails on this 2-lane highway) are numerous, and the response time is limited by the fact that the LifeFlight helicopter can't land on many spots of Highway 129 due to dense tree cover. Despite admirable efforts from the Blount County and Graham County EMS, crews still take almost an hour to reach the most remote areas of this stretch of highway. All that said, it's a beautiful drive and puts you within striking distance of some excellent scenery and hiking (Joyce Kilmer National Forest, Citico Creek Wilderness, and the remote southeastern trailheads of the Smokies.) Just take the motion-sickness pills before you go, and be sure to buckle up.

Port-wine stain (or *nevus flammeus*, if you like the fancy term) is a medical condition due to a vascular malformation of the capillaries in the skin. The birthmark grows as the person grows, but may become darker red or purple over time, and sometimes the skin will become bumpy or thickened. Treatment includes the use of cosmetic coverings, pulsed-dye laser, cryotherapy, or excision and grafting. Many of the treatments can be quite painful and run the risk of scarring. Due to discomfort, most procedures are performed under anesthesia. Patients who are born with port-wine stains sometimes will need further testing such as a brain MRI, to ensure that the birthmark does not indicate the presence of genetic syndromes that affect blood vessels in other places such as the brain.

The second story about Sina and her Eel is a well-known Samoan myth, passed down through generations. The story seems a little creepy to me with the whole stalker eel situation, but it served its purpose in my novel! The original story concludes with Sina burying the head of the eel/king, not the body, but I wasn't prepared to introduce decapitation in a story told to second-graders. That's a step too gruesome even for me! Regarding the coconut, it is not native to Western Samoa or to American Samoa, nor much of Polynesia. Cultural anthropologists explain that anywhere you find a coconut in the far reaches of Polynesia, this indicates human occupation, much like the presence of potsherds or stone tools in the Americas.

A few notes about the *tatau*, which is the term from which the English word, *tattoo*, derives. The traditional myth of the Samoan *tatau* is that two Fijian sisters (Siamese twins joined at the lower spine until they were separated) brought the art of *tatau* to Samoa—they were taught that it was for women. However, right before the sisters landed on the shores, they got confused and the new story was that men should get the *tatau*. (Some Samoan tradition cites the origin of the *tatau* as purely Samoan, not Fijian. Given similar practices in Fiji that date back numerous centuries, this remains a point of debate.)

The name *tatau* comes from the sound the instrument makes as the design is being hand-created.

The instrument is a boar tusk sharpened into a comb-like configuration with sharp points to drive the pigment into the skin. The boar tusk is affixed to a sea turtle shell which in turn is attached to a stick that gets tapped. The pigment comes from the soot of the candlenut burned in a coconut shell and scraped out for use. The process is lengthy, painful, and can create soft tissue damage or scarring. The *tatau* is also a mark of adulthood, honor, and acceptance of the Samoan culture. It can take weeks or months to complete the full design. Receiving a *tatau* traditionally involves payments of cloth or mats and utilizes the artistry of the *Tafuga*, the artist who applies the *tatau*. He or she is assisted by apprentices who stretch skin and wipe away blood. Oftentimes, family members will sit with the person receiving the *tatau* and sing during this rite of passage.

The men's *tatau* is called a *pe'a*. The design is dense and extends from the lower back (where the Siamese twins were originally joined) around to the flank, to below the waist area and then down below the knees. The designs and patterns have various and significant meanings. There is always a special design around the navel, and without this mark, the *tatau* is considered incomplete.

For women, the *tatau* is called the *malu*, and it is placed from the upper thigh to just below the knees and sometimes also on the backs of the hands and lower abdomen. The design is more delicate and less ritualized than the *pe'a* but is still deeply meaningful as a visual depiction of one's life, cultural identity, family, and values. In the past, the *malu* was given only to the highest-ranking woman in the village, the *taupou*, which holds similar position as the high (district) chief. In the past, the women who had a *malu* became something of local celebrities. More contemporarily, the *malu* is available for any woman who wishes to have it applied. It's felt to be an acceptance and embodiment of Samoan culture.

I have tried to be thorough, accurate, and sensitive in my use of these and other cultural depictions in the novel. Any incorrect information or errors are mine.

EVERNIGHT PUBLISHING ®

www.evernightpublishing.com